Beneath a
Dakota Cross

**Center Point
Large Print**

**This Large Print Book carries the
Seal of Approval of N.A.V.H.**

ॐ श्री गणेशाय नमः

Beneath a
Dakota Cross

Stephen (A.) Bly 1944 -

Center Point Publishing
Thorndike, Maine

This Center Point Large Print edition
is published in the year 2001 by arrangement with
Broadman & Holman Publishers.

The text of this Large Print edition is unabridged.
In other aspects, this book may vary from the original
edition. Printed in Thailand. Set in 16-point Plantin type by
Bill Coskrey.

Cover photo used with permission of freestockphotos.com.

ISBN 1-58547-083-X

Library of Congress Cataloging-in-Publication Data

Bly, Stephen A., 1944-
   Beneath a Dakota cross / Stephen Bly.
     p. cm.
   ISBN 1-58547-083-X (lib. bdg. : alk. paper)
     1. Black Hills (S.D. and Wyo.)--Fiction. 2. Large type books. I. Title.

PS3552.L93 B46 2001
813'.54--dc21

                                             00-065679

For
the March sisters
and
all
their
adventures

Author's Notes

The migration of people groups across western North America began when the first intrepid Asian hunter and his family stepped off the ice bridge across the Bering Strait.

Native American tribes located and relocated as they fanned out and filled the diverse, awe-inspiring, and physically challenging landscape we now call the West.

The parade of settlers diversified when the Spanish rode north on majestic horses and French trappers paddled their way into mountain ranges so mysterious few would believe their early reports.

Then came mission-founding priests, burly Missouri mountain men, hardworking farm families, and shrewd New England businessmen, to name a few.

The wave of emigrants intensified after the Civil War in the East left many seeking a fresh start. The twentieth century and the demise of prospecting did not change the migration pattern so firmly established. From the dust bowl exiles of the 1930s to the high-tech work force of today, the West still beckons and challenges.

Its lure has always been great. Settlers answered the call to majestic open spaces, beaver-filled creeks, unclaimed government land, and the most irresistible magnet of all—gold.

Of all the nineteenth-century pilgrims following the siren call of mineral fortunes, very few found a bonanza of wealth. But most of the hearty ones who chose to stay in the West found a richness of lifestyle and companionship that sat well in their hearts and in their spirits.

A majority of the early pioneers were quick to acknowledge Divine Providence in their journeys. Many left their homes and headed for this unknown land believing that the Lord had personally called them to this special place.

Henry "Brazos" Fortune was one such man.

The restlessness in his spirit to find the exact place God wanted him to be is a longing that most of us experience to this very day.

Beneath a Dakota Cross is the beginning novel in a saga that explores that restlessness and one family's finding their place among the narrow, treasure-filled gulches of the northern Black Hills.

While Brazos Fortune is a fictional character, his response to this inspiring land, the burden of his love for family, the loyalty of friends, and a heart that seeks to please his Lord and Savior is all very much real.

I know.

As a third-generation westerner born to the land, it is the cultural and spiritual baton that I carry daily. Perhaps this series of novels, in some small way, will be my method of passing the call of the West on to the next generation.

Stephen Bly
Broken Arrow Crossing, Idaho
Spring of '99

For I know the thoughts that I think toward you,
saith the Lord,
Thoughts of peace, and not of evil,
to give you an expected end.
Jeremiah 29:11 (KJV)

Chapter One

On the banks of Rio Leon, Coryell County, Texas,
April 24, 1875.

Two dark sorrel horses leaned into their rigging and pulled the loaded buckboard up the muddy embankment.

Brazos Fortune refused to look back.

There were no tears in his eyes.

That one fact surprised him.

Wheels squeaked.

Worn boards groaned.

Pots and pans rattled.

But there was no conversation.

Brazos ran his hand through his neatly trimmed, gray-flecked beard and glanced out of the corner of his eye at the young girl in the long, yellow dress sitting next to him.

She was looking back.

He felt her glove-covered hand reach up and hold on to the sleeve of his canvas coat.

"Is that all we do, Daddy? We just drive off?" Her voice fluctuated somewhere between that of a ten-year-old and a girl of fifteen. "Shouldn't we say good-bye, or something?"

With calloused, bare fingers he rubbed caked dust from the time-plowed furrows at the corners of his eyes, then slapped the reins on the rump of the lead horse. "Darlin', we said our good-byes when we left the house."

Two long braids pulled her light brown hair back and seemed to enlarge her blue eyes. "We'll come back, won't we? We just have to come back someday." She sniffled.

"Dacee June, we prayed that through already. The Lord has someplace else in mind for us, and we're going there."

The wagon leveled off on the east side of the Rio Leon. Brazos allowed the wheels to slip into the dried mud ruts of the Waco road. There were no trees or buildings in sight.

"But we have to go back, Daddy. We have to take care of Mamma's grave."

The image of a stark, lonely plot under a live oak tree flittered across Brazos's mind. "It's got a nice black iron fence around it. Your Aunt Barbara's going to look after it. She'll do a fine job. You know what beautiful flowers she raises."

"But . . . but," Dacee June protested, "it's like we're going off and leavin' Mamma."

Brazos took a deep breath and stared across the empty prairie. "Where's your mamma right now, Dacee June?" His blue-gray eyes were not nearly as stern as his voice.

"She's in heaven with Jesus."

"And where's heaven?"

"Just a step away from us." She answered like a beginning catechism student.

He leaned forward until his bony elbows rested on

10

worn, denim-covered knees. "So, we really aren't leavin' Mamma in Texas, are we?"

"No, I guess not. But could we come back to see her grave anyway?" Her smooth, round cheeks perfectly balanced a small but full mouth.

Brazos reached over and patted her knee. "We'll come back, darlin'. But I just don't know when. It won't be easy for me to come back and see someone else living in our house and runnin' cows on our ranch."

"Daddy, the Lord's leading us somewhere else, isn't he?"

"I told you about the dream I had, Dacee June. We're going to find that ranch under a big cross. I just know it."

"Well, if it's a home for both of us, how come I didn't have a dream like that?"

"Maybe it's because daddies need to make the decisions, especially when girls are little."

"I am not little," she huffed. "I'm medium. I'll be twelve my next birthday."

"You're right, Dacee June. You're not little."

For several minutes the buckboard rumbled along, free of conversation. The road wound through gently rolling, treeless hills covered with short, green grass and scattered congregations of bluebonnets. The sky was light blue, with high, streaked white clouds.

"Daddy, I'm sorry for making you melancholy." The voice was so soft, Brazos had to lean down to hear the words.

He slipped his arm around her thin, narrow shoul-

11

ders and hugged her tight. "Darlin', you can talk about your mamma any time of the day, any day of the week. Now, it might make me a little melancholy, but that's because I loved her dearly, just like you do. So don't you ever stop thinkin' of her or talkin' about her. 'Cause I know I won't."

"It's been over three years, you know," Dacee June added.

"Three years, two months, seventeen days . . ." He pulled his wide-brimmed, beaver felt hat low over his eyes and glanced up at the position of the sun. "And about four hours."

"You really miss her, don't you?"

"Dacee June, some days it feels like someone just cut me right down the middle and threw half away."

"I miss the way she hugged me," Dacee June announced. "Do you miss that?"

"Yep. And I miss hearing her sweet voice."

"Do you miss talking to her?"

"Well, I sort of end up talkin' to her ever' day as it is. What I miss is hearing her voice reply."

"What do you talk to her about?"

"About you . . . Todd . . . Robert . . ."

"And Samuel—you talk to her about Samuel, don't you?"

"You know I do. We talk about all you children."

Dacee June tugged at the lace collar on her dress. "Do you talk about Veronica and Patricia?"

Brazos stared out over the lead horses' ears. He took a big deep breath but couldn't keep the tears from streaming down his tired blue-gray eyes.

"Now, I've gone and made you melancholy again." Dacee June moaned as she dropped her chin to her chest. "Forgive me, Daddy . . . I'm only eleven . . . I say the wrong things."

"Your sisters are up in heaven with Mamma, so I don't worry about them like I do the four of you. But I reckon it would be good to change the subject." He sat straight up on the wagon seat and tried to stretch a cramp out of his back. He knew that under the jacket, shirt, and long johns was a bruise the size of a grapefruit from a horse kick the day before.

Dacee June locked her gloved fingers together and rested them on her lap. "Are we really going to live in Wyoming? Billy Fred said that Wyoming was full of wild Indians and we'd surely get scalped if we moved there."

"No one will get scalped. Things are calming down up there. Why, they have a railroad that runs from Omaha to San Francisco. Besides, I didn't say we were going to Wyoming."

"I know, I know . . . we're going wherever the Lord shows us some big old cross. Will it have beautiful sunsets and rolling green hills and bluebonnets? Will it have bluebonnets, Daddy?"

"Probably not, darlin'. But we won't be disappointed. That's the important thing. The Lord will lead us to a place that won't disappoint. Remember what we read this mornin'? 'For I know the thoughts that I think toward you . . . thoughts of peace, and not of evil, to give you an expected end.'"

"I wish I could go with you to find it." She stared at

him with wide eyes. "Why can't I go?"

"Young lady, we've been through this before. You need to be in school. And while you live with Aunt Barbara, you can go to school with your cousins."

"What if I don't like our teacher? What if she's mean?"

"Then you'll treat her nice, anyway. Just like your mamma would."

A stagecoach rumbled straight towards them, and Brazos drove the rig off the road to the right to allow the stage to gallop past.

Dacee June held on to his arm as they drove back onto the road. "Daddy, is Todd mad at you?"

"Darlin', Todd's not angry with me. We have a difference of opinion on the ranch, that's all."

"He told me he thought we should get Robert to come home from the army and chase those people off with guns."

"Dacee June, I can't shoot my neighbors. My daddy and their daddy settled this land when there was nothin' here but Comanches and famine. They made ranch country out of it. If we have to keep it by killin' neighbors and bankers and such, it's just not worth it."

"But it's our ranch!" she wailed. "They stole our cattle, run off our horses, burnt the hay barn, and then took it when we couldn't pay taxes that no one else had to pay anyway. That isn't fair."

Brazos glanced down at his worn, blue denim trousers and realized they were his best pair. "Dacee June, life isn't always fair," he mumbled.

"I don't understand."

14

"We just can't go around killin' people." He reached over and patted her narrow knee. "Mamma would understand."

"I wish Mamma was here."

"So do I, darlin', so do I."

A gunshot fired somewhere behind them. Brazos reined up and spun around, lifting the converted .50-caliber, saddle ring, Sharps carbine to his shoulder. When he saw the rider wave his hat from a hundred yards down the trail, Brazos lowered the gun and sat back down.

"Who is it, Daddy?"

"It's Big River Frank."

"Why do they call him 'Big River'?" She shaded her eyes with her hand and stared back down the trail. "He's a very short man. I'm almost as tall as him."

Brazos pushed his dark brown felt hat to the back of his head and waited for the approaching rider. "Well, darlin', cattlemen sometimes talk about a man who is such a good drover and such a courageous friend that he'd be a good man to cross a river with. Well, Frank has twice the courage and twice the loyalty as most, so they started sayin' he's a good one to help you across a big river. The name stuck. Ever'one calls him Big River Frank."

"What's his last name?"

"Well, I don't reckon I know that. He never told me."

"But he's been your friend for years!"

"I don't figure it's polite to ask."

"I'll ask him."

"Don't you dare, Dacee June. That would be a quick

way for you to get a spankin'. Don't ever ask personal questions."

"Is asking a person's name a personal question?"

"Sometimes it is."

The black Texas horse that Big River Frank rode was not more than fourteen-and-a-half hands, but it still seemed large next to the small frame of the rider. He had a thick bedroll tied on the cantle and a small sack of grain lashed in front of the fork of his saddle. A '73 Winchester carbine bounced in front of the saddle horn. His narrow face sported a three-day beard and a thick mustache. Big River's small brown eyes seemed locked in a permanent stare.

"You look like you're goin' on a trip," Brazos challenged.

"Me? Look at you. Got your belongings in the wagon and the pride of Coryell County ridin' beside you." Big River tipped his black felt hat. "Mornin', Miss Dacee June. You look as lovely as a river rose."

Dacee June grinned. "Thank you, Mr. Big River Frank."

Brazos slapped the reins and drove the buckboard east. "You didn't answer my question. Where are you headed?"

Big River Frank trotted the black horse alongside the wagon. "Where are *you* goin'?" he challenged back.

"I don't know," Brazos mumbled. "North . . . across the plains . . . out of Texas."

"What a coincidence. That's exactly where I'm goin'!" Big River beamed.

"You travelin' with me?"

"I heard you're leaving this fine young lady in Waco with her aunt."

"Just until he finds us a ranch," she insisted.

"Well, I figured without Miss Dacee June around, someone would have to look after the old man, and I'm volunteerin'."

"Old?" Brazos boasted. "I know some twenty-five-year-olds I can still whip."

"And I know a twenty-five-year-old who calls you Daddy," Big River countered.

Brazos took a deep breath and smiled. "Well, you're right about that."

"And I'm comin' with you. There's no way to get rid of me, and you know it."

Brazos unfastened the top button of his cotton shirt and rubbed his neck. "What about that freight job?"

"Quit the job and drew my back pay," Big River Frank announced.

"But you don't need to leave Texas."

"Neither do you. It's a big state. I know they stole your ranch because you opposed secession. But the war's been over for ten years. Other people around the state don't hold that kind of a grudge."

"You're whippin' a dead horse there, Big River. The question of leavin' Texas has already been decided."

"I know. . . . That's why I packed my gear. I always wanted to see that north country."

"I'm glad you're going with my father, Mr. Big River Frank," Dacee June said. "He'll need someone to talk to."

"Well, he's goin' to have his pick."

17

"What do you mean by that?" Brazos quizzed.

"Guess who I ran into down in Austin City last week?"

"Santa Anna?"

"Grass Edwards."

"Grass is in Austin City? I thought he was tryin' a hand at prospectin' out West."

"Yep, he's been in Nevada, but he's back. I invited them both to go north with us," Big River said.

"Both?" Brazos quizzed.

"He's got a partner named Hook Reed. He knows minin' claims like the back of his hand."

"Minin' claims? Why do we need to know that? I'm lookin' for a ranch, not minerals."

"Unless you inherited a bonanza I don't know about, we need capital," Big River reminded him. "If we're goin' to buy a place up north, we need money. We aren't going to make a dime of profit drivin' cattle for someone else. So I figured we'd find ourselves a gold claim and build up a little stake."

Brazos rubbed the sweat and grime off the back of his neck. "Where we goin' to find gold? Every square inch of the West has been picked through."

"Not every place. This guy Hook Reed knows a man who was with General Custer last year in the Black Hills of Dakota. Said there was gold in the streams just waitin' to be shoveled up and dumped into sacks."

"Nothin' is that easy."

"Maybe not, but this man, Hook Reed, has a map of the area and a gold strike marked right on it. It's a sure thing."

"Where'd he get such a map?"

"Won it in a poker game down in Tucson."

Brazos rubbed his eyes, then stared across the light green hills. "I read in the newspaper that Custer said there wasn't much gold in the Black Hills."

"What does the army know about prospectin'?"

"Well, if you and I know about it, so do others. There won't be any left on the ground when we get there."

"That's not true. Them hills is off-limits. It's Sioux land. Most men are afraid to ride in there for fear of gettin' scalped."

Brazos glanced down and could see worry in Dacee June's eyes. "And just how are we goin' to manage?" he probed.

"Old Hook's map shows a secret trail to get in followin' draws and gulches without giving away our position."

"I'm not really lookin' for a gold mine. I want a ranch," Brazos reiterated.

"Well, there ain't no one in the world that is going to hand us one. We have to buy it, and we need money for that. So unless you plan on robbin' banks, stages, or trains, we're going to need a stake."

"No bank robbin' for me . . . one Fortune in that business is one too many."

"Is Sam still on the run up in Indian Territory?"

"If he hasn't got himself killed." Brazos glanced down at Dacee June's wide eyes. "I didn't mean that, darlin'. Your brother is too good with a gun to get himself killed."

Big River Frank yanked his pant leg up over his boot

and scratched. "Are your other boys goin' with us?"

"Not this trip. Todd's drivin' cattle up to Dodge City for Ol' Bill Wilson, and Robert is still in the cavalry, stationed at Fort Abraham Lincoln."

"Where's that?"

"In Dakota Territory, up on the Missouri River."

"Well, that settles it. We'll look for gold, and you can visit your boy. That sounds like a nice summer."

"Daddy needs to find us a home!" Dacee June insisted. "He promised me that."

Big River Frank stared at her as he rode beside the wagon. "You're right, li'l darlin'. Did you ever know your daddy to break a promise?"

"Uh, no . . . not really."

"Neither have I. Him and me is from the old school. If we tell you we're goin' north to find you a home, jist as sure as the sun sets in El Paso, you're goin' to have a new home."

"Daddy's looking for a ranch under a big cross."

"Well, how do we know it's not in the Black Hills?" Big River insisted. "Grass and Hook will join us in Fort Worth, Brazos. They said we can pick up some minin' gear in Denver or Cheyenne City."

"I didn't say I was goin' prospectin'."

"I know," Big River pushed his pant leg down, then picked his teeth with his fingernail. "But, jist in case we decide to get rich, we'll be ready."

The home of Dr. and Mrs. Milton Ferrar was the largest one on the confluence of Rio Bosque, three miles northwest of Waco. The upstairs, alone, contained eight bedrooms. Most times, all the rooms were filled.

Besides raising nine children of their own, numerous relatives, guests, and occasional strangers stayed the night at the Ferrar place. Brazos figured his sister-in-law, Barbara, just might be the hardest-working woman in Texas.

He knew, for sure, she was the most organized and gracious.

Barbara did not follow the rules of Texas society. She made the rules. In the Ferrar household, children ate first, not last, leaving the adults a more leisurely meal. And Barbara insisted that the men could not excuse themselves to the parlor after supper, but must remain in the dining room and visit with the ladies as well as each other.

She preferred that the men wore suits and ties at the evening meal. However, her sister's husband, Brazos Fortune, looked so ill at ease in a suit, she allowed him to have supper wearing a vest instead of a jacket.

And a tie.

Big River Frank left for Fort Worth after a quick cup of coffee, and Dr. Ferrar was still in town. The kids laughed and shouted in the yard. That left Brazos alone in the dining room with his sister-in-law. Four kerosene lanterns flickered above the table as Brazos studied the china and silver.

Barbara Ferrar buzzed out the swinging door that separated the kitchen from the dining room. She carried linen napkins and silver napkin holders.

"You're makin' a lot of fuss tonight for the likes of

me," Brazos complained.

His sister-in-law was the only person, other than his wife, who ever called him by his Christian name. "Henry Fortune, you listen to me." Her long skirt rustled, and he smelled sweet rose perfume as she sashayed around the long room. "You are leaving the sweetest daughter on the face of the earth to go off, Lord knows where, and have no idea when you will return—if you do at all. You will probably eat undercooked food out of poorly washed tin plates, if you eat off a plate at all. We are certainly going to use the best china!"

Though she was ten years his junior, he felt properly scolded. "Yes, ma'am," he replied. "But I am comin' back for Dacee June. Soon as I get us a place up north. It will probably be in September, but I didn't tell her that. Don't want to make a promise I might not be able to keep."

"I can't understand why anyone would want to leave Texas. Milton says you should take them to court to get the ranch back. They have no legal right to do what they've done."

"No local judge is going to help me, and it would take years to get it to an appeals court. By then Dacee June would be a grown woman, and the boys with families of their own. I think this is best."

She stopped her fussing and stood next to him. "You could just shoot them all."

He looked into her perfectly round green eyes. "Now, do you think Sarah Ruth would want me to do that?" Her eyes began to tear up.

She reached up, hugged his shoulders, and kissed his

cheek. Then she wiped her eyes with a rolled-up, white linen napkin. "I miss her, too, Henry."

His voice was almost a whisper. "I know."

She continued setting the table. "When I was in the East, I read an article in a New York newspaper about a medical procedure that, when perfected, might cure cancers forever. They said it was five years away from being usable."

"That makes it eight years too late."

"And you're right about Sarah Ruth. She would never want you to start a war over that ranch. All that girl ever wanted in her life was to live a quiet and godly life, taking care of her children and her man. Oh my, how she loved you, Henry Fortune."

"I still love her."

"I know . . . I know. Did I ever tell you how she made me stay up with her all night on the day you two met?"

"All night?" Brazos replied. "As I remember, I brought her home from that church supper by nine o'clock."

"Oh, you brought her home. But she claimed to have such an ache in her heart for you, that she was afraid it would stop beating in the night and she would very probably die. I had to sleep with her and check to see that her heart was still beating."

"You're stringing me along, Barbara Ferrar."

One glare from his sister-in-law made the hair on the back of his neck curl. He knew she was extremely serious.

He changed the subject. "You're settin' up for eight of us. Not includin' the kids, I count you and Milt,

Granny Young, Reverend Smithwick, Miss Adaline Crosley, and me. That's only six. You having other company tonight?"

"Didn't I tell you the March sisters are stopping by?" she hummed.

Brazos tugged at his black tie. "Eh, no . . . you seemed to have forgotten to tell me about the March sisters."

"Well, they saw me at the grocery store in town, and when they found out you were going to be here for supper, they practically invited themselves. You know how the March sisters were such good friends with Sarah Ruth."

"They haven't been 'March' sisters in over thirty years."

"Isn't that strange how we still remember some people by their maiden names? They were our next-door neighbors for fifteen years. When was the last time you saw them?"

"I reckon at Sarah Ruth's funeral. I don't remember much about that day," he admitted.

"You didn't attend Leonard Driver's funeral?"

"That was when I was up in the Territory, tryin' to find Samuel, remember?"

"It was a very nice service. Not like Sarah Ruth's, of course. But nice, nonetheless. I was nine months along with Flora Doe when Mr. Speaker was laid to rest. You and Sarah Ruth went, as I remember."

"We surely did."

"What with their children all grown and living in the East, the March sisters mainly just have each other. It's too bad, both of them losing their husbands at such a young age."

"Young? Both of them are only a few years behind me," Brazos reminded her.

"That's what I mean," she purred. "Way too young to spend the rest of your life unmarried."

"Why do I get this feelin' I should have left for Fort Worth with Big River Frank?"

"Hush! I'll expect you to be cordial and gregarious for the March sisters. Do you understand?"

"Yes, ma'am."

Louise March Driver was one year and one day older than her sister. From the day their mother died, Louise had assumed the role of supervisor and counselor to Thelma. Louise had worn her long, straight black hair wrapped tightly on top her head since her school days. Her small brown eyes always sparkled, and her narrow-lipped smile revealed straight white teeth and a warmth that disarmed many a cold, tough male. She stood several inches taller than her sister.

Thelma March Speaker often allowed her curly, sandy blonde hair to billow down her back. In her late thirties her hair began to show a little gray, but no one had seen a gray hair on her head since . . . nor did they ask why. Her young-girl-smooth skin was the envy of most women over forty in central Texas. Her wide, full-lipped smile and her ability to properly fill out a dress still often turned men's heads in a crowded room, some much younger than Thelma.

At the far end of the table sat Dr. Milton Ferrar, who

spent the entire day doctoring people and every evening talking politics to anyone who would listen and to many who didn't.

To his right was Barbara's place setting. However, she spent most of the evening scooting between the cook and the table. Next to her was her mother, affectionately called Granny Young. She had decided to stop wearing her false teeth on her seventy-fifth birthday, and to cease talking on the seventy-sixth. She always seemed happy, with her pleasant, toothless smile and voracious appetite.

On Milton Ferrar's left was a seminary-trained, twenty-six-year-old Methodist clergyman, Reverend Rodney Smithwick. Other than the few moments he bowed his head to say grace, he never took his eyes off Miss Adaline Crosley, the recently appointed schoolteacher and permanent houseguest, who sat next to him and seemed to delight in the attention she received.

As Brazos expected, Barbara seated him at the far end of the table—with Louise Driver on one side, Thelma Speaker on the other.

Milton Ferrar, finding no one near him to talk politics, spent most of the evening shouting bits of conversation down the full length of the table. "Brazos, did you read about those doings in Europe?"

Brazos stared across a forkful of pot roast. "I don't reckon I did. They didn't start a war, did they?"

"Not yet, but who knows," Milton called out. "They're having riots over there in Bosnia and Herzegovina against the sultan. Those Turks should never be in Europe in the first place!"

"I don't suppose there's too much anyone can do about that," Brazos called back.

Louise Driver reached her hand over to Brazos's arm. "You know, Mr. Fortune, I think it is terribly exciting what you're doing."

"Exciting?" he said.

"Imagine packing up and moving to the wilds of Montana! It's very courageous. Why, the most adventuresome thing Thelma and I ever do is our yearly train ride to the East Coast to visit the children."

"I'm not sure, exactly, where I'll find a place," Brazos replied. "It might not be Montana. Perhaps it will be in Wyoming, or Dakota . . . or even Idaho."

"Idaho?" Thelma Speaker gasped. "Good grief, who would move to such a primitive place as that?"

"Now, Thelma," Louise cautioned. "We know people who have moved to Idaho."

"Who?"

"Our neighbor, Mr. Abbney, remember?"

"He was a cattle rustler and a murderer!"

"Yes, dear, but he took very good care of his garden. Remember those carrots he brought us?"

"Brazos," Milton Ferrar hollered, "what kind of job do you think this man, Disraeli, will do as prime minister in England? It sounds rather chancy to me, a man of his age."

"I've never really understood English politics," Brazos shouted back. "I thought he was prime minister once before."

Milton stabbed a large bite of mashed potatoes and brown gravy. "He was . . . back in '68. It didn't work

27

out. I know what you mean! My sentiments exactly. They need American democracy over there, that's what they need!"

Thelma cleared her throat, then blurted out. "I hear that since his wife died, Mr. Disraeli has been seeing Lady Chesterfield."

"Oh no, dear," Louise corrected. "He's quite smitten with her sister, Lady Bradford."

Brazos focused on the pot roast.

Louise's hand still on his left arm, Thelma Speaker reached over and took his right hand. "Mr. Fortune, how long will you be gone north?" she asked.

"He's going to move, dear," Louise informed.

"Well, he's not officially moved until he comes back for sweet little Dacee June. When do you intend to come back?"

Brazos looked at Thelma, then Louise. "In a few months."

"That will be nice," Louise tugged on his left arm. "You will have to come over and let us cook you some supper on your return."

"Yes, indeed," Thelma echoed.

"Well, if I have time, I'll certainly plan on that."

"Oh, that will be marvelous. Do you like homemade noodles?" Louise asked.

"Yes, and I . . ." he tried to raise his fork to his mouth, but Thelma Speaker didn't release her grip.

"Let's see, several months . . . oh . . . we will have fresh fruit by then. Would you like a berry or a peach cobbler?"

"I, eh . . . ladies, don't go to any trouble . . . I don't

know if I'm even goin' to . . ."

"Oh, for goodness sake, Thelma," Louis insisted, "we'll just make one of each!"

"Yes, yes . . . that's what we'll do!"

"Brazos, have you ever read anything by this young man, Twain?" Doc Ferrar boomed across the room. "He's written a book or two. He's quite humorous, you know. All those Missourians are."

"Other than the Bible, I haven't had time to read anything in the past couple years." Brazos glanced over at the Reverend who was oblivious to all conversation, other than the muted whispers of Miss Adaline Crosley.

Finally, the ladies released his arms. He and the pot roast renewed their acquaintance.

"You know, Louise," Thelma began. "We should just take a little trip out west ourselves."

"You mean go to San Francisco?"

"Well, at least we could go to Denver, Cheyenne . . . Helena," Thelma suggested.

"Doesn't Helena sound like a lovely place? It sounds so cultured . . . so Grecian."

"Actually," Brazos corrected, "if you want to pronounce it correctly, you put the accent on the first syllable."

"Oh, my!" Thelma's hand flew up to her mouth. "Dear me," she began to giggle. "Perhaps we shouldn't go there."

"Some of the West is still pretty undomesticated," Brazos cautioned.

"Now, Mr. Fortune, if it's tame enough for Dacee

June to go live, it would be tame enough for us to visit."

"You have a point there," he conceded.

"Brazos," Ferrar called out, "did you know they started a medical school in London just for women?"

"Sounds very progressive."

"Too blasted progressive, if you ask me," Dr. Ferrar hollered.

"I think it's marvelous," Barbara Ferrar added, as she carried the silver tureen full of steaming vegetables towards the far end of the table.

"You know," Thelma Speaker suggested, "if you, Dacee June, and the boys were settled in Wyoming when we take our little western excursion, I'd stop by for a visit."

"Don't you mean, we'd have to stop by?" Louise corrected.

"Oh, yes . . . of course that's what I meant."

"Ladies, I'm not at all sure where we'll have our place or where it will be, but you are *both* invited to come for a visit," Brazos offered.

"That settles it. We'll come for a sojourn," Louise rejoiced, then looked across the table. "I do hope you aren't having those spells still," she nodded to her sister.

"Spells?" Brazos asked.

Louise leaned forward in a hushed whisper, "Thelma's going through the Change of Life, you know."

Brazos flushed and was thrilled to hear Milton's baritone voice boom out, "I hear there's a rebellion down in Cuba. That island always seems to be the

30

center of turmoil. Have you ever been there, Brazos?"

"No, but then I've never been to Florida, either."

"Don't go to Florida. If the mosquitoes don't carry you off, the alligators will! It's a worthless land. One big swamp and a little sand. I don't know how the Spanish ever suckered us into takin' it off their hands. An ol' boy from New York City came out here tryin' to sell me a hundred acres of beach. Can you imagine the gall? Can't farm sand, I told him. Can't graze cows in the swamps. It will never be good for anything."

"I'll remember that."

"Pass Mamma the potatoes," Barbara signaled. "I believe she's still hungry."

"Granny Young hasn't been full since '59," Milton roared.

Everyone at the table laughed.

Including Granny.

Brazos hugged a teary-eyed Dacee June Fortune in her bed before daylight the next day and rode north towards Fort Worth. He hoped to make the nearly one-hundred-mile journey in one day. He'd have to push his dark sorrel geldings to reach town before dark.

It felt warmer than April should be. He pulled off his coat before noon. The traffic on the road increased a little as he rode north out of Hill County. Most of the day he kept wide of the others on the trail.

His Sharps carbine bouncing on his lap, he trotted north, his mind wandering from Wyoming to Waco.

Lord, leavin' Dacee June was the second hardest thing I've ever done in my life. I told her over and over ever'thing's fine, but you and I know it truly could be the last time I ever see her.

Where did this thing go wrong?

It was supposed to be me and Sarah Ruth, some babies, and a nice little spread down on the Leon River. We weren't goin' to bother no one. Just work and love and go to church on Sundays. A simple life.

Then came the war. A man had to choose.

The war cost ever'one somethin'.

It cost me the lives of two beautiful little girls who died of smallpox down on the border. Sarah Ruth lost the sparkle in her eyes in Brownsville. Too ashamed to come home, Sammy went on the owlhoot trail. It's like we lost a son, too. We came back to squatters livin' on our ranch. Neighbors who hated us. A bank that was set to ruin us.

Then, Sarah Ruth came down with the cancer.

Now Lord, I'm not sayin' that it's not fair. No, sir. Fairness is your business, and I probably couldn't spot it if it stared me in the face.

Sometimes I think I'm goin' north just to speed up things.

There are worse things than dyin'. Like losin' my Sarah Ruth. And sayin' good-bye to Dacee June.

If a man is given a certain number of tough times, I think I used mine up already.

Take care of my baby girl, Lord. She's the reason I get up in the mornin' and keep pushin' myself.

I'm gettin' tired, Lord. Way too tired for a man of forty-nine.

Big River Frank, Grass Edwards, and a extremely thin man introduced as Hooker Reed were waiting on the bench in front of the Ranger's Roost Cottage when

Brazos rode into Fort Worth. They spent half the night pouring coffee and poring over maps of the North. After selecting a route through the Llano Estacado and up to Denver, then on to Cheyenne City, they eyed the 40-by-120-mile stretch of western Dakota called the Black Hills. The entire area was marked "Sioux Indian Reservation."

"It don't seem right to go in there, if the government says we can't," Big River mildly protested.

Hook Reed jabbed his fingers at several places on the map. "They're going in from Cheyenne, Sidney, from Fort Pierre and Fort Abe Lincoln. Trust me, boys, the government don't care. Shoot, it was Custer who went in there and brought out the report of gold. He ain't goin' to come kick us out. I say if we don't get in there by Christmas, there won't be any claims left. I was too late to the Comstock, too late to Alder's Gulch, and too late to the Salmon River. I ain't goin' to miss this one."

"I heard they might open it up by this summer. Could be that question is solved by the time we get there," Grass Edwards added.

Big River Frank rubbed his freshly shaven, pointed chin. "What do you think, Brazos?"

Brazos tugged off his gold-framed spectacles and rubbed the bridge of his nose. "Boys, somewhere up there is a place the Lord has for me. I'm goin' north to find it. Might be Wyoming. Might be Montana. Might be the Black Hills. I'll know it when I see it."

"Brazos got a sign from the Lord," Big River reported.

"What kind of sign?" Grass Edwards asked.

Brazos stared across the room. "I don't want to sound fanatical, but I had this dream about a big cross and . . ."

"A cross?" Hook Reed shouted. "You're lookin' for a cross? Look here!" He unrolled a crude map etched out on buckskin. "This gold claim is beneath a Dakota cross! Right out on the bluff above the creek this old boy drew a cross. Do you see that!"

Brazos studied the map. "That's not exactly what I envisioned. Some gulch on Indian Reserve Land isn't ranch country."

"But it is a cross!" Hook insisted.

"Might be a good place to start lookin'," Big River offered.

"I suppose headin' for one destination is better than havin' none at all," Fortune admitted.

Brazos had never been in two barns that were exactly the same.

But every barn had the same smell.

Leather.

Hay.

Sweaty horseflesh.

Manure.

For him it was the smell of home. It was still mostly dark when he led his packhorse, Mud, out of the livery stable and tied him to a corner of the corral. Coco, the other dark sorrel gelding, pranced at the touch of the saddle blanket on his back. He snorted when the cold bit was slipped into his mouth and tugged back at the feel of the girth yanked tight.

With the morning drift from the north a little chilly,

the blanket-lined coat felt comfortable. As Brazos waited for the other three to saddle, he pulled off his dark brown, wide-brimmed hat and ran his fingers through his clean hair that looked increasingly gray.

Well, I'm ridin' out of Texas, Daddy . . . and I hope you understand why I just couldn't stay. For you it was the promised land, but the Lord's promised me something else.

He untied Mud's lead rope, then swung up in the saddle on Coco. He pulled his carbine out of the scabbard and laid it across his lap, just as Big River Frank rode out of the barn. "Well, Brazos, are you ready for a long trip north?"

"Are you Brazos Fortune?" It was a high-pitched, nervous voice.

Brazos turned back towards the street. He spotted a medium-built man in a custom wool suit, vest, tie, crisp bowler hat, and a silver badge pinned to his pocket.

"I presume you ain't been in Texas too long," Big River called out. "You pronounce his name Braa-zis . . . just like the river."

The well-dressed man ignored Big River Frank. "I'm from Illinois and unfamiliar with Texas rivers, but that don't matter. I asked you a question. Are you Brazos Fortune from Coryell County?"

"I reckon that's me. What can I do for you, Deputy Constable?"

As the policeman watched Grass Edwards and Hook Reed ride up alongside Big River Frank, four guns became visible.

"Eh, well . . ." He pulled a paper out of his vest pocket. "I have a telegram here from the sheriff of

Coryell County saying I should detain Mr. Brazos Fortune in Fort Worth, pending his arrival."

"What on earth for?" Brazos asked.

"It mentions failure to pay some sort of loyalty tax."

Brazos took a deep breath, then stared up to a mostly clear, breaking daylight sky. He rode his horse forward past the lawman, and the other three swung in beside him.

"Where do you think you're goin'?" the deputy constable shouted.

"We're leavin' Texas," Brazos called back.

"You can't! You have to wait for the sheriff of Coryell County!"

Brazos stopped and turned in the saddle to face the man who now had a .32 caliber revolver in his hand, pointed down at the dirt. "I have strict instructions to keep you in town and to impound your saddle, horse, and gear, including that Sharps. They will sell them at auction to repay the back taxes."

Brazos rubbed his hand across his mouth, glanced over at Big River Frank, then back at the constable. "Son, I appreciate your enthusiasm. I'm a law-abidin' man myself. As Big River can testify, the folks down in Coryell County ran off my cattle, burnt my barn, and illegally appropriated my ranch. This horse and this gear and this gun is about all I have left in the world. I'm not givin' them up to you. I'm not givin' them up to any man." The carbine across his lap pointed in the general direction of the deputy constable. Brazos cocked the hammer with his thumb.

The deputy took a couple steps back, but left his

own gun in hand, hanging at his side.

"You cain't leave town! You're a wanted man!"

"Son, I don't know if you're goin' to lift that gun and pull that trigger or not. If you are, hurry up and do it. But I guarantee that when that gun gets pointed at me, I'm goin' to pull this trigger."

"Are you threatenin' me?" he screamed.

"No, sir. I'm just trying to avoid either of us gettin' hurt. Do you think this horse and saddle are worth either of us gettin' shot?"

"Eh, no . . . I reckon I don't."

"Good," Brazos said. "Now, we're goin' to ride out of town. Why don't you go have a cup of coffee to settle down those shakes of yours?"

All four men and the packhorse rode past the constable, who now trotted down the dirt road beside them.

"But . . . but . . . what will I tell the sheriff of Coryell County?" he cried out.

"Tell him you chased me out of Texas and threatened to arrest me if I ever set foot in Fort Worth again."

The deputy stopped his jogging. "Yeah . . . that's right . . . I did, didn't I? And don't you come back to Fort Worth again!" he shouted.

A slight grin broke across Brazos's face as he eased the hammer down on the carbine and kicked his spurs into Coco's flanks.

Chapter Two

Near Lightning Creek, southern Black Hills,
Dakota Territory, August 2, 1875

"Wake up, Brazos, I think I'm in love!" The voice rolled across camp like a gravelly serenade.

If it had been May or June, Brazos Fortune would have grabbed his Sharps carbine and yanked back the hammer before investigating the shout. Reaching the Black Hills unscathed, the quartet had been confident of rapid riches. In those early days, a big gold strike was just around the corner, untold wealth only hours away, and every disturbance a signal of a possible intruder, a thief . . . or both.

But now such enthusiasm was buried somewhere in the muck and the mud of western Dakota Territory.

Brazos slowly pulled himself out of his damp bed. For sixty-seven straight days he had risen to the sound of rain dripping from the roof of the dirty canvas tent onto his damp, mildewed bedroll.

On this day, it finally stopped raining.

It snowed.

Brazos briefly thought about combing his hair, then jammed his mud-caked-brown felt hat down on his head. His hair felt dirty and greasy. "You find yourself a woman, Grass?" The words broke out of his mouth like thin ice cracking underfoot after a light freeze.

"Not yet, but I got evidences," Edwards shouted back.

"Evidences of a woman?" Brazos contemplated an image of a blue silk dress . . . a sweet, shy smile . . . and a sailboat ride on Galveston Bay.

"Yep. I've got evidence here in my hand. I'll build up the fire. You come on out, and I'll show ya the proof!"

The peace of the east Texas portrait faded from Brazos Fortune's mind. *Sarah Ruth, you always were one handsome woman!*

With narrow, blue-gray eyes creased by nearly fifty years of outdoor work and worry, Brazos peered out at the snow-covered ground west of the creek. Their tents were pitched at the base of the rimrock on the west side of the gulch. Even though the sun was blocked by East Mountain, daylight had broken, and an inch of fresh, clean snow radiated light from the unseen sun. Still sleeping in the tent was a gaunt, black-bearded Hook Reed, his filthy, gray wool blanket pulled up to his chin. His eyes were so sunken, his cheeks so caved in, that he looked more like a corpse than a prospector.

Brazos squeezed his own right wrist with calloused fingers, trying to wrench the tightness out of his joints, then rubbed his beard away from narrow, chapped lips. *Darlin', I'm sure you got better things to do up there than torment my mind. Now, you run along and tell Veronica and Patricia "good mornin'" for me.*

In the neighboring canvas tent, Brazos heard the erratic gasps and snores of Big River Frank. The cascade of a little stream, bouncing through sluice boxes and over granite riffles, bubbled in the background. Across camp he heard the crunch of Grass Edwards's boot heels in the snow. Brazos pulled his own boots out from under the India rubber sheet that had almost kept them dry during the night. He sorted through a brown leather satchel and yanked out a pair of worn, slightly dirty socks, then sat on his bedroll and began to pull them on.

Now, Lord, I ain't arguin' with you. I followed your leadin' out of Texas to a place I didn't know. And I'm livin' in a tent in this promised land like a stranger in a foreign country. I haven't found my cross . . . I haven't found my ranch . . . we haven't even found Hook's Dakota cross. We're strugglin' just to survive day by day. If we would discover a little more color in the stream, we'd be rich enough to leave. This isn't exactly somethin' to write home about, let alone move your family to.

A sharp pain shot through Fortune's lower back. He stood and stretched just outside the tent flap. As usual, both his knees locked up stiff. It would take a half-mile of walking before they limbered up. He gingerly stooped back into the tent and plucked up his Sharps carbine, then hobbled over to the fire.

Both men had floppy beaver felt hats pulled down tight on unwashed hair. Edwards's long, full mustache drooped down past his chin and made him look permanently depressed. He was two inches shorter than Fortune and toted a Colt .44, hung by a wire loop to his leather belt. His hat forced his ears out, which widened his face and narrowed his round brown eyes.

Brazos tugged the coffeepot off the hook and plopped it down on the flames of the fire. "Now, what's this deluded shoutin' about being in love? Have you been isolated so long you're starting to believe your dreams? None of us has seen a woman in three months."

"One hundred and six days, unless that includes the Chief's wife, but she was covered up by a blanket and don't count," Grass informed. "Now, look at this!" He shoved a folded beige sheet of stiff paper into Fortune's hand. "What do you think?"

"A letter?"

"A notice," Edwards said.

"Where'd you get it?"

"Down at the post office tree."

"You're supposed to leave those notices posted," Brazos reminded him.

"I ain't sharin' her with no one else," Grass insisted. "And the only reason I'm tellin' you is because you're a widower and still consumed with your Sarah Ruth."

"You're beginnin' to sound desperate, partner. I hope the C hief doesn't bring his wife through here again." Brazos handed the notice back to Grass Edwards. "I don't have my specs on, so read it to me."

"You can see that fancy writin', can't you?"

"The penmanship is quite impressive." Brazos rolled a stump over to the flames and plopped down to stretch out his legs and massage his knees.

Grass cleared his throat, then hooked his left thumb into the pocket of his tattered leather coat.

41

"Listen to this."

My dearest friends,
If you know the whereabouts of my brother, Vince Milan,
please inform him that his baby sister is waiting in
Cheyenne with a surprise for him.
With much sincere affection and gratitude,
Jamie Sue Milan

A wide, easy smile broke across Brazos's bearded face. "You fell in love with a notice like that?"

Edwards stared at the handbill and sighed, "I've fallen in love with Jamie Sue."

"I believe you fell for her handwriting." Brazos tugged suspenders off his shoulders, then leaned over to rub rough and dirty fingers above the campfire's flame. "Maybe she can't write and had the man at the train station pen that note."

"Don't talk about my Jamie Sue like that," Edwards snapped. "I just know she's well educated, slim, and has long, curly yellow hair . . . and freckles."

"Where in that handbill does it say all that?"

"I'm readin' between the lines," Edwards insisted.

Brazos felt his stiff denim trousers begin to warm. "How do you know she's not sixty years old and fat?"

Grass Edwards leaned forward, elbow on his knee, chin on his palm. "After one hundred and six days, sixty and fat don't sound all that bad," he grinned. "Anyway, I'm keepin' this notice, and next time we're in Cheyenne, I'm lookin' up my Jamie Sue. The rest of you might want to live like hermits the rest of your lives, but I'm the marryin' type."

"You waited a long time to decide that," Brazos teased.

"How old were you when you married Sarah Ruth?"

"Twenty-two."

"See, that proves it. Ever'body knows I'm twice the man you are, so I should wait until I'm forty-four."

"Well, you'd better hurry. That leaves you less than a year."

"I reckon I'll wait until the next time I'm in Cheyenne."

"You figure Jamie Sue's the one?"

"It's destiny."

"What were you doin' down at the message tree, anyway?"

"Lookin' for dry wood."

"Did you see either of the Jims stirring around?" Brazos probed.

"Just Quiet Jim."

"Did he say anything about fixin' my pick?"

"Quiet Jim don't ever say nothin'. But it's a good thing I went down there. There's a miners' meetin' at Sidwell's posted for today."

"Today?" Brazos snatched up a tin cup with his left hand, and the coffeepot with his right, then poured himself a steaming cup. "That don't give us five days' notice."

"Nope. Must be an emergency meetin'. You want me to go wake Big River and Hook?"

"Let them sleep until breakfast is fryin', anyways. With snow on the ground, it doesn't feel like August."

Several of Grass Edwards's fingers poked through his leather gloves as he poured himself some coffee. "We done jumped from spring rains to fall snow. You reckon these Black Hills just don't have any summer?"

Brazos Fortune's canvas coat was nearly frozen stiff as he beat it against his legs to loosen the sleeves, then pulled it on. "It's bound to get better. Can't go on like this much longer."

"That's what you've been saying ever since we left the Staked Plains," Grass Edwards reminded him.

Brazos brushed his fingers through the hair hanging over his ear and picked out a pine needle. "Well, one of these days I'll be right."

Edwards whisked some weeds off a stick of wood, then shoved it into the fire. He plucked up a weed and waved it at Fortune. "Did I tell you the *spartina pectinata* is starting to mold?"

Brazos took a slow sip of coffee and let the radiant heat warm his face. "I believe you've mentioned it, day and night, for two weeks."

Edwards pulled off his dark brown hat and waved it at the picket line of horses. "Well, if we can't cut cordgrass for winter feed, them horses is goin' to have a rough winter."

Brazos studied the low-hanging clouds. "Unless we have some sunlight in the sky, and more gold in the streams, we're all goin' to have a rough winter. I don't know how I let you three talk me into comin' up here anyway."

Grass Edwards yanked off his stovetop boots and tugged off his dirty wool socks. "You figure we'll winter it out up in these hills? The Jims and some others are talkin' about pullin' out in November."

"I was thinkin' about just cuttin' a swath across Wyoming and Montana. There's a cross waitin' up there for me someplace. And underneath it, there's a ranch."

"What about that Dakota cross on Hook's map?"

"We haven't come close to findin' it."

"Maybe we should go to Texas for the winter. I don't mind tellin' you a warm gulf breeze would feel mighty fine about now."

"You all can go back, but I don't think anyone wants to see me in Coryell County, Texas. Or anywhere else."

Grass Edwards's penetrating stare seemed to be locked onto Brazos's eyes. "I understand there's a young lady in McLennan County that wants to see you."

Brazos Fortune felt extremely tired. "Yeah, you're right. I'd go back to Texas to see Dacee June."

"Now, that's where you got us all beat, Brazos. Ever'one of us would give our right arm to have a daughter like that pinin' for us."

"Don't get me in a sentimental mood, Grass. I'm liable to saddle that dark sorrel and ride south."

"You wouldn't go alone. But if we weren't scalped, we'd probably starve to death before we got to Kansas."

"I don't think I could ever leave her again. That's why I can't go back now," Brazos admitted. "I need to find that ranch, then go fetch Dacee June."

"Gold diggin's a disease. We barely find enough to

survive, but it always seems like a big strike is just around the corner. So we keep holdin' on like the last leaf of winter," Grass said.

"And this is summer."

"That's snow on the ground, Brazos."

"Well, it keeps the place from gettin' too crowded, doesn't it?"

Grass glanced up at the morning sun that was barely peeking over the east rim of the gulch. "Hard to imagine the Lord leading anyone to a place like this, ain't it?"

"I don't reckon this is the destination . . . just a rest stop on the journey."

"Rest stop? I ain't ever worked harder than I have the last two or three months. Look at you. I've seen better lookin' specimens on the prairie after longhorns stampeded over them."

Brazos rubbed his eyes. There was a deep, throbbing ache in his legs. "I didn't sleep much last night."

"You ain't slept more than four hours a night since we left Texas."

"Just old age, I suppose."

"You ain't that old."

"How many men older have we met in the Black Hills?" Brazos challenged.

Grass Edwards rocked back on the stump and studied the flames. "Well, there's Pop Richards, for one."

"And?"

"Well . . . I'm, eh, sure there's others."

"Pop's two years younger than me," Brazos said.

46

"You don't say?" Grass Edwards stuck his little finger in his ear as if trying to improve his hearing. "Ever'one of us is going to age in a hurry if we have to go through the winter in these tents."

"If we find some rich diggin's, we can pull up a cabin come fall," Brazos said.

"Sure, and maybe we'll find enough gold by November so that we'll need an army escort across the plains!" Grass draped his socks over his bare toes, then roasted them over the campfire. "It would help if the government would open this land up, and keep the Sioux back out in the badlands."

Brazos circled the rim of his blue, enameled tin cup with his bare fingers. "They open this reservation land up and there'll be ten thousand bummers rushin' up and down every gulch in these hills. We got here at the right time, if there's anything to get."

"There are still some new ones movin' in," Grass added. "There was four sets of tracks around the message tree. I didn't recognize the prints. They looked like big, old Montana horses."

"Shod or unshod?"

"They wasn't Indian ponies, if that's what you mean."

"Where did they trail to?"

"North towards the pass," Grass said.

"There aren't any more decent claims left open up there," Brazos reported. "You figure they just rode by us in the night?"

"I reckon it was near daylight. There wasn't much snow in their tracks," Grass Edwards reported.

47

"Probably in a hurry to find their spot. Maybe they're going to open a new district. Everybody seems to have a secret location only they know about," Brazos said.

"Like Hook and his fool map?"

"Yep."

Grass Edwards leaned across the fire and whispered, "Don't tell the others, but I'm beginnin' to doubt Hook's story. If there's a big strike somewhere's under a Dakota cross, what in the world are we doin' camped out in the snow right here?"

"I figure it's like havin' an ace up your sleeve. You don't want to cash it in until you're sure it will win the pot," Brazos pondered.

"Well, Hook ain't talked much about his treasure map in the past few weeks."

Although the clouds above hung low and heavy, the snow ceased and the fire began to draw steam out of Fortune's damp, denim trousers. "He hasn't talked much at all about anything for days."

Grass Edwards leaned close and again spoke softly. "Hook ain't lookin' so good. You reckon he's gettin' dysentery or ague?"

"I don't know what he's got," Brazos admitted. "Ever'day he seems to be worse. I sure wish he would've gone down to Utah in July like he said. Maybe those hot, dry days would suit him better." Brazos finished his coffee and plopped his tin cup on a rock. "I'll stir up some fry bread. You tell Big River and Hook about the miners' meeting. Maybe we ought to ride on down to the stockade after the meeting and see

48

if some supplies have come in. We're runnin' low."

"I'll wake 'em." Edwards tugged on his boots, then folded the paper and crammed it back into his coat pocket. "But don't you tell them about my Jamie Sue."

A small patch of blue sky broke through the heavy, gray clouds as Brazos Fortune, Big River Frank, and Grass Edwards plodded horseback along the trail down Lightning Creek. Thirty- to forty-foot Ponderosa pines were scattered ten to fifteen feet apart along the trail. As they serpentined around each claim, other prospectors joined in their descent, making it look like a miners' parade.

Yapper Jim rode his swayback pinto mare beside Fortune. His neatly trimmed sideburns swung down to his chin and blended with the whiskers on his chin, from a distance resembling a circus clown's painted smile. "Brazos, how's Hook this mornin'? He didn't die on us, did he?"

Fortune allowed the wooden forearm of his Sharps carbine to rest on the saddle horn. "Nope, he's not dead, but he's got the chills this mornin', so we wrapped him in mostly dry blankets and left him in camp."

"I once had a friend in Bannock who was as healthy as a horse, took a chill one night and by sunrise he was deader than a New England camp meeting." Yapper Jim pulled a plug of unwrapped tobacco out of his vest pocket and bit off a sizable chew.

The dirty cotton shirt rubbed under Brazos's suspenders. "I reckon he'll pull through. Hook's a tough man."

"Ain't that the truth? Last fall, me and Hook was sitting in a card room down in Tucson, when Doc Kabyo and that bunch starts a ruckus right there at the poker table. Before the gunsmoke cleared, Hook had taken two bullets in the shoulder, and I had one in my foot. But you should have seen Kabyo hightail it out of there . . . now stop me if I told you this one before . . . why even though he carried two bullets, Hook was . . ."

"I've heard it."

"You have?"

"A dozen times," Brazos said.

"You don't say? That story does get around."

"Hook never mentions Kabyo," Brazos informed. "You told it to me."

"All twelve times?"

"Yep."

"You want to hear it again?" Yapper Jim pressed.

"Nope."

Yapper Jim studied Brazos's face. "You know, that reminds me of the time I was in the Bulldog Saloon in Wichita when J. B. Hickok told me that I'd better . . ."

"I heard that one, too, Yapper Jim."

"But you ain't heard it as often."

Brazos studied the heavy, dark clouds that had held back their moisture since daybreak.

"Am I right?" Yapper Jim insisted. "You ain't heard the Hickok story as often as you heard the Doc Kabyo one?"

Fortune didn't answer but spurred his dark brown horse to catch up with Big River Frank.

Yapper Jim trotted up alongside of him. "You ain't much of a talker, are you, Brazos?"

"Sorry, Yapper Jim, I'm worried about Hook," Fortune reported. "If you want to gab, ride up there with Grass Edwards and ask him about the *spartina pectinata*."

"The what?"

"Cordgrass."

"Shoot, all he talks about is them blasted weeds. I've heard all of them stories a hundred times before. A man is lucky to slide one or two words between the cracks."

"Don't rate yourself so low, Yapper. I figure you can talk circles around Grass Edwards."

A wide grin broke across the big man's lips and yellow teeth. "You're right about that. I am a mighty good talker. See you at the meetin', Brazos."

Fortune tipped his hat to Yapper Jim and watched him ride up the trail. Big River Frank, whose boots covered his trousers almost up to his knees, waited astride his lanky black horse for Brazos to catch up.

"You figured out this meetin' yet?" Big River asked.

"I'm guessin' another bunch is pullin' out of the hills and wants a few more guns to keep them company across the plains," Brazos speculated.

"If that's all it is, they shouldn't have called a meetin'. We could be workin' our diggin's a few hours without it rainin' or snowin'."

"We haven't had a meetin' in three weeks," Brazos added.

"And we didn't need a meetin' that time, neither . . .

51

they was done scalped before we got to them."

"Maybe it won't be wasted. If someone brought in supplies to Gordon's Stockade, we'll ride on down there."

For the first time all morning, Big River's face lit up. "Wouldn't that be nice? What if they have some sugar?"

"Might as well hope for the best," Fortune said.

The Discovery claim on Lightning Creek was about two miles above its confluence with French Creek. A wide meadow stretched along the stream, providing a much more open landscape than the narrow gulch along Texas Camp, as Fortune's claim was called by the other miners. At the Discovery claim, the only log building in the Lightning Creek Mining District had been erected. It was a ten-by-fifteen-foot log house occupied by Ernie Sidwell, Beartooth Adair, and Old Dan Blackwell. On occasion, they brought supplies up from the stockade and it served as an extremely informal business establishment.

During storms, all mining district meetings were held inside Sidwell's cabin. If the weather was tolerable, the men met outside around the fire pit. When Brazos, Grass Edwards, Big River Frank, and the others reached the cabin, most of the prospectors were already gathered around the bonfire located only steps away from the uncovered front porch of the cabin.

About two dozen men were present by the time they loosened the girths and turned the horses out into the crude corral. There were only a half dozen animals in the pen. Most of the men had hiked to the meeting.

Brazos studied the tired eyes, and dirty, unkept faces

of the men who warmed their bones and dried their clothing around the fire. They came in different shapes and sizes, but each one displayed worry on his face and a weapon in his hand.

It was the district president, Ernie Sidwell, who climbed up on the stump and quieted them.

"Have we got us a hostile war party comin' this way, Ernie?" Yapper Jim shouted.

"Let your guns rest easy, boys. I don't think we're in for a fight just yet. I know we ain't had five days' notification of this meetin', and therefore we won't be changing any laws or doin' any votin'. But I decided these matters wouldn't wait."

"Those six Alabama boys ain't here yet," someone called out. "Maybe we ought to wait for them."

Sidwell pulled off his mud-splattered, black felt hat, revealing a tangled mass of gray hair and a bald spot on top his head. "They ain't goin' to be here. We got word from the stockade that two freight wagons left Fort Laramie and were headed this way. The Alabama men went all the way down to Cheyenne Crossing to help 'em ford the river. But Black Bear and his band attacked the wagons just as they was in the water and ever' last man, includin' our Alabama boys, was killed. One of 'em lived jist long enough to give us a report."

A roar crested in the crowd like a tidal wave at sea.

"Are we goin' after them?" someone shouted.

"That was six days ago. No tellin' where Black Bear is now. We surely ain't goin' out on the plains after that bunch. That would be like chasin' Br'er Rabbit into the briar patch."

"We need the army to move in here and protect us," someone else shouted.

Sidwell tried to quiet the crowd. "The army's not going to protect us as long as the map calls this Sioux Reservation. We all knew that when we moved in."

"You reckon we'll get more supplies before winter?" a tall, Arkansas man asked.

Big River Frank climbed up on the woodpile, where he towered above the others. "If you had a load of freight sittin' in Cheyenne City and heard about a massacre just south of the hills, would you come up here?"

Grass Edwards pulled out Jamie Sue's faded notice from his pocket, then shoved it back. "Maybe we should send a contingency to Cheyenne to buy our own supplies. I, for one, would volunteer."

"Good. Now we just need a hundred more guns to make it safe," a fat man shouted from the back of the crowd.

"We've got to get some flour, salt, and coffee," Quiet Jim mumbled.

"We need more mercury," Eggs Martin shouted. "I cain't separate my gold if I don't get more mercury. Any of you got any to sell?"

"If we don't find more color, we'll have plenty of mercury to sell," someone shouted from the cabin steps.

Sidwell waved his arms. "Boys, do your barterin' and jawin' later. Here's the important news. We was brought a handbill that I will post on the cabin, but you better hear it right now. It comes from Brigadier General George Crook, who is camped with his troops somewhere up near Bear Butte. I'll read it to you word for word."

Proclamation!
Whereas the President of the United States has directed that no miners, or other unauthorized citizens, be allowed to remain in the Indian reservation of the Black Hills, or in the unceded territory to the west, until some new treaty arrangements have been made with the Indians:

And whereas, by the same authority, the undersigned is directed to occupy said reservation and territory with troops, and to remove all miners and other unauthorized citizens, who may now, or may hereafter come into this country in violation of the treaty obligations:—

Therefore, the undersigned hereby requires every miner and other unauthorized citizen to leave the territory known as the Black Hills, the Powder River, and Big Horn country by and before the 15th day of August next.

"Are they kickin' us out?" Yapper Jim yelled.
Sidwell stared down his long, hawkish nose like a schoolteacher on the first day of class. "Let me finish."

He hopes that the good sense and law-abiding disposition of the miners will prompt them to obey this order without compelling a resort to force.

55

It is suggested that the miners, now in the hills, assemble at the military post about to be established at Camp Harney, near the stockade on French Creek, on or before the 10th day of August.

That they then and there hold a meeting, and take such steps as may seem best to them, by organization and drafting of proper resolutions, to secure to each, when this country shall have been opened, the benefit of his discoveries and the labor he has expended.
George Crook, Brigadier General, U.S.A.
Company G, Department of the Platte
July 29, 1875

After a moment of mumbling, everyone seemed to shout at once.

"They're kickin' us out!"

"I ain't goin'."

"Is them army boys going to escort us to Fort Laramie or all the way to Cheyenne City?"

"They can't do that. I'm goin' to hit it big any day now."

"We all knew we was in here illegal."

"But it's unoccupied land. There ain't no hostiles livin' up here."

Sidwell held his Winchester '73 above his head as if to fire it, but the crowd silenced before he pulled the trigger. "There are worse things than havin' the army lead us out to safety."

"They're takin' away our claims. What fate could be worse than that?" Yapper Jim shouted.

"Ask those Alabama boys." Brazos Fortune's words

56

silenced the crowd.

"We ought to vote," Grass Edwards suggested.

"This ain't a votin' meetin'. Besides, we ain't going to win if we fight the U.S. Army," Ernie Sidwell cautioned. "I was with General Custer's survey party when they came in here last year with a thousand men. They'll all be back with a thousand more if we put up a fight. So pan out as much as you can and mark your claims well. Maybe by next spring, ever'thing will be settled."

"They can't just chase us out of our claims!" a deep voice shouted.

With his Sharps across his shoulders, and his arms looped over it, Brazos Fortune replied, "I reckon they can shoot us, if they want to."

"Not without a fight!" Yapper Jim insisted.

"You aimin' to take on the entire United States Army?" Grass Edwards chided.

"It won't be the first time!"

"Yeah, but you lost that war, remember?"

A blast from Sidwell's '73 silenced the crowd. "We've only got two weeks before they root us out. I don't aim to waste my time standin' on this stump. It ain't rainin', and it ain't snowin', and I saw a patch of blue up in the sky. I've got a claim to work. I aim to pull out enough color to tide me over 'til spring."

"You reckon they'll really let us back next spring?" Big River Frank pressed.

Sidwell jumped off the stump. "Yep. The government will get them Indians settled down by then. Them Sioux ain't goin' to attack the entire U.S. Cavalry, that's for certain!"

Brazos Fortune, Big River Frank, and Grass Edwards made the rounds of visits with the other prospectors before cinching their saddles and pulling out for camp. They rode single file most of the way, with Brazos in the lead. The clouds broke up enough to melt the light snow, and the trail remained muddy and slick. Just past #14 Above Discovery the path widened. Brazos dropped back to ride alongside the other two.

"Don't trample on the *ceanothus velutinus!*" Edwards called out.

Brazos Fortune stared down at the dense, upright clusters of white flowers on the green-leafed shrub. "Are you talking about this buckthorn?"

"It ain't buckthorn. It's mountain balm. Them leaves is evergreen, and it will make mighty good feed for the horses this winter when we run out of moldy cordgrass," Edwards lectured.

Big River Frank cradled his rifle across his lap and searched the trail ahead of him as if expecting an ambush. "Brazos, did you ever wonder whether Grass is tellin' us the truth with all his stories about weeds and plants?"

"I reckon it don't matter." Brazos reached up and combed his horse's mane with his glove-covered fingers. "It's more entertainin' than yakkin' about the weather."

"And it ain't nearly as frustratin' as talkin' about women," Big River added.

Grass Edwards yanked his hat low over his forehead. "Why did you bring up the subject of women?" he snapped.

"Boy, he's jumpier than a drover at the dance hall after all the girls is pledged," Big River teased. "Except for Ol' Man Fortune, we could all use a trip to Cheyenne City."

"Cheyenne City?" Edwards quizzed. "Why did you mention Cheyenne?"

"He's surely soundin' like the littlest dog when there's one bone short," Big River laughed.

"I reckon he's pinin' for his girlfriend," Brazos added.

"Girlfriend?" Big River leaned back, letting his left hand rest on the rump of his horse. "You mean that little señorita down at Mamma Gordita's in Castlerock?"

Fortune refused to look Edwards in the eyes. "I think this one's a little closer."

"Brazos, I warned you!" Grass huffed.

Big River Frank raised his bushy, black eyebrows. "What are you two talkin' about? Is there a woman in the hills?"

"Grass is right," Brazos grinned. "I promised not to say a word."

Big River brushed his bearded mouth with the palm of his tattered leather glove. "If there's a woman in these hills, we all get to go take a look at her. That's the rule."

"She ain't . . ."

A volley of three rifle reports echoed down from the

direction of Texas Camp. Big River Frank stood in his stirrups and stared north. "Did that sound like hunters?"

Brazos pulled the heavy hammer back on his converted Sharps carbine. "Too close together to be huntin'."

"It could've came from our camp," Edwards added. "Maybe them Sioux snuck over the pass and crept on down the creek." By the time he had finished the sentence, Brazos and Big River cantered up the trail, guns pointed, eyes peeled.

High above them, jagged peaks of Dakota Territory sandstone pushed their way heavenward past the tops of dark green Ponderosa pines. At that altitude, Lightning Creek was no more than ten feet wide, depending on the sluice boxes it had to run through. Banks were lined with boulders and river rock, almost devoid of vegetation, due to the aggression of the prospectors. The mountain grasses, what was left of them, still held a light summer green and were beat down by the constant rain.

The narrow trail was sloppy, and an occasional splatter of mud flew off Brazos's horse's hooves. When they reached the stand of whitewood trees just below their claim, Brazos reined up and waited for the other two to catch up.

Big River Frank had the deepest voice of any 120-pound man Brazos had ever met. The little man stood in the stirrups. "You hear any more shots?"

"No, but let's ride in slow." Brazos held the saddle ring carbine in his right hand and waved the barrel to each side of the creek. "Big River, you take the east bank. Grass, you skirt the tree line up there on the west. I'll ride right up the trail. Fire a shot if you see danger and take cover."

A small, white column of smoke drifted up from the campfire, fifteen feet from the two canvas tents. Brazos studied the campsite as he slowly walked his horse forward. There was no movement. Hook Reed's buckskin stallion was picketed and saddled like they left him—halfway between the fire and the diggings. The iron skillet was still propped on the rocks. Two wooden crates were pulled up to the fire circle, and deer meat still hung in the trees, covered by an India rubber sheet. The axe was still wedged in the pine round, next to the smoldering fire. The thicket of small whitewoods a hundred yards up the slope of the mountain revealed nothing more than a solid fence of light green, quaking leaves.

In the corners of his eyes, Brazos could see Big River Frank to the east and Grass Edwards moving along the tree line to the west.

Indians would have stolen the horse, pans, and grubstake. Maybe those shots came from on up the mountain. Maybe it's the newcomers. Didn't notice any at the miners' meetin'. I don't see Hook prowlin' around. No matter how sick a man is, there are some things you don't sleep through.

Then Brazos spotted the blackened tin coffeepot sitting on the rocks next to the campfire. He reined up and raised his carbine high above the head as a warning to the others.

Someone's been in camp! There is no way on earth that

Hook Reed would let the coffeepot get cold on the rocks! It's hung on that iron rack day and night since the day we made camp three months ago. But I don't see any hoof-prints. If they walked in, they must have been from the north.

Brazos slipped down out of the saddle and let the reins drop in front of Coco. He reached into his canvas coat pocket with his left hand and felt the cold brass and lead of a half-dozen .50-caliber cartridges. Then he grabbed the reins and led the horse towards the tents, keeping the dark sorrel gelding ahead of him as a shield from the grove of whitewood trees.

If anyone is still here, they're in our tents . . . or up in that aspen grove.

As he approached the campfire, he thought he heard a horse whinny up the mountain. He paused near the fire to peer over the top of his saddle horn.

Pointing the Sharps towards the trees, he glanced over at the closest tent. Three holes the size of his thumb punctuated the flap, two showed black powder burns on the outside. The other a clean puncture. Gunsmoke lingered inside.

The mechanical click of a gun hammer checked inside the tent. Brazos left the horse by the dying fire and squatted down next to the tent. He avoided the front flap and the bullet holes.

"Hook . . . it's me . . . Brazos," he spoke softly. "Are you all right?"

He scanned the grove of trees while he waited for an answer. Brazos glanced over at Grass Edwards, who was off his horse and crouching behind several large boulders on the far side of the creek. Brazos pointed his carbine barrel towards the grove of whitewoods.

Finally there was a faint reply from inside the tent. "They done shot me, Brazos!"

On his hands and knees, Fortune scooted around to the tent flap in front. As he did he exposed himself to the grove of trees. The puff of smoke, the report of the rifle, and the tumbling of the newly punctured coffeepot caused the horse to bolt towards the creek. Brazos ducked inside the tent. Edwards and Big River blasted away at the grove of trees. Then the shooting stopped.

Hook Reed lay sprawled on top of his brown canvas bedroll, blood soaking up his dirty wool shirt near his right shoulder blade. His right hand clutched the bronze receiver of his '66 Winchester rifle.

Sweat rolled down the creases of his unshaven face. Blood trickled down his chin where he had bitten his lower lip.

Tired brown eyes stared through the lingering gunsmoke at Brazos. "I knew you would come. I ain't goin' to die alone. No, sir . . . that wouldn't be right," Hook insisted.

"You're not goin' to die at all," Brazos said. "I'll fix you up. You hang on, partner. How many men are out there?"

"I only saw three, but there could have been more."

"Who were they?"

"Doc Kabyo and some others."

"What's Kabyo doin' in the hills? I thought he spent his time robbin' stages." Brazos dropped flat on his stomach beside Hook Reed as several more shots crashed through camp from the whitewood trees.

"Hook, we're goin' to chase down these boys that shot you, then I'll be back to doctor that wound." Brazos pulled a wool blanket out of his own bedroll and stretched it over Reed. Then he jerked a folded cotton shirt out from under the rubber sheet. "This shirt's fairly clean. Press this up against that wound and lay still."

Hook tossed his rifle down and reached up and grabbed Fortune's wrist. "Say a prayer over me, Brazos."

"You're goin' to pull through, Hook. We'll nurse you back."

"No, I mean right now. Say a prayer over me right now." His thin, bony fingers felt ice cold on Brazos's hand.

Fortune raised up on his knees and laid his left hand on Hook's forehead. But he didn't take his eyes off the tent flap while he prayed.

When he finished, Hook Reed dropped his arm back down on the gray wool blanket. "You goin' to kill 'em, Brazos?"

"I don't reckon Kabyo's the type to surrender."

"I didn't tell Kabyo nothin'."

"What did they want to know?"

Hook's voice was faint. "About the big claim beneath the Dakota cross. He was there in Tucson when I won it in a poker game."

"That's what I heard."

"Said he's been on my trail since Arizona."

"Did you give him the map?"

"I cain't feel nothin', Brazos. Do I still have on my boots?"

Brazos glanced down at the foot of the tent. "Yep."

"Then he didn't get the map. It's in my left boot."

"You hang on, Hook. We've got to take care of the bushwhackers in the whitewoods."

"You and the others will have to find that Dakota cross without me."

"Oh, no . . . you're goin' to lead the way, partner. Right now, we have a little justice to serve up."

A wide, pained smile broke across the wounded man's face, revealing tobacco-stained teeth. He nodded his head and closed his eyes. Brazos heard noise outside the tent.

"Is Hook dead?" Grass Edwards called.

Brazos crawled to the tent flap on hands and knees and poked his head out. "No, but they shot him."

"Who are they?" Big River Frank called. He was now perched just behind the second tent.

"Doc Kabyo and them."

"Kabyo? What are they doin' in the hills?" Edwards grumbled. "They ain't prospectors. They're murderers and horse thieves."

Brazos kept his eyes and his gun focused on the grove of whitewood trees. "They wanted Hook's treasure map, he said."

"Did he give it to them?"

"Nope."

"You boys need some help?" someone hollered from the rocks below camp.

65

"Is that you, Yapper Jim?"

"I've got Alamo McCoy and Quiet Jim with me."

"We've got bushwhackers in the whitewoods. It might be Doc Kabyo, so don't get yourself shot."

"We'll flank them east of the creek," Yapper Jim hollered back.

Brazos, still on hands and knees, crawled through the mud behind the tent and motioned to Big River and Grass. "You flank them on the west. I'll drive them out of the woods."

"How you goin' to do that?" Big River challenged.

"I'll ride straight at them," Brazos said.

Grass Edwards continued to point his gun at the aspen grove. "By yourself?"

"Me and Mr. Sharps."

Big River Frank shoved his hat back. "You're crazy, Brazos!"

"Ever'body in these Black Hills is crazy, Big River . . ."

The first shot from the Sharps carbine hit the aspen tree about six feet above its base. The bark exploded, and twenty-five feet of treetop toppled over as if felled by an axe. Two more rapid explosions from the single shot brought down two more aspens.

Suddenly, four horseback riders bolted out of the back of the grove and galloped towards the pass, east of Thunderhead Mountain.

Chapter Three

The bright August sun was straight above the three men who squatted around the low, crackling campfire. Brazos Fortune was the only one still sipping coffee.

Grass Edwards rocked back on his heels, his cheeks freshly shaved, his mustache neatly trimmed. "I still say it seems strange to ride off and leave you two."

Brazos idly poked at the fire with a short stick. "Hook can't last another night. I'll catch up to you tomorrow."

His floppy, felt hat hanging on his back by a braided leather stampede string, Big River Frank ran his fingers through his clean, black hair. "And I say we can all three wait one more day. A man don't ride off and leave his friends."

"It's a business decision," Brazos insisted. "Tomorrow morning they're drawin' up the papers on all our claims. We need you two to be at the stockade on French Creek to represent us. If we don't get in on that, we're liable not to have a claim when we come back. General Crook and the troops should already be there."

"I ain't never rode off and left a partner in a tough pinch before," Big River insisted.

"I'm not in any danger. These hills are deserted. Ever'one else has gone down to the stockade. We've almost waited too long as it is," Brazos reminded him.

"Word is, the army is usherin' us out of the hills on

Wednesday." Big River plucked a cocklebur from his pant leg and dropped it into the fire. "If you ain't down there by then we'll come back lookin' for you."

"If I'm not there by then, push on to the crossing of the Cheyenne River. I'll meet you there."

Grass Edwards drew letters in the dirt with his finger. "You can't go through Red Canyon by yourself."

Brazos thought he spotted a *J* and an *S* among Grass's letters. "You two quit your worryin'. You're beginnin' to sound like a couple old maids fussin' over the dog."

"Wouldn't mind findin' a couple old maids . . ." Big River mused.

"I cain't believe they're really makin' us all leave," Grass bellyached.

A wide smile broke across Brazos's face. "Think of it this way: we'll be in Cheyenne within a week, and not all the gals there are old ladies."

"Why did you look at me when you said that?" Edwards protested.

Brazos shrugged, then winked at Big River Frank. "Figured you were lookin' forward to doin' some visitin', that's all."

"What's all this talk about visitin' young ladies in Cheyenne?" Big River Frank challenged. "You two ain't keepin' secrets, are you?"

"Brazos!" Edwards's word stabbed the air like a fork into the last pork chop at a boarding house.

Fortune sipped the dregs of his coffee, straining the grounds with his teeth. He stood as his blue-gray eyes

68

surveyed the claim. "Boys, we have her all buttoned up real nice. From ridge to ridge across the gulch, three hundred feet of prime Black Hills mineral rights. We've got most of our gear packed, the property line marked with stone pillars, camp torn down except for me and Hook's tent. We even have enough gold in our pokes to do a little explorin' of some Wyomin' ranch country. I reckon that's better than when we pulled in here."

Grass stood up beside him, his thumbs laced in his vest pockets. "For a man who thought his future was under that there Dakota cross, you're surely takin' all this leavin' peaceful."

"I didn't say it was under a Dakota cross, just a cross." Brazos glanced down near Edwards's boots and definitely saw the name Jamie Sue scratched in the dirt. "Anyway, even the children of Israel went into exile in Egypt before they returned to the promised land," he muttered.

Big River Frank stood up by the other two, a good six inches shorter than Brazos. "Maybe the Lord's exiled you from Texas. You ever think maybe he's going to call you back there?"

Brazos pointed down at the flames. "The Hebrew children were in Egypt for four hundred years."

"I know better than to get you in a Bible quotin' contest," Big River conceded as he glanced around camp. "I suppose we've done all we can do."

Edwards rested his right hand on the walnut grip of the Colt revolver that hung from a wire hook on his belt. "There's one more thing I wished we could have finished. I wish we could have caught up with Kabyo and them that shot Hook."

Brazos gazed to the west. "We chased them down out of the hills and straight for the Big Horns. The Sioux and the Cheyenne will have to take care of them out there. That's too dangerous land for any of us."

Big River Frank spat a wad of tobacco clear over the top of the fire. "You know the thing I can't figure? Kabyo and them risk their lives comin' all the way to the hills 'cause they is convinced Hook's got a treasure map. Now, it don't seem likely that they just up and rode off because we threw a little lead at them."

"If you had a mind to rob trains and stagecoaches, how much would you want to tramp up and down these mountains lookin' for a gold claim no one's ever seen. Truth is, it just might not be worth the effort."

"Strange thing is, I've never seen this man Kabyo," Big River added. "I wouldn't know him if he rode up."

"And none of us knows him," Grass Edwards concurred.

"Yapper Jim does," Brazos reminded them.

Big River Frank pointed his calloused, bronzed hand to the two saddled horses. "I suppose we ought to ride south."

Brazos dumped his coffee grounds onto the dirt, then scattered them with the toe of his worn, brown boot. "I'll see you down to French Creek before you pull out. If not, I'll meet you at the crossing."

Big River Frank looked over at the one remaining tent. "I still think we ought to stay and help you bury Hook. That's what family's for."

Brazos stared into Big River's trusting brown eyes.

He means it, Lord. Up here in the hills, we're the only family any one of us has. Brazos cleared his throat. "We've got the grave dug. Only one of us needs to hang back, and that's me 'cause I promised I'd pray over his grave. That's the kind of promise a man has to keep."

Edwards used his boot to erase the words in the dirt. "Then why on earth are we draggin' around like this is a final good-bye? Come on, Big River," he slapped the shorter man on the back. "Let's go make sure them miners hear from Texas Camp on upper Lightnin' Creek."

"Cover his grave so the wolves won't get in," Big River Frank cautioned, reaching out to shake Brazos's hand.

"I'll bring the rest of our gear down on Hook's buckskin." Fortune walked the other two to their mounts. "Listen, boys, I have one favor to ask of you." Brazos reached in his pocket and pulled out two envelopes. He handed one to each man.

"What is this, your last will and testament?" Edwards protested, staring at the address on the envelope.

"Nope. Just one letter to Todd and another to Robert."

"This don't sound like you plan on seeing us tomorrow," Big River said.

Brazos pulled a third letter out of his pocket. "Sure I do. I've got one to send myself. But crazy things happen. We could get split up somewhere along the trail. I haven't got a letter out to the children in over a month. I just wanted to let them know I'm doin' fine. I need to send three, just to make sure one gets through."

"Then we can all mail them at the same time when we get to Cheyenne City," Big River Frank proposed.

Grass Edwards swung into the saddle, then pointed back to a flat, sandstone rock. "Hand me up that *Monarda fistulosa* I found this morning."

Brazos snatched up the large, lavender-flowered, green-stemmed plant. "Now, tell me again what you're goin' to do with this Horsemint."

"Boil it up," Edwards replied. "The fumes cure the vapors. Yes, sir, just a whiff or two of this and the chest clears right up."

Big River Frank mounted his black horse, leaned across the saddle horn, and spat a wad of tobacco into the dirt. "How do you know it works?"

Grass folded the plant and tucked it into his saddlebag. "You ever seen an Indian with a cold?"

Big River punched his heels into the flank of his horse and started down the trail. "I ain't never got close enough to see one with freckles, either, but that don't mean they don't have them."

Brazos watched as the two men trotted down the creek, arguing the merits of herbal medication. He stared at the backsides of their horses until both men dropped over the rise and disappeared from sight. He snatched up his Sharps carbine and studied the three-hundred-foot claim from border to border. His eyes locked on to every Ponderosa tree, every sandstone rock, every ripple in the creekbed, every blade of cordgrass, every low-growing gray sage.

The animals and the snow can knock down the markers. We've got to have this place memorized. It's going to get hectic if they open this land up. Not only will the miners move back, but so will the saloon keepers, the gamblers, the bankers and merchants, and families. Won't it be somethin', Lord, when this country is filled with families?

Brazos reached into his vest pocket and pulled out gold wire-framed spectacles, perched them on his nose, and wrapped the earpieces behind each ear. Then he tugged out the letter he had shown to Big River and Grass. He squatted down next to the barely glowing fire and scanned the India ink scrawled note.

August 13, 1875—Dakota Territory

Dearest Dacee June,

I am missing you something terrible. Thoughts of your smile and the twinkle in your blue eyes keep me warm most every night. I imagine you, your cousins, and Aunt Barbara will be putting up preserves about now. I know you are a big help to her, and I'm grateful you can stay with her and Uncle Milton.

Well, your daddy hasn't exactly found that ranch under the cross . . . yet. But we just might have a bonanza in gold. The prospect looks good.

It's an amazin' land up here, darlin'. There are white rock mountains, and millions of trees pointin' straight up to heaven. The creeks are tiny, but clean . . . and the water is so sweet they could bottle it and sell it at the state fair.

The hills have been rainy this month, but one smile from my Dacee June and I'm sure the clouds would run away. The summer storms have put me behind

73

schedule a little. You'll need to go ahead and start school in Texas in the fall. I'll make ever' effort to be there by your birthday.

Yes, there are still buffalo up here. I can't wait to show them to you. But, most of all, I can't wait to hug my little girl again.

Promise me you won't get married until after I come home!

With sincere affection always,
Daddy

Brazos tucked the letter back into his pocket, took a deep breath of warm air, wiped a single tear out of the corner of each eye, then sauntered over to the lonely looking tent. He stooped his six-foot frame down to enter the four-foot tent flap. Lying motionless under three wool blankets was Hook Reed.

Eyes closed, sunken.

Mouth open, sagging to the right.

Forehead flushed, sweating.

"Well, I sent the boys on down to French Creek to attend that miners' meetin', Hook. You and me will catch up with them tomorrow or the next day, whenever you are up to it. The air tastes summer fresh, if you know what I mean. I reckon our rainy days are over for a while. You'll be plumb excited to get out on the trail."

Reed didn't respond.

He hadn't responded for over ten days.

Brazos reached under the top blanket and held onto Reed's ice cold wrist. The faint pulse continued its erratic rhythm.

He just keeps hanging on, Lord. It seems to me it would be in his best interest to get well or pass on. But I guess it's not in your best interest. Comfort his soul, Lord. I know his body can't hold out much longer.

Brazos took a rag off the empty powder crate that served as a bed table, dipped it in a coffee cup of clean water, then wiped Reed's forehead.

"Hook, it's a mighty beautiful day out there today. In fact, the weather's been pretty since the day you were shot. If your hands and feet weren't so cold, I'd open the flap and let you taste that summer breeze."

He reached over and patted Reed on his good shoulder. "Now, you go on and take a nap. I'll cook us some supper after a while. If you're up to it, I'll let you cook breakfast. Who knows, by mornin' you just might feel like a new man!"

Brazos crawled out of the tent. *By morning, maybe he'll be walkin' the streets of glory.* He carried his Sharps carbine with him as he hiked across the deserted camp toward the whitewood trees where the two horses were picketed. He plopped down on a stump, studied the solitary tent in the distance, then glanced up at the blue Dakota sky.

It's quiet here, Sarah Ruth. If there were no hostiles and no miners, this would be a peaceful, quiet land. Just the kind you'd like. I reckon the same could be said for any place on earth.

But someplace . . . is our place.

A place for me, Dacee June . . . maybe Todd, Robert . . . and someday, Lord willin', even Samuel. Lord, keep the

75

prodigal safe today. Bring him to his senses.

We can't stay in Texas.

Mr. Houston was right. The war brought ruin to Texas. But they chased him out of the Governor's mansion . . . and now they chased me out, too. Lord, forgive them.

Now, Sarah Ruth, I promised you on your deathbed that I'd raise our boys to honorable manhood and Dacee June to respectable womanhood, and I aim to do it. We got one that is more trouble than the others, but I won't give up on him.

He stretched out on the ground and closed his eyes. He couldn't remember when he'd had his last full night of sleep.

And he knew that he would not sleep on this day, either.

Brazos had spent the war working out of Browns-ville, Texas, making sure supplies from Europe could break the Union blockade and reach families up and down the Rio Grande. He, Big River Frank, and six others got the assignment of leading the Union ships in decoy chases, while the supply boats slipped in behind them. Over the course of four years, he watched seven boats and several friends sink in the surf of the Gulf of Mexico. In one incident, when their ship capsized, he spent twenty-eight hours floating atop two crates of dynamite that miraculously refused to sink.

It was the only time in his life that he had felt more lonely than he did at this moment. It had been four days since he said good-bye to Big River Frank and Grass Edwards.

He lay across the top of his bedroll, which he had

spread out in the trees near the horses. Fifty feet up the hill a few coals glowed in the campfire. The unseen smoke wafted in his nostrils. Beyond the fire, the bright summer stars dimly reflected off the canvas tent that contained an unconscious Hook Reed.

Brazos lay on his back, his head propped on the Texas saddle. The Sharps carbine lay alongside, his right hand on the smooth, cold receiver. He tried to close his eyes, but they kept flipping open like a school-yard gate during recess.

General Crook has moved the miners by now . . . they're probably at Cheyenne Crossing already. If I rode hard all night through Red Canyon, I might catch them before they reached Fort Laramie. Probably, I'd just catch some Sioux arrows or bullets.

But I can't up and leave Hook to die, and I surely am not goin' to speed it up. If I hadn't doctored that wound of Hook's, spoon-fed him, wrapped him up when he's cold, wiped him down when he's feverish, he would have died two weeks ago. So I've kept him alive for two more weeks.

For what?

Two more weeks of unconsciousness? Two more weeks of suffering?

Lord, sometimes doin' good don't make sense. If I cooled him off right now, then pulled his covers off and let him sleep outside, he'd catch a chill in the night and be dead by mornin'.

If he was dead, I could head down to the Cheyenne River. And Hook, he could waltz through the pearly gates.

But I can't do that.

You know I can't do that.

*So, here we are . . . me nightguardin' camp and keepin'
him alive, and both of us waitin' for him to die.*

What if the Sioux come stormin' through here?

*That's why I need to stay awake all night and keep
watch.*

He fingered the carbine at his side.

*It's a strange feeling, Lord, to know I could fire this .50
Sharps as a warning shot, and absolutely no one would
hear it.*

No one but the unconscious Hook Reed.

And you.

But you know I'm going to stay.

I'll stay until Hook's dead. Or I am. Or both of us.

But I won't sleep.

I can't.

Coco's cautious snort woke Brazos. The sun had
broken over the eastern pine-covered hills, and the
well-used canvas tent took on new brightness in the
light of early dawn. It was the first morning in three
months that Brazos hadn't been up and around before
the sun rose.

Without raising his head off the saddle he slowly
pulled the Sharps carbine up across his chest and fingered the trigger. The heavy dual clicks of the hammer
being pulled back echoed above the gurgle of Lightning Creek behind him.

Slowly, he scanned the region to the north of camp,
towards the whitewood grove that had been a hiding
place for Doc Kabyo two weeks before. *Something
made Coco whinny and his ears stand up.* High above the

limestone outcrop on the ridge to the west, a brown hawk coasted in a morning drift.

There was no other movement.

Until the tent flap flew open.

"Hook?" Fortune's response to seeing Hook Reed crawl out of the tent on his hands and knees was more of a croak than a statement. Having kept night watch fully dressed, Brazos leaped to his feet, still clutching his carbine, and tried to straighten out his legs and back.

Barefoot, wearing only dirty long underwear and a blanket still draped on his shoulders, Reed struggled to straighten up, barely able to keep his balance.

"Hook! You shouldn't be up. What are you doing?" Brazos called as he shuffled towards the campfire.

When Reed turned to face Brazos, he also was facing the bright morning sun, and the sight made Fortune stop and stare.

Hook's face isn't hollow . . . his eyes are bright and alert . . . he looks thirty . . . he is thirty! Lord, you've healed him!

"I think I'll go on home, Brazos." The voice was so strong and clear that it made the hair on the back of Fortune's neck stand up.

"Sure, Hook, when you feel good enough we'll . . ."

"Well," Reed shouted, staring off at the sunlight behind Brazos, "ain't that a wonderful surprise!"

With his carbine at his shoulder Brazos spun around to view the object of Hook's gaze. But he saw nothing but the morning sun, the stream, and two horses still picketed in the tree. *What's a wonderful surprise?*

The sound was like a 120-pound sack of barley

being tossed out of the hayloft onto the barn floor—dead weight hitting dirt.

When Brazos spun back towards the tent, Hook Reed lay crumpled on the ground next to the slightly smoldering campfire.

Brazos had no urge to run over to Hook.

He didn't call out.

He knew.

Like the aroma of sweet perfume from a pretty lady, deep peace seemed to waft across the camp.

Well, Lord . . . I reckon you did heal him, didn't you?

Brazos walked over and knelt down beside the body.

Again the face was sunken.

Eyes wide open, shallow, lifeless.

And there was no pulse on the ice-cold wrist.

Brazos stared at the unshaven face.

Well, Hooker Davis Reed . . . you found your gold now. The streets are paved with it. I did what I could, Hook . . . sorry I couldn't do more . . . and forgive me if I did too much.

By the time the sun was straight above Lightning Creek, Brazos packed camp on the back of the buckskin stallion and carefully covered Hook Reed's grave with river rock and dirt.

He climbed up on Coco and stared down at the gravesite that blended in completely with the trail down to French Creek.

Hook, I wish I could have buried you beneath that Dakota cross of yours, wherever it is. There's no marker here, because I don't want no one disturbing your grave.

80

Neither the four-legged nor the two-legged wolves can get to you now.

I read over you from the Bible and said prayers like I promised. And I committed you into the hands of God Almighty. We didn't catch up with Doc Kabyo yet . . . but I will someday. The Lord likes justice, and so do I.

Brazos tipped his hat. "Good-bye, pardner. We'll be back in the spring."

Fortune had ridden down the gulch past Sidwell's cabin to French Creek and over to Gordon's Stockade several dozen times in the past three months. But this time the trip was completely different. Always before, camps lined up one after another on each of the three-hundred-foot claims. There had been men in the stream or huddled under an awning in the rain. Scattered about were always gold pans, sluice boxes, rockers, and Long Toms. There were always horses and mules hobbled in the tiny meadows, the noise of hard work in the air.

He never rode fifty yards without smelling a campfire, meat frying, coffee boiling, bread baking. Tents and lean-tos had littered the flat, west side of the stream. There had always been a "howdy," a "mornin' Brazos," a "pick me up some flour at the stockade," or some similar request.

But this day, the men were gone.

The animals gone.

The tents and equipment cached or packed off.

Just markers, notices, and a half-worked little stream remained.

"They're all gone, Coco. It used to feel so crowded. Now it's empty. They aren't 'dreary Black Hills' today. They're empty hills."

Brazos reined up the horse and surveyed up and down the trail. *'Course, I don't know if they're completely empty.*

A deserted Lightning Creek gulch had made Brazos feel lonely. But the totally vacant French Creek mining district brought a feeling of depression and doom.

With the lead rope of the buckskin in his left hand and the carbine and the reins in his right, he plodded along the deserted creek towards the abandoned Gordon Stockade.

The stockade sat like a tiny ghost town. Ten-foot-tall walls were deserted bastions in the corners of the eighty-foot square fort. Peering past the twelve-foot opened doors, Brazos Fortune gazed at the six small, empty log cabins.

Captain Mix drove out Gordon and the others in April.

Now, General Crook swept though cleaning out all the rest.

Who will come in next, and how long before they're driven out?

He stared off to the west.

I got two more hours of daylight. Trailing that mob will be easier than following railroad tracks. But I'd surely like to know how far ahead they are.

Fortune gazed off to the north.

Maybe I should ride up the slope of Buckhorn Mountain. Some say you can see the mouth of Fourmile Canyon from there. At least they ought to be sendin' up a dust cloud.

'Course, if they're already out on the plains . . .

The two saddled horses grazed on clumps of silver-green Junegrass as Brazos Fortune leaned against the trunk of a one-foot-thick Ponderosa pine. He chewed on a grisly piece of deer jerky, the carbine flung across his lap.

He gazed over at the horses. "You two reckon we should just unpack and spend the night up here on Buckhorn? Can't see anything, or anyone, in any direction. That was a steep, rocky trail, and we covered our tracks. Good chance no one will find us up here. 'Course, there's no one around to follow us, anyway."

Lord, here I am talkin' to the horses again. Other than those words from Hook, I haven't talked to anyone in days. I wonder if this was what it was like for Adam. This is a beautiful land. It's not a Garden of Eden. But it's Eden to me . . . not Canaan land, but a promised land. It's some-place new, fresh, different, unsettled—a break from the past. It has the potential for peacefulness . . . and violence.

Adam must have known how to talk if he named the animals. But without someone to respond . . . without Eve . . . it must have been like drowning in wonder.

Eve.

He gazed to the western sky and the dying sun.

Sarah Ruth, what am I doin' here?

Sometimes I don't know if I'm following the Lord's leading or just running away.

He spied a slight dust devil to the southeast.

But there was no breeze.

Maybe someone else is late. If there's several of them, we might have a chance out on the plains. Providin' it's not Doc Kabyo and them.

Fortune stepped over to his saddlebags and pulled out a small, brass spyglass. He returned to his perch, then shoved his spectacles into his vest pocket and positioned the spyglass.

He could see nothing but dust.

Sitting back down, he dropped the block on the Sharps single shot, pulled out the .50-caliber bullet, inspected it, then shoved it back into the chamber. *Right at the moment I'm mighty glad the army converted these over to cartridge guns.*

The dust column seemed to be approaching, and yet was still at least three miles away. He didn't bother cocking the hammer. The dust cloud dissipated at the eastern edge of the meadow. He fought back the urge to stand up and stare.

I'm not givin' them a silhouette or a shadow. Not until they show themselves. They're stopping near the Dutchman's cabin . . . maybe some pilgrim just comin' in that hasn't heard of Crook's edict.

He again peered across the valley with the spyglass. The first thing he spotted were flames lapping up the shake roof of the cabin, then billowing smoke, then several dozen mounted warriors. He jumped to his feet and threw the carbine to his shoulder.

The cabin on fire? No one would burn it down . . . except for Sioux! They must have just been waiting to take this land back.

He lowered the Sharps.

I reckon it's their move. The miners are gone. They'll torch

Gordon's Stockade, too. I can't contest that. Must be two dozen of 'em . . . and I'm over a mile away from the stockade. I ought to be further away.

He marched over to the horses and began to tighten the girths. "Well, boys . . . I do believe we'll ride north. The Sioux have just reclaimed their precious Pahá Sápa, their Black Hills. And I'm very glad we came up this mountain. Maybe they'll be so occupied with burning the stockade, they won't see us slip over Buckhorn."

Keeping back among the two-foot-thick trunks of the Ponderosa pines, Brazos saddled up and gazed down at Gordon's Stockade, the most permanent symbol of the white man's intrusion into the Black Hills.

With a Sharps rifle, I suppose I could put a little scare into them from up here. This carbine would be doing good just to hit the side of the wall. That's just what you need, Fortune . . . two dozen Sioux chasin' you through the mountains.

"OK, boys," his voice just above a whisper as he addressed the horses. "Let's bid a fond farewell to French Creek."

Staying back in the trees, Brazos circled the mountain to the west. As he reached a clearing he realized he could now look southwest down the mouth of Fourmile Canyon. The dust from several riders caused him to rein up.

Soldiers? Miners? More Indians?

The spyglass revealed only the dust and a vague outline of dark-colored horses.

85

Those aren't Indian ponies. And they can't see the Sioux at the stockade yet, nor can the Indians see them. But when they crest that draw, it will be too late!

If I ride off this mountain to warn them, the Indians will spot me and kill me and them both. Lord, I left Texas to avoid conflict.

And I've had conflict since the day I left.

I've got to do something . . . but what can I do? I can't just sit here and watch this. I've got to get out of here.

Brazos rode fifty feet through the trees to the north. Then, he stopped to stare up at the fading August sky.

I can't do it, Sarah Ruth. I just can't make myself ride off and let someone get ambushed. I know you understand.

Brazos turned the horses and rode back to the southern point of the mountain. This time he rode right out onto the limestone rocky clearing near the peak of the mountain as the Indians began to torch the stockade. He lifted the carbine to his shoulder.

I hope I know what I'm doing. And I trust I'm not saving the lives of the likes of Doc Kabyo.

The report of the .50-caliber Sharps amplified off the rocks. The startled reaction of the Indians at the stockade signaled that he had, indeed, slammed the lead bullet into the vertical log wall. Before any could mount their horses, he had hurled two more bullets from the single-shot carbine. Without climbing down to retrieve the empty brass shells, he spurred the horse and rode north.

If I can't figure out how to outrun those Sioux, I surely won't need to reload that brass.

Glancing up as he circled slightly west, he could see four horses sprint for cover in the rocks at the mouth of Fourmile Canyon.

Well, they heard it, all right. Maybe they have a chance if they're in the rocks.

That's the best I can do, boys, whoever you are.

Brazos spurred the brown horse and tugged the lead rope of the buckskin.

"If we can make it to the Needles before dark," he told the horses, "we can hide in there 'til daylight." *I reckon if I'm still alive at sundown it will be an act of God.*

Rather than drop down into Lightning Creek Gulch, Brazos kept riding in the trees on the ridge of the mountain. The cocked carbine was in his right hand, the reins and the lead rope to the packhorse in his left. He repeatedly looked back.

I'd make better time if I abandoned Hook's buckskin, but he's got what supplies I have. There's no way I'd make it out of the mountains without my outfit.

After several miles along the highline, he dropped down into a shady gulch and let the horses drink from clear, running water that was no more than two feet across.

He stared back at the trail he had just made through the trees. *Lord, this is a beautiful land. I can't hear a sound . . . an ideal setting. Yet back up that mountain there are people right now planning to kill me . . . and I'm tryin' to figure out how I can kill them first.*

I guess that's the story of mankind.

With the horses refreshed, he pushed them at a canter back into the forest. The downed trees and deadwood of the untrailed woods slowed his progress, but he knew it would slow his pursuers as well.

Up ahead, somewhere to the northeast, were the eroded granite outcroppings of the Black Hills' crystalline core. Like monumental fingers pushing out of the batholith, they were labeled "the Needles." Brazos had been there once, weeks before. At the time he figured a person could hide a hundred men among the crevices.

Today, he just wanted to hide one man.

And two horses.

Brazos considered it a major accomplishment to reach the Needles before any shots had been fired. The ancient nature of the Black Hills loomed among the granite spires that had been worn down by the weather so much that large aspen trees grew in the decomposed rock and dirt at their bases.

The combination of vertical rock and strong, healthy trees made it almost impossible to ride through the Needles. Both he and the horses, however, were greatly encouraged to press on when the sound of a distant rifle sent granite chips flying behind them.

Finding a shaded spot deep in the interior, Brazos stopped the horses and slid to the ground.

"Well, boys, we made it in. 'Course, they'll surround us, and there's no way out. But we'll take one disaster at a time."

Brazos yanked the pack and saddles off the horses, tying their lead ropes to the trees. Then he climbed up into a pocket of rock about ten feet higher than the surrounding ground level. Three rock needles surrounded him. From there he could watch the horses and most of the path that he had taken. There was no view to the north, but a limited one east and west. The Needles were a giant maze. Indians could sneak up any of the rocky paths through them and remain unseen until they burst around the corner.

There's no tellin' when, where, or how many. But they don't know which one of these I'll be hidin' in either. I'll get a jump on the first one. But after that, my position will be exposed. If they're smart, they'll perch outside the Needles and wait for me to make a move.

A few hours after dark the moon comes out. I could leave the horses, pull off my boots, and try to slip out.

Which sounds absolutely stupid.

Without a horse, barefoot, running around the Black Hills.

They'll come in after me.

Brazos pushed his hat back and could feel the sweat rolling down his face.

I should have brought my canteen up here. What was I thinkin'?

I was thinkin' about being shot.

An hour later Brazos crouched with cramping legs and aching back among the granite rock formations, when he heard a rifle report and the ricochet of lead among the pinnacles.

He thought the sound was wonderful.

Those shots are coming from the hillside! That means they stopped and are just spraying in a few bullets to get me to reveal my position. They wouldn't random shoot if their own men were crawlin' in here. They aren't comin' in! At least, not right away.

Brazos squirmed down out of the pocket and scooted cautiously to the horses and supplies. He snatched up both leather-covered canteens and a small, cotton sack with jerky, then backtracked to the miniature rock fortress.

As he scrunched back down, he chewed a piece of jerky and glanced down at the crudely embroidered "Daddy" on the side of the cotton sack.

Not bad for a seven-year-old, Dacee June. Of course, you stitch much better now.

With his carbine in the crotch of the rocks, he stared across the granite maze to the south.

You're goin' to be twelve and I'm not going to be there. How I miss you, little darlin'.

Fortune's thoughts shifted to his oldest son.

Todd should be in Kansas by now, sellin' another man's beef and workin' for wages. He ought to be drivin' Circle-F beef. It ain't right, Lord. The oldest son should have a ranch to inherit.

He surveyed to the east and west, then pulled off his hat and wiped the sweat from his forehead. One more shot rang out, this one from the east.

They're circling around, but still not coming in.

He replaced his hat, took a swig of tepid water from the canteen, then wiped his mouth on the back of his hand.

Maybe I ought to shave this beard off. It's mighty hot in the summer. Of course, if I'm goin' to get scalped, who cares about a shave?

He raised up to peer out of all three granite turrets. There was a slight breeze from the southwest, but absolutely no air movement when he crouched back down.

Don't worry, Sarah Ruth. Todd will make it. So will Robert. I've never seen a young man who likes discipline like him. Strikingly handsome. He's his mamma's boy when it comes to looks.

I know . . . you want to know about Samuel. Mamma, what can I say? He thinks his father's a Texas traitor. He's livin' in the Indian Territory with a bunch of cattle thieves and outlaws.

If he's still alive.

He hates his daddy. Yet in some ways, he's just like me. Bullheaded. Quick-tempered. Judgmental.

But I can tell you one thing, Sarah Ruth, he loves his mamma.

Darlin', they love you even stronger than the day you died.

You seem to be still in the center of ever' conversation.

When we have conversations.

Brazos thought he heard a noise to the south. He peered over the rocks. When he could see nothing, he squatted back down.

Darlin', if those Sioux come round these rocks bunched up, I'll be standin' alongside of you before nightfall. But that would mean leavin' the children to shift on their own.

Now I know you wouldn't want that. So I'll try to get out of this.

The explosion to the south brought him straight up to his feet. It was followed by two other explosions in

91

rapid succession.

It sounds like a cannon.

There are no cannons in the Black Hills.

There aren't even any troops this side of the Cheyenne River, are there?

Did General Crook turn around?

This doesn't make sense at all. Did the Indians capture a cannon? But they wouldn't know what to do with it, would they?

He heard sporadic gunfire to the south and east. It grew more distant with each shot until there was no more.

They're shootin' at each other, and someone left.

Who?

What about the cannon?

Brazos climbed out of the granite perch. He left the canteens and jerky near the saddles. Vest pockets stuffed with heavy .50 caliber cartridges, he toted the carbine and sneaked among the Needles to the south, nearly crawling to keep out of sight. He peeked carefully around the last granite needle and caught sight of several horses at a distance in the trees.

The deep voice sounded familiar.

Extremely familiar.

"You jist go in there to relieve yourself, Brazos, or did you move in permanent?"

"Yapper Jim, is that you?"

"Me, Grass, Big River, and Quiet Jim."

Brazos stepped out from his hiding place and strolled to the trees. A wide smile framed his white teeth. "What are you renegades doing back here?

92

You're suppose to be on your way to Fort Laramie and Cheyenne City."

Big River Frank lumbered out to greet him. "When you didn't show at Cheyenne Crossing, we decided to come back and look for you and Hook."

"I buried Hook this mornin'."

"We never figured he would hang on this long," Quiet Jim said.

"Did the boys in blue miss you when you left?" Brazos said.

"We had a bunch of miners meet us at the river, and it got confusin' as we crossed. We jist dropped back in the reeds and waited for them to disappear," Yapper Jim reported.

Grass Edwards remained on his horse, staring off to the southeast. "It was a good thing you fired that Sharps when you did, or we would have run straight into those Sioux."

"How did you know it was me?" Brazos said.

"Who else has a Sharps and is a complete fool?" Big River Frank whooped. "Now how did you know it was us down there at the mouth of Fourmile Canyon?"

"I didn't know it was you, but I figured someone needed a warning."

Quiet Jim stared down at his boots and mumbled, "You took a mighty big chance revealing your position."

"As did you, coming after them. What did you fire from the mountain?" Brazos quizzed.

Yapper Jim threw his arm around Brazos's shoulder. "Big River rigged up several sticks of dynamite in tandem. Took a chance it would scare them off."

"And it worked," Grass boasted.

Quiet Jim's voice was soft. "At least for now."

"I figure there's trouble in the east, west, or south," Brazos reported. "So it looks like we'll ride straight north through the Black Hills."

Yapper Jim remounted his pinto. "What if we run into some more of those army boys?"

"We'll tell them we're on our way out, just tryin' to avoid the Indians."

Quiet Jim swung up into his saddle, his '73 Winchester perched across his lap. "What if we run across some Sioux?"

"We'll just have to hope our dynamite holds up," Brazos hooted.

Grass Edwards turned his horse to the north. "And what if we run across a stream with gold jist waitin' to be plucked?"

Yapper Jim let out a big laugh. "Why, shoot, boys, then we'll jist pitch a tent and camp for the winter!"

Chapter Four

"Of all the memories of the past that come like a summer breeze . . ." Quiet Jim's soft tenor voice and perfect pitch seemed to float on the chill September air as he continued the familiar refrain, concluding with the words, "the good-bye at the door."

"Dadgum it, Quiet Jim, you keep singing that song and you'll turn us all melancholy," Yapper Jim hollered.

He rode second in line, behind Big River Frank.

"We are all melancholy already," Grass Edwards insisted. He was just ahead of Brazos, who rode at the rear of the procession. "It's been over a month since the army rounded up the miners, and we are still in these hills. We haven't found any more gold, nor Hook Reed's Dakota cross. Shoot, we cain't even find a safe trail out of here."

Big River Frank leaned back on his horse but continued to lead the plodding procession. "Make you feel like the last rats on a sinkin' ship, don't it? What do you think, Brazos? Is it time for us to make a run and try to save our scalps?"

"It's dangerous to stay, dangerous to leave." Brazos said. "The Sioux know we're up here. They're not waitin' for us to give 'em an easier target."

"Maybe we ought to all go get some jobs in town," Grass suggested.

"What town?" Yapper Jim challenged.

"I was thinkin' of Cheyenne, myself," Grass replied.

"Ain't no jobs in Cheyenne," Yapper insisted. "Why there's ten bummers hangin' around ever' street corner for one honest job as it is."

"Well, maybe we could pass through Cheyenne on our way somewheres. I surely would like to meet my sweet Jamie Sue," Grass pined.

"No offense, but I'm gettin' a little tired of starin' at the same four dirty faces ever'day, myself," Quiet Jim added.

"Well, boys," Brazos laughed, "the situation is desperate when Quiet Jim is willin' to admit he misses the ladies."

"Not just ladies in general," Quiet Jim added. "One special lady."

"Whoa!" Yapper hollered so loud every horse instantly pulled up. "Do you mean to tell me Quiet Jim has a special lady on the side that none of us knows about? This is a momentous day!"

Quiet Jim tugged off his dirty felt hat and ran his hands through his light brown hair, thin enough on top to foreshadow a bald spot. "I didn't say I had a special one lined up," he mumbled.

"You most certainly did," Yapper boomed.

"What I meant was, I know the Lord has a special one for me. I guess what I mean is, I'm not interested in just any dance hall girl."

"Good," Yapper shouted, "that'll leave two for me!"

"Three, I reckon," Grass mused. "The ol' man here is still a grievin' widower."

"You ever think about gettin' remarried, Brazos?" Yapper Jim asked.

"Nope."

"Never?"

"Nope."

"You reckon you ever will start to think about gettin' remarried?"

"Nope."

Yapper Jim's unshaven beard now covered up his previously neatly trimmed sideburns and goatee. "How about you, Big River?" he called. "Are you the marryin' type?"

"Well, I do have a fondness for Mexican señoritas . . .

but I don't reckon I'd make much of a husband. Don't seem fair to stick some lady with the likes of me."

"Why, I don't know, Big River," Grass Edwards chuckled. "You seem like a mighty fine catch to me. Providin' the woman was short. What do you think, Brazos, does Big River have marryin' qualities?"

"Yep. Hardworkin', loyal, truthful . . ."

"'Course, if that's all she wanted she could jist get herself a dog!" Yapper hooted.

Quiet Jim began to sing, and Brazos leaned forward to hear his soft voice.

Grass Edwards's voice cut through the melody. "I hear down in Colorado they have this hundred-foot cross up in the mountains that forms ever' spring melt. The snow just stays in them rock crevices in the shape of a gigantic cross. I wonder if this here Dakota cross is somethin' like that?"

Quiet Jim continued to sing.

"Trees cover most ever'one of these hills. Them that is bare is worn smooth. If you want a marker in these mountains you'd have to carve 'em, yourself," Big River Frank called out.

"The whole thing about a cross could have been made up by some down-and-out gambler in Tucson who wanted a stake for a game," Brazos added.

Quiet Jim stopped singing. "Maybe we ought to rest the horses in this little meadow. It's more grass than we've seen in two days."

"It ain't no ordinary grass," Edwards insisted. "This here red one is *Agrostis stolonifera,* and that one that

97

looks like wild wheat is *Agropyron smithii*."

Yapper Jim turned his horse around and rode back to Brazos, but he talked loud enough for all of them to hear. "You know, if Edwards would have got snowed in that winter with a mining engineer instead of some fool botanist, we'd all be rich by now."

Quiet Jim glanced up with his normal, expressionless face. "If that had happened, we'd probably have to call him Mother Lode Edwards."

Brazos watched the others dismount.

"You ain't gettin' down?" Big River inquired.

"I'm going to ride on up over that next ridge, just to see what's on the other side."

"You thinkin' about mamma . . . or daughter?"

"Both, I suppose," Brazos said.

"Let's get out of these mountains and go back to Texas."

"I've thought about it." Brazos nodded toward the ridge. "If I'm not back after you take a rest, follow my tracks up the hill."

The loose limestone shale on the steep hillside made every step a gamble. Brazos continually spurred Coco to convince him to keep climbing. The downed trees, caught in the fairly thick stand of pine, acted as a random corral wall and prevented any semblance of a straight trail. As Brazos picked his way up the steep incline, he gave up his seat on the saddle and hiked, tugging his reluctant dark sorrel gelding.

Well, Lord, the only good thing about this country is that no one in their right mind would work this hard to follow us.

Brazos struggled to make it ten steps up the steep hillside, then stopped to rest.

Lord, I can't bring a family into these gulches. I can't even bring a horse in here. Wherever it is you're leadin', I think I made a wrong turn someplace. Hook's Dakota cross got me sidetracked.

Brazos hiked up ten more steps. His calf muscles cramped up, and he stopped to rest.

I don't reckon many men ever hiked this hill. Maybe I'm the first, ever.

I suppose the old-time trappers worked this land. But not this mountaintop. They would've stayed to the creeks and basins.

He glanced back down the steep hillside at his tracks, still evident in the loose rock and dirt below him.

Maybe I'm the first one to ever set foot here. From the time you created it, Lord, until this moment, it's just been sittin' here . . . growin', livin', dyin', snowin', and growin' some more. Maybe you made this whole mountainside just for me to see!

Brazos tugged the horse another dozen steps up the loose shale, then leaned over and rested his hands on his knees. "Coco, I'm too old for this." He could feel a cramp coming on his right side. His long-john shirt was holding cold sweat against his chest under his heavy canvas coat.

It's like Adam and Eve in the garden lookin' at things for the very first time.

Well, it's like Adam lookin' at things . . .

In my case, there is no Eve.

Only fifty feet from the tree-covered crest, Brazos

split the difference and pushed himself to the halfway point. Sliding downhill, he jammed his boot against a pine tree with a six-inch trunk.

Sarah Ruth, what would you say about this land?

No place to raise children?

Well, the boys are raised.

And Dacee June? That girl would follow her daddy anywhere. But I can't bring her in here. Can I?

Brazos glanced down the steep hillside.

His words interrupted the rustle of a slight breeze about the pine top. "Dacee June, can you hike up this hill?"

Somewhere in the back of his mind he heard the crisp, clear voice of a twelve-year-old. *Yes, Daddy, I can make it! Just watch me!*

"Well, come on, girl," he mumbled to the wind. "Let's see what's up there."

When he reached the top, he found it to be a razor-back ridge no more than six feet across. Lightning-burned pines were scattered along the northern slope, so thick they prevented any view of the next gulch. After a small swell to the east, the ridge seemed to ascend to an outcropping of white limestone rock about a half-mile away.

"Time for a little break, Coco," he explained as he tied the horse to a pine. "I'll hike this on my own." He pulled the Sharps carbine out of the scabbard.

When he finally reached the rock outcropping, it was forty to fifty feet still higher than the ridge. He searched for a path to the top, but realized it would be a hand-over-fist ascent.

Brazos carefully shoved the carbine down his back, between his shirt and his coat, hooking the barrel on his belt. He yanked off his spurs and dangled them from his suspenders. His calloused fingers clutched the cold, rough rock as he pulled himself up, one step at a time.

Brazos, you're a fool for doin' this. An old fool. It'll be four times tougher climbin' back down. I surely hope there's somethin' worth seein' up here.

The top of the huge rock he was climbing was not the crest of the mountain, but merely a platform on which to catch his breath. He continued the ascent on another rock that jutted up and out to the north.

He took a swig from his canteen, adjusted the carbine at his back, and continued the climb. Cresting the final limestone boulder, he found a swell in the rock the size of a small bench. From the highest point he could look out over the Black Hills to the badlands to the east. There was one more tall ridge to the north, then it, too, looked as if it sloped down to the plains.

Brazos pulled off his sweat-drenched spectacles and gazed to the south and west. In both directions, there was nothing but wave after wave of steep, pine-covered ridges. The wind whipped across from west to east, turning the sweat into ice water. He yanked his carbine from his coat, then hunkered down on the limestone bench. The boulders blocked some of the breeze.

Brazos hunted for a dry spot on his shirttail to try to wipe his spectacle lens clean. Carefully placing the gold wire frames back on his broad, bent nose, he folded his arms across his chest and began to survey the gulch in front of him.

Movement in the creekbed far below him to the north caused him to leap to his feet, barely able to catch the carbine before it tumbled off the rocks.

"Men? Tents? Miners?" The words knifed through the breeze like a woodpecker on a dead tree. *There are prospectors down there workin' that stream! Who are they? Where did they come from? Why didn't they leave with the others? Are they havin' any luck? Are there any more claims left?*

For half an hour Brazos perched on the limestone peak and studied the proceedings below. He was too far away to count men, or even distinguish claims. But he could trail the creek from the east up to a fork where the gulch split into two smaller ones. There was hardly any room on the south side of the creek. The mountain seemed to drop straight down into the brush and deadwood along the creekbank. The north side was wide enough for a cabin or two, then swooped up a pinescattered ridge almost as tall as the one he was on. To the west, he spotted scattered, dark clouds that seemed to be tethered to the horizon.

Goose bumps formed on his chest and arms as the cool breeze continued to swirl around the peak. He took one more studied 360-degree survey, then started down. The descent proved as treacherous as he had thought, but the excitement that raced through his heart and mind kept him moving down the rocks at a steady pace. Twice he slipped and crashed into some boulders, scraping and leaving a welt on his temple.

He was trotting down the razorback when he realized the other four were standing next to their horses at the pine where Coco was tethered.

Big River Frank hiked towards him, his '73 Winchester in his hand. "Brazos, you get hurt?"

"No, no . . . just a scratch."

"There's blood all over your—"

"There's a couple dozen men a few miles north of here, workin' the next gulch!" Brazos interrupted.

"Which gulch?" Yapper Jim hollered.

"Follow this razorback around to the east, then you drop down into a little creek," Brazos reported as he tightened the girth and climbed into the saddle. "I tell you, boys, they're workin' it like they found gold!"

"Don't that beat all! For over a month we've figured we're the only ones in the entire Black Hills, and they've been up here beatin' us to pay dirt," Grass Edwards complained. "How come the army didn't round them up?"

"The same reason they didn't corral us," Brazos replied. "I think there's even a cabin or two."

"How do we get off this ridge?" Big River Frank queried.

"Not up that way. It drops straight off on the other side of those white rocks. Let's slant down off this razorback to the east, pick up the south creek, and—"

"There's two creeks?" Big River probed.

"They fork down there near where they're working," Brazos explained.

Yapper Jim spurred his horse to catch up with the others. "If there's two creeks, there's bound to be a claim left."

"We don't want just any claim." Quiet Jim's voice was just above a whisper. "We want one with gold on it."

It was noon the next day before they hacked their way through the brush and rode up to three startled prospectors with gold pans working a placer claim on the south fork of the creek. Within minutes an impromptu meeting was called at a cabin about half the size of Sidwell's. Two dozen men huddled to explain to Brazos and the others the mining laws and point out what claims were still available. They were given five days to prospect any one claim in.

Within two days they paid their two-dollar recording fee for each of five claims. No. 14 Below Discovery and No. 18 and No. 19 Below Discovery on Whitewood Creek showed the most promise of placer gold. No. 20 and 21 Above Discovery on Deadwood Creek showed some possibility at bedrock depth or deeper.

Huddled around the evening campfire, Big River Frank yanked the coffeepot off the hook, then replaced it without pouring any in his cup. "I've drank spring water that's had more taste than this coffee."

"We can make tea out of the *Ceanothus herbaceus*," Grass Edwards reported.

"I ain't drinkin' no weed tea," Yapper Jim protested.

"I reckon if we get desperate enough we'll be steeping pine nuts," Big River Frank said.

Quiet Jim nodded agreement.

"That ain't the only supplies runnin' low," Big River added.

Grass Edwards tried to bite off a chunk of jerky, but it was so tough he just shoved the entire wad in his mouth and mumbled, "We can buy a few supplies from Frank Bryant and that gang."

"Word has it that by November the creeks is froze and all placer work is finished until spring," Yapper Jim informed.

"The ones that has hit bedrock are plannin' on diggin' underground during the winter," Big River said.

Brazos poked at the flames with a short stick. "The army could show up any day and move us out of here, too."

Yapper swizzled his coffee around in his cup and stared at the grounds. "Or the Sioux could just ride up the gulch and scalp us all."

"I think they're too smart to come to these hills in the winter." Brazos could feel the flame lap at his face. "The ol' boys on No. 15 Above have a two-man saw in camp and no one who's ever bucked one. They said it's so dull they can't cut kindlin'. They'll trade it to us, if we cut some boards for them. Quiet Jim's a sawyer, and any of us can get down in the pit and buck the other end. You've got a file on ya, don't you, Jim?"

Like a bass note feather in a soft breeze, Quiet Jim's "Yep" floated across the fire.

"You sayin' we should go into the timber business instead of findin' gold?" Yapper Jim protested.

Brazos scooted back on a stump. "I'm sayin' with two of us workin' timber and three in the creek, we can have a little poke of gold and a decent cabin within three weeks. Maybe we can trade wood for supplies." He tried to rub the stiffness out of his wrists. "We aren't going to buy many supplies with gold. These boys have gold by the sacks. They can't get out to spend it. What they're worried about, right now, is keepin' these claims through the winter."

Yapper Jim poured the contents of his coffee cup into the dirt next to the fire. "The very first thing we are tradin' for is some coffee."

The Texas Company cabin was twenty-four feet by twelve, the biggest structure in Whitewood Gulch. It contained two identical rooms, with rock fireplaces at both ends. The fire in the bedroom end barely glowed, but the one in the other end blazed.

Brazos Fortune entered the cabin with a stack of firewood balanced in his left arm, the Sharps carbine in his right. He pulled off his boots inside the door; his denim trousers were water-soaked from the knees down. He could feel the stiff material rub raw on his legs. "Did you boys hear the tally on the vote to name this burg?" he asked.

"If they decide to call it Muckleville, I'm leavin'," Yapper Jim piped up.

"Deadwood City."

"Well, that got my vote, but it isn't much of a city," Big River Frank reported. "Shoot, it don't even have one store. It didn't even have three cabins before Quiet Jim opened the saw pit."

Quiet Jim waited for a break in the conversation. "Did you see Albien and Verpont about salt?" he asked.

Fortune squatted in front of the fireplace and shoved several sticks into the flames. "I saw 'em. They said they couldn't give us any salt, no matter what the trade."

"We might could make it to January, but we'll never last to March," Big River reminded them.

"We keep wadin' in that creek, we'll all die of pneumonia long before January." Brazos turned his back to the flames, and felt his pant leg beginning to warm. "We're breakin' ice ever' mornin' now. One of these days we'll have to shut it down for the winter."

Yapper Jim broke off a hunk of stale bread and waved it around as he talked. "How can we quit when we're pannin' a hundred dollars a day out of No. 14 Below Discovery?"

"Not to mention Quiet Jim clearin' twenty dollars a day on sawed boards," Big River pondered.

Brazos rotated his stream-soaked pants and now faced the fireplace. "What about a couple of us makin' a run for supplies?"

Yapper Jim pushed his long-handled shirtsleeves up to his elbows. "Two can't get through the Sioux."

"We snuck into these hills following the draws and arroyos. Maybe we can slip out to the north the same way," Brazos proposed. "We could divide the gold—leave half with those who stay, and half with those who go."

"That way, when the fools goin' for supplies get themselves scalped," Yapper blurted out, "the ones back here still have some gold."

"Yeah, something like that," Brazos continued.

"Those who go for supplies can try to make it back in here before the snow flies. The ones that are left will have fewer mouths to feed. With any wild game at all, they should be able to survive most of the winter, even if the others get bushwhacked."

"I ain't really interested in survivin' *most* of the winter," Quiet Jim reflected. "I was countin' on survivin' *all* of the winter."

Grass Edwards leaned back against the wall as he ran a cleaning stick with a rag tied to it down the barrel of his pistol. "It don't make sense for all of us to sit in here hoardin' gold, then starve to death."

"I say for them that leave, take all the gold," Big River Frank suggested. "We don't need any gold here in Deadwood."

"But what if they get scalped, like Brazos said?" Yapper protested.

"Then we lost a whole lot more than some gold. The more we send out, the more supplies and equipment we can bring in. The more we bring in, the more gold we dig next spring," Big River Frank proposed.

"Who is it that tries to make it out?" Yapper quizzed, as he continued his stroll across the room.

"Brazos ought to be one," Big River insisted. "He's the best shot among us. Besides, he's got his boy, Robert, out at Fort Abe Lincoln."

Quiet Jim rubbed his full beard. "Being the sawyer, I better stay to keep sawin' boards as long we can."

Brazos could feel his pant legs growing ice cold again. He returned to the fireplace. "Who do you want to stay in the pit with you?"

Yapper Jim waved his arms. "Me, of course. Ain't no one can work that bottom cut like me."

Quiet Jim concurred. "I do enjoy the silence."

"What silence?" Yapper Jim demanded.

Quiet Jim didn't crack a smile. "With all that sawdust tumblin' down, Yapper has to keep his mouth closed."

"Laugh all you want to, but I'd just as soon stay. Don't feel much like gettin' scalped anyways," Yapper pouted.

"Grass knows more about buyin' minin' equipment than I do," Big River suggested. "I reckon that means I stay."

"Do you think we'll have time to go down to Cheyenne?" Grass Edwards asked.

"Nope. We'll make a run straight for Fort Pierre. It's the closest place, providin' we don't get lost," Brazos said.

"Speakin' of lost," Yapper Jim tugged his suspenders down over his shoulders and let them hang towards the ground. "Did you see that notice posted on Muckle's cabin? They're searchin' for some man who's lost in the hills."

"What's his name?" Brazos asked.

"Vince somethin' or other."

Grass Edwards jumped to his feet. "Vince Milan! That's my sweet Jamie Sue's brother! Is she still in Cheyenne?"

"It said to contact her in Fort Pierre," Yapper said.

Grass Edwards began to prowl the room. "My Jamie Sue's in Fort Pierre? Why, in a week or so, she could be in my arms."

"I would surmise that Jamie Sue has a little somethin' to say about it," Brazos teased.

"She won't be able to resist me, boys. You ain't never seen me when I turn on my charm." Grass Edwards's smile seemed wider than his ears.

By 10:00 the next morning, Brazos and Grass Edwards had ridden past the lowest claim in the district. They tried to follow Whitewood Creek out of the mountains, but found its steep gulches so checkered with dead trees and abandoned beaver dams that they slowly climbed the pine-sloped hill on the north, and picked their way through the tree line for two more days.

On the third day out, they broke through the pines into the great plains of Dakota Territory.

Grass Edwards waited as Brazos rode up alongside him. "Look at that . . . prairie as far as the eye can see. I've been in them gulches so long I forgot what it was like to look out over a quarter mile at a time. It's goin' to be mighty tough takin' freight back in this way."

"Quiet Jim said if the ground froze up, they'd try to log off some trees along the trail. Maybe it will be a little easier on the return."

"You plannin' on droppin' down there and followin' the north fork of the Cheyenne River?" Grass quizzed.

"Nope."

"But it looks like it's the easiest grade, now that we've gotten out of the hills."

"Too easy. It will be the trail everyone takes."

"But there ain't no one around. What 'ever'one' you talkin' about?"

"Cheyenne and Sioux," Brazos said.

"Where?"

"If we could see them, it would be too late. Let's head northeast through that white, crusty-looking land."

Grass Edwards cupped his hands and blew warm breath into them. "Fortune, you're just gettin' senile in your old age. There ain't nothin' out there! I'll bet there ain't a stalk of *Elymus canadensis* for twenty miles. There won't be any water in there, no feed, not a scrap of firewood, and no trees to hide behind. No one in his right mind would ride through that."

"Good." Brazos retied his black bandanna around his neck, then glanced at Grass. "That way no one will bother us."

By nightfall they had crossed the north fork of the Cheyenne River and made a cold camp at the base of a small gorge that led down to a dry creekbed. For the last two hours of the day they had seen nothing but the crusted rolling prairie of baked-hard, white alkaline dirt. As the clouds piled up above them, the north wind increased, swirling with it the flour-fine white dust.

Hats pulled low, bandannas over their noses, covered in white dust, they crowded near the base of the small cliff, trying to block the wind. They picketed one horse on each side of them, facing south. Sitting beside each other, their backs against the dirt, they pulled Brazos's canvas bedroll tarp partially over their heads. Carbines tucked in their laps, huddling close, they tried to drink a little water from their canteens.

"This surely is a lovely camp, Fortune."

"Thank you," Brazos said.

"Ah, but you was right. Not one Sioux followed us in here. Boy, we sure are smart. The wind blows away our tracks and no one on the face of the earth knows we're here. Wherever we are."

"It could be worse," Brazos added.

"Worse? How can it be worse?"

Brazos pointed to the evening sky. "It could rain."

"What's wrong with rain? That would clear the air of this dust."

"This alkali turns to a gumbo in a heavy rain. It would be so slick and sticky, we couldn't ride ten feet without boggin' down."

"You figure we ought to keep ridin' tonight?"

"Nope. We'd probably just circle around with all these clouds above."

"You plan on sleepin' sittin' just like this?"

"Nope. I don't plan on sleepin'. Me and sleep don't do too good."

About midnight it began to snow.

Tiny flakes dropped like crumbs off a boardinghouse table for about fifteen minutes, then a blast of frigid wind followed. Finally, the clouds disappeared, and a blanket of Dakota stars covered the coal-black night sky.

"Brazos, are you awake?"

"Yep."

"Ain't that something the way them stars light up the snow? It's almost like daylight. Not that the color of the badlands is any different. They was white with alkali. But at least now the air is clean."

"When the snows melts it's going to get real gummy," Brazos reported. "And if we wait for the gumbo to dry, it will be another dust storm and we still won't have water or wood."

"What are you saying?"

"I'm saying we take off right now," Brazos said.

"That's mighty fine with me." Edwards stood up and stretched his legs. "Gives me the feelin' I'm walkin' on the moon."

Both men pulled the blinders off their horses and yanked the girths down tight. Brazos waited in the saddle for Grass Edwards to mount up.

"Brazos, do you figure there's people livin' on the moon? I read this here book one time about moon people."

"I don't know, Grass. The Lord created the sun and the moon for light for the earth. It says that in Genesis. You'd think he'd have mentioned people up there."

"I reckon the Almighty can do anything he wants."

"If he ever needs some people to live on the moon," Brazos offered, "I'd be tickled to recommend a few."

The night got so cold that Brazos clutched his carbine in his lap by the wooden stock, not the metal receiver. Even then his gloved fingers ached. They rode straight east, but the cold wind that pushed the clouds away continued to blow from the north.

"I have half a mind to turn around in the saddle and ride backwards," Grass called out. "That way my right side can freeze on equal basis with my left."

"I have been thinkin' about breakin' out the bedroll and pullin' it over my head," Brazos said.

"It will make us look like squaws."

"If they stay warm when they ride at night, they're smarter than we are," Brazos added.

Hats tied over their ears, wool blankets hanging down from their heads like shawls during fiesta, the two plodded through the night.

Right before daylight, Grass Edwards tried clapping his gloved hands to restore circulation to them. The noise startled his horse. He broke into a series of bucks that landed Edwards in the dirt.

Real dirt.

"Brazos, do you see this?" Edwards yanked a plant out of the ground and waved it up at Fortune. "Do you know what this is?"

"A dried weed?"

"It's *Distichlis spicata*, that's what it is . . . inland salt-grass. That means we made it to the edge of the badlands!"

Brazos tugged the blanket off his shoulders and rolled it up. "Well, I think we better find some water."

As the sun rose over the flat eastern horizon, sage and grass appeared as scattered clumps in the gently rolling, treeless prairie. The only evidence left of the light snow was the clean air and dustless ground. Cresting a long, steep incline, the prairie dropped off into a ribbon of yellow-leafed cottonwood trees running north and south.

"There's a creek down there." Edwards pointed to the tree row.

"Or at least a mud hole."

The trickle of water in the creek was no more than two feet wide, mostly clear, and very cold. A four-foot-wide patch of Canadian wild rye, brown and with full head, banded the creek. The horses grazed and drank as the men filled their canteens and built a small fire to boil coffee.

"It's a wonder there ain't a band of Sioux and Cheyenne camped here," Grass said, squatting next to the fire.

"The creek's too small, and there isn't any game. Besides that, there's not enough protection from the wind and blowing snow. Not exactly the kind of place I'd want to winter," Brazos replied.

A movement in the leaf-shedding cottonwoods startled them. Brazos lifted the Sharps carbine to his shoulder. Grass yanked his revolver off his belt. Both men followed the noise through the brush, looking down the sight of their guns.

A thin, hatless man staggered into the open space on the other side of the creek. He clutched a bloody rag held tightly to his chest. "Thank God, you're here!" he groaned, then collapsed into the short, dry grass.

"You check on him. I'll see if there's more," Brazos ordered as he leaped the creek and scrambled towards the brush, his carbine cocked. He found no trace of any others and jogged back to a kneeling Grass Edwards, who was giving the injured man a drink from his canteen. "How is he?"

Water dribbled down the man's unshaved face, as he squinted in pain. "I'm fumed, boys. Don't mind me.

115

It's them Sioux you have to watch out for!"

"Where are they?" Grass quizzed.

"North of here."

"North? We thought they were south."

"So did I. I figured on makin' a run to Fort Pierre, but they ambushed me yesterday evening just east of here. I hid out in a buffalo wallow all night and finally had the strength to make it to the creek."

"Were there others with you?" Brazos plied. "This is a dangerous trail by yourself."

"I should have knowed better. But I was in a hurry. Are you two goin' to Fort Pierre?" The man's narrow gray eyes searched wildly around the camp.

"If we can avoid the Sioux," Brazos said.

"You got to do a favor for me."

"What can we do?"

"Take my poke to my sister who's waitin' for me in Fort Pierre."

Grass Edwards gently gave him another drink of water. "A poke?"

"You two are carryin' gold out of the hills, ain't ya?" he asked.

"Maybe . . ." Grass answered.

"That's what I figured. I knew I could trust a couple of miners like myself."

"Where's your gold?" Grass asked.

"I cached it right before the fight with the Indians. About a mile east of here, I piled up three rocks as a marker, in the clearing in the middle of the boulders."

Brazos studied the man. *This might be the first mortally wounded man I've seen who didn't sweat.* "We

116

haven't seen a boulder since we left the Black Hills."

"There's some just east of here. You got to go get my poke and take it to my sister in Fort Pierre." The blood on his bandage had already dried.

"How will we find your sister?" Edwards asked.

The wounded man pointed to his coat pocket. Grass removed a yellowed handbill, slowly opening it up. "Jamie Sue! My word, man, are you Vincent Milan?" Grass choked.

"You've got to go tell her what happened and give her the money," the man gasped.

"We'll do it!" Grass promised.

"Let me look at that wound, partner," Brazos said.

"Cain't move my hand," Milan protested. "It's keeping my guts from spillin', boys. Just let me die peaceful in the grass, knowin' my bones will be buried and my sister will get my gold."

"Grass, you go get his gold and bring it back here. I'll stay here and take care of him," Brazos suggested.

"No!" the man insisted with a clear, strong voice. "You'd both better go. Those Sioux might be hiding near those boulders. It would be safer for you to go together."

"He's got a point about that," Grass concurred.

Brazos stood up, then looked down at the man. "We can't go off and leave you here."

"The only thing that will bring rest to my soul is that I know you have my poke in hand."

Grass Edwards stepped across the stream and retrieved the horses.

"We'll leave you a canteen," Brazos offered.

"Thank ya . . . and when you come back . . . bury me deep. But hurry . . . you've got to find that gold before them savages do."

As they trotted east, both men kept their guns cocked. Their eyes scanned the horizon.

"My dearest Jamie Sue's brother. This is providential, Brazos! I reckon she'll be a-grievin' when you tell her about her brother's death," Grass called out.

"Me tell her? She's your sweet Jamie Sue."

"I figure you can do the tellin', and I'll do the comfortin'. Look, there's the boulders, jist like Milan said. I wonder if the Sioux is in them rocks?"

"I don't know why they should be. They stole his horse, gun, and saddle. Milan was wrong to think the Indians would steal his gold. They have no use for it."

"I was thinkin' the same thing," Grass said.

"It's a wonder they didn't steal his boots and clothes."

"He must've got away before they stripped him. I'm going to get that gold for my Jamie Sue." Grass spurred his horse into the boulders.

Brazos hesitated, then followed.

In a clearing, about twenty feet across, Grass Edwards leaped down and walked his horse towards a small pile of stones. "This must be it!"

Brazos's hand was still on the receiver of his carbine that lay across his lap, when he heard a hammer cock only a few feet behind his head.

"Oh, there's gold in here all right, boys, but it's in your pokes, not that ground," a deep voice boomed.

Brazos cocked the big hammer on his Sharps but let it lay in his lap.

A man in a black long coat stepped from behind the rocks, a Smith & Wesson pistol pointed at Grass Edwards on his knees by the pile of rocks. Brazos couldn't tell if there were one or two men behind him. He didn't turn around to look.

"Well, I'll be . . ." Grass dropped his hand to the grip of his revolver.

"Don't try it, boys," the voice behind Brazos insisted. "We've got the drop on you, and you know it."

"It was a trap, Brazos . . ."

"I reckon it was."

"I cain't believe Jamie Sue's brother would do this to us, wounded like he was."

"Maybe he wasn't wounded," Brazos suggested.

The injured man from the creek rode into the clearing on a stout bay horse. The bloody rag hung from his saddle horn. He displayed no sign of an injury. "You two is the most gullible we've had in a month," the man sneered.

"Drop those guns in the dirt!" the man behind Brazos insisted.

"I'm not going to do that," Brazos replied.

"We can shoot you right where you are."

"And one of you will have a hole the size of a watermelon in his gut when this .50 caliber hits him."

"But you'll be dead!"

"So will the man with the hole in his guts."

"You don't need to shoot anyone," the man behind him said. "You get down, and we'll just take your

119

horses and packs and leave you here with your guns. That's a deal, and you know it."

"It's a lousy deal. I'm not gettin' down," Brazos replied.

A fourth man strolled into the clearing leading a string of saddle horses. On the last horse was an Indian woman, bound and gagged.

"You stealin' women, too?" Brazos quizzed.

"That ain't no woman, that's a squaw. We found her all doubled up and sick. We nursed her back to health, and now she helps us locate water holes."

Brazos glared at the man across the clearing. "Is that why she's tied up?"

"We got tired of her kickin' and bitin' us," Milan replied. "Now, are you goin' to drop those guns, or do we shoot you?"

Brazos gave Grass Edwards a look. Grass dropped a quick glance down at his revolver, dangled on a wire from his belt. There was a barely visible nod at the man standing nearest him.

Brazos gripped the receiver of the carbine tight in his right hand. *I agree with you, Grass, we aren't lettin' go of our gold, let alone our lives, without a fight. They have no intention of letting us go.*

Lord, have mercy on us all.

"Well?" the man behind him shouted.

Still mounted, Brazos held his hands up, the carbine in his right hand, the barrel parallel to the ground, pointed over the top of his head to the north.

"I said, drop the—"

Brazos opened his hand as if to let the gun drop,

instead he twirled it to the back and pulled the trigger without looking behind him. At the sound of the blast of the .50-caliber Sharps, Grass Edwards yanked his gun and fired a quick round at the man standing closest to him, who promptly dove behind the boulders.

Brazos threw himself low on Coco's neck and spurred across the opening, frightening the cavvy of horses held by the fourth man. He had dropped the lead ropes in order to pull his own gun, and the horses, including the one the Indian woman rode, bolted to the open prairie to the east.

The scream from the man behind him let Brazos know he had wounded the spokesman. Whipping around fifty feet beyond the boulders, he fired a second shot. Grass Edwards swung up into the saddle, galloped out of the boulders, riding so low on the horse's neck he could hardly be seen above the saddle horn.

Brazos sprinted off to the east with Edwards. Several shots rang out, but they didn't slow until they crested the next roll of the prairie and the boulders dropped out of sight.

"Are you all right?" Brazos called out.

"I ain't shot, if that's what you mean."

"Did I hit that guy behind me?" Brazos asked.

"I reckon. He dropped to the rocks like a rotten apple topplin' from a tree in winter."

"I think you wounded one, too," Brazos added.

"I didn't aim too much. I was in such a hurry to mount up. We ain't going back after them, are we?"

"Nope. They're in the middle of Sioux land on foot,

several wounded. I surmise that's punishment enough."

"There's their horses!" Edwards pointed to the next ridge.

Brazos grabbed his spectacles out of his vest. "Is the woman still riding one?"

"Yep."

"She can sit a horse, if she stayed on during that romp, all tied up like that."

"You reckon we should unbind her?" Grass asked.

"That's what I'm thinkin'."

The loose horses trotted further out on the prairie as they approached, but the woman's horse stood fastened by a lead rope that had snagged a sage.

Brazos rode alongside her and untied the bandanna around her mouth, her hands still fastened behind her back. The moment the dirty red cloth dropped from her mouth, she let out a high-pitched, blood-curdling scream.

Brazos held up his hands. "Quiet, we aren't going to hurt you," he shouted.

She continued to scream.

"Put the gag back on her!" Edwards shouted.

"What?"

"The gag!"

Brazos reached back over with the gag, and she snapped at him like a bobcat cornered in the barn.

But she did stop screaming.

"Look, lady, we aren't going to harm you," Brazos insisted. "Do you speak English? What is your name? Where do you come from?"

She looked at him, then Edwards, then back at Brazos with her fiery brown eyes. "Táku eníciyapi hwo? Tuktéta ŋha ŋ yaú hwo?"

"What did she say?" Edwards probed.

A sly smile broke across her face. "I said, 'What is your name? Where do you come from?' Don't you speak Lakota?"

"No, ma'am," Brazos admitted. "Let me untie your hands, and we'll be on our way, and you can go on yours."

"You will let me go free?" she said.

"I reckon you've got family around here."

"Yes, these men kidnapped me when I was at the creek drawing water. They demanded I tell them where the next water was to be found."

"Did you?"

"Oh, yes. It is about ten miles straight east of here." As Brazos leaned over to untie her hands she looked back at the boulders. "But I did not tell them there would be two hundred lodges of Lakota camped there."

"Two hundred lodges?" Grass stared at Brazos. "I reckon we're not going east."

"Are you going to Fort Pierre?" she asked.

"That was the plan."

"My people are scattered from here to there. It is better you go north to Bismarck."

"She might be right," Brazos admitted.

"She might be lying," Edwards added.

"She has been taught at the mission school not to lie."

"How do you know I've been to the mission school?" she asked.

"You speak good English."

She rubbed her wrists, then leaped to the ground and untangled the reins from the sage. "It was a very good school."

"Are you going to take their horses?" she asked as she remounted by grabbing the horse's dark mane and yanking herself to the saddle in one motion.

"Nope. We won't steal a man's horse, no matter how despicable he might be."

"I do not steal horses either. However, if they happen to follow me into our camp, there is nothing I can do about it," she grinned.

After two steps Brazos turned back and laid his hand on the horse's rump. "Ma'am . . . is there a water hole to the north?"

"Yes, ride northeast under the noon sun, and you'll find water at Tatá ṇka Wiwíla."

"Where?"

"Buffalo Springs."

"Will we find buffalo there?"

"No, but there is plenty of *Buchloe dactyloides.*"

Grass Edwards jerked back as if he'd been kicked in the shins. "Buffalo grass? Where did you learn the proper names?"

"I told you, the mission school was very good."

Brazos and Grass Edwards rode northeast for several minutes then stopped to look back.

"You see anyone?" Grass asked.

"Nope. How about you?"

"Nope."

"I reckon she got those horses to follow her," Brazos mumbled.

"Yep," Grass concurred. "Horses is funny that way."

Chapter Five

The Streets of Bismark, Dakota Territory, were filled with men.

Railroad men.

Army men.

And, especially, gold-seeking men.

No one talked openly about going to the Black Hills. After all, it was Indian land. Off-limits. Sioux territory. The army had cleared everyone out. Just a mountain ridge of hidden treasure protected from exploitation by the United States government.

But everyone was making plans to go there.

As soon as they bought supplies, they banded together with others, gathered up courage, and slipped out of town.

Just a dozen here.

A dozen there.

A trickle.

A stream.

Not a flood.

Not yet, anyway.

The biggest deterrent now seemed to be the weather. Bulging numbers of gold rushers resigned themselves to wait for spring.

Brazos knew it was absolutely crucial to get back to Deadwood as soon as possible.

Wearing a new suit, sporting a freshly shaven face, Grass Edwards surveyed the stack of crates crammed into the corner of the warehouse. "You reckon we bought too much?" he asked.

Brazos rubbed his neatly trimmed gray-and-dark-brown beard and pulled off his spectacles, slipping them into his worn, leather case. "Prices were high, but not nearly as high as we figured."

"It's that train that done it," Grass reported. "The Northern Pacific makes a run in here ever' other day. One ol' boy said he sent a telegraph order to Chicago and got the goods within seven days. Seven days from Chicago! Don't that beat all?"

Brazos studied his hands, clean for the first time in six months. Dark age spots were sprinkled across the suntanned surface. "It will take a little longer than seven days to get back to Deadwood."

Edwards's shirt collar was so starched, his head reminded Brazos of a lollipop. "I don't see how we can do it at all. We could load it in two freight wagons," Grass offered, "but there's no way to get a wagon into Deadwood."

Brazos wiggled his toes inside his boots and felt the comfort of new, store-bought socks. "That's no problem, pard . . . we'll probably be scalped before we ever reach the hills."

"You know, I was thinkin', if you and me hadn't run across that Lakota woman, we'd have kept going straight into two hundred lodges of Sioux," Grass said.

"Must've been Divine Providence for that gang to try and bushwhack us."

"That's exactly what I was thinkin'. Now, if the Lord led us out, don't it seem cruel for him to let us be slaughtered on the way back in?"

Brazos folded the long inventory and shoved it back into his pocket. "For I know the thoughts that I think toward you . . . Thoughts of peace, and not of evil, to give you an expected end."

Grass plopped down on one of the crates. "Where did you find them words?"

"Jeremiah 29:11."

"Yeah, but does that mean the Good Lord will give us our expected end," Edwards spun his new, wide-brimmed hat in his hands, "or *his* expected end?"

Brazos rubbed his beard as if brushing some invisible crumbs. "Does it matter?"

"No . . . I don't reckon it does."

"Then I say we take freight wagons," Brazos suggested. "We'll buy a couple of six-up teams for each. With our saddle horses, that gives us fourteen animals. We'll take the wagons as far as they go, then use the horses for a pack string, and freight it in the rest of the way, even if it takes ten trips. Who knows, maybe the Jims will be cutting logs out along the trail, and we can snake the wagons part of the way through the hills. We could disassemble the wagons and bring them to town, too. Sooner or later we'll have a road into Deadwood City."

Grass strolled around through the crates, surveying the goods. "How much you figure this would be worth

127

in the Black Hills?"

"If we make it back before Christmas, I would guess about five times the money."

"Fifteen thousand? Don't that beat all? A man could make more money sellin' goods than diggin' gold. Three thousand dollars for each of us . . . that's more money than I ever made in five years of pushin' cows."

"I think if we hold on to our claims until spring, then sell out when all these rushers finally find their way to Deadwood City, we should end up with twice that amount," Brazos suggested.

"Six thousand dollars? I bet there's many a nice ranch that can be bought for less than six thousand cash dollars. If you find one under a cross, you could have your Dacee June up here by July."

"That's what I told her in that letter I sent out with the Swedes last month. It might take most of next summer to find the right place."

"Shoot, with six thousand dollars in each of our pockets, we could stick a cross up on some windy hillside ourselves."

"I don't think that's what the Lord has in mind," Brazos corrected. "But it might not be around this country. I heard the Sioux turned down the government's offer for buying or renting the Black Hills at that Grand Council they held in September."

"Yeah, I heard there was ten thousand Indians down there in Nebraska at that meeting," Grass said.

"I heard twenty thousand."

"You reckon that's part of that big band we almost stumbled into?"

"That's what I surmise."

"The army likes to fight out on the prairie, and so do the Sioux and Cheyenne. Maybe them mountains is the safest spot," Edwards offered.

"The Black Hills are either a fortress or a trap, depending on how many Indians come up the gulch," Brazos concluded.

"You get them telegrams of yours sent?"

"Yep. Dr. Ferrar bought a steam sawmill east of Waco, and he's just lettin' it sit in his barn. Told him Deadwood would be a great place to open a mill, if we had a way to ship it north. Told him to wire me right back, and we'd start makin' the arrangements."

Grass unbuttoned his tight collar button and his face resumed a more normal color. "Did you find your boy Robert?"

"I learned he's still stationed at Fort Lincoln, but he's been transferred to the Seventh Cavalry."

"General Custer's outfit?"

"Colonel Custer's outfit."

"I thought Custer was a general?

"He was a brevet general during the war. He's a Lt. Colonel now."

"You don't say?"

"Some figure he's lucky to hang on to that rank. Anyway, they said Robert's on personal leave," Brazos reported.

"Maybe he went back to Texas to visit ever'one."

"Maybe so, but I don't think he had that much time. Then again, maybe he does. If a man went downriver he could take the train most of the way back."

"Wouldn't that beat all?" Grass hooted. "You comin' all the way to Fort Lincoln, and he goes home. 'Course, it could be he went downriver a couple of days to drink and chase the ladies. You know them soldier boys."

"Not Robert. He does everything by the book."

"Army rule book?"

"The Good Book."

"Well, if you cain't visit Robert, you can come with me to Fort Pierre while I find my sweet Jamie Sue. I could tell her you're my father."

"I wouldn't want to give her a bad image of your kin," Brazos chided. "Besides, I may be old, but I'm not nearly old enough to be your father."

"I suppose I could tell her you're my older brother and a little touched."

"Some folks probably think I'm a whole lot touched." Brazos grinned. "I think I'll stay here in Bismarck. Robert might return. Besides, I've got to hunt around for two teams and wagons."

"It's kind of a strange time, Brazos. Ever'one knows that land is going to open up, but those that wait will miss the rush. California . . . the Comstock . . . we just heard about those from a distance. This time, we're there, partner. You reckon they'll mention us in the history books?"

"Only if we get massacred in a particularly gruesome fashion, or freeze into statues during a blizzard."

"If fame is that expensive, I believe I'll pass," Grass added. "I'm going to pack my satchel and buy a present for my Jamie Sue. The boat goes down to Fort

Pierre about noon. If you change your mind, meet me there."

"I'm goin' over to the depot. I've been thinkin' about telegraphin' a mail order into Chicago and have them send Dacee June one of those great big mail-order dolls for Christmas."

"I reckon that ought to work," Grass concurred. "Bet they can have it to her in seven days!"

The stern-wheeler, *Far West,* sat high in the water. Its cargo had been unloaded the previous day. There was very little to ship back downriver: buffalo hides, buffalo bones, and a few passengers.

The wooden ramp creaked and sagged as Brazos Fortune led a saddled Coco onto the main deck. He had just checked the horse into the horse pen, when a voice called down from behind the railing of the second deck.

"You changed your mind?" Grass called out. "I knew you was dyin' to meet my Jamie Sue! I was just tellin' this . . ." Edwards's words faded with one glance from Fortune.

Brazos pushed his hat back and marched toward the purser. By the time Grass Edwards reached him, he had purchased his ticket, paid for horse passage, and was standing near the ship's bow, waiting for it to cast off.

"Brazos, what happened? You look like you was hit in the stomach with an axe handle."

Fortune yanked a telegram out of his pocket and stared out at the Missouri River.

131

"From home? Oh, Lord . . . it ain't about your Dacee June, is it? She didn't get the dysentery or pox, did she?"

"I should have never left her," Brazos replied. "I knew better. I was runnin', Grass. I didn't want to fight, so I just ran off."

"What's it say?"

"It's from Milt. Dacee June got the letter I sent out with the Swedes. When she read about me maybe not comin' home until next summer, she . . ." Brazos could feel tears begin to swell in his eyes. "She ran off, Grass . . . my baby girl ran away!"

"Run away? She cain't run off, she's only eleven!"

"She's twelve now . . ." Brazos mumbled. "What in the world am I doin' here? I'm two thousand miles away, standin' in some icy, muddy creek, in a gulch unfit for human habitation . . . fightin' Indians, bush-whackers, and the cold . . . tryin' to make myself rich. Good Lord, what am I doin' here?"

"Where did she go?" Grass Edwards tried looking over Fortune's shoulder at the telegram. "Did Dr. Ferrar say where she took off to?"

"She left a note sayin' she's goin' to find her daddy."

"The Black Hills? A little girl on her own is goin' to them hills? Did he tell you what direction? Is that all he said?"

"He said he didn't know how to get ahold of me, so he wired Robert last week at Fort Abraham Lincoln."

"That's why Robert ain't there! He went searchin' for Dacee June."

Brazos nodded, then hiked out to the extreme point

of the bow. The steamboat whistle blew, and they pulled away from the shore.

"I'll help you look for her," Grass called.

"We've got men in the hills whose lives count on us to get that freight back."

"Ever'one of 'em would understand. You got to find your girl."

"She's my last girl, Grass. I can't lose her, too. Not like this. Not when it's my fault."

"A little girl in Texas jist can't up and travel on her own all the way to Dakota."

"I told her in my letter that I was goin' to try to get to Fort Pierre for supplies, and I'd mail her a present from there."

"You reckon that's where she's headed?"

"Dr. Ferrar thought maybe so."

"Do you think Robert went down to Fort Pierre to look for her?"

"I imagine, if Milt told him the same thing."

"What if she's not in Fort Pierre? Has she had time to make it up from Texas? How far does the train go? They don't let unaccompanied children ride on trains, do they?"

"I don't know, Grass!" Brazos barked. "I don't know anything!"

Grass Edwards backed away. "Whoa, partner . . ." His voice was quiet, but shaken. "I reckon I'll stroll the deck."

Brazos tried to say something, but he couldn't get any words out. He just waved his hand. As the boat reached the main current, he stared straight ahead at the silt-laden river.

*What have I done, Sarah Ruth? I need you, darlin'. I
need you bad, right now.* He pulled off his hat, then
wiped the tears on the dirty sleeves of his old, brown
canvas jacket. *I never was any good without you. A man
like me should never raise kids on his own. I'm too unstable.
Too undependable. What was I thinkin'?*

*I go off and leave her like it's some big noble cause. Oh,
I'm followin' God's will . . . I'm a modern Abraham . . . I'm
goin' to the promised land . . . my calling is holy and spiritual. You're a fool, Brazos Fortune. All the treasure you ever
wanted in your life is with your girls and with your boys.
What in God's name are you doin' here?*

*Lord, have mercy on her. I want my girl, Lord Jesus.
She's got to be safe. This world is full of a lot of evil. At least
a girl should have a father to look after her!*

Your daddy was right. You married a fool, Sarah Ruth.

If I find her, Lord . . . I mean, when *I find her, Lord, I'll
never leave her again.*

*Of all the children, she's the one just like me. You told me
that yourself, Sarah Ruth.*

Just like me.

But I didn't run away from home when I was twelve.

*If I were that age, how would I get to Fort Pierre? I'd sell
something and buy a ticket on the Missouri, Kansas &
Texas Railroad all the way to Kansas City. Then, I'd go
book passage on a steamboat out of St. Joseph . . .*

But she's only eleven.

I mean, twelve.

She wouldn't have the money for that.

Maybe she's already made it to Fort Pierre. Maybe she

found some bummers trying to go west to the Black Hills. They wouldn't let her go with them. It's too dangerous. Unless she sweet-talked them.

My, how she can sweet-talk!

If she went straight west from Fort Pierre, she'd ride right into that big band of Sioux!

Grass Edwards tapped him on the shoulder. Brazos turned away from the bow. "They got some food for us upstairs. You want to eat?"

"I'm not hungry."

"Well, you cain't stand out here the whole trip. You'll freeze to death."

Brazos pulled his hat low in the front and shoved his hands into his pockets. "There are worse things that can happen to a man."

Like Bismarck, Fort Pierre swarmed with men who waited.

Some waited for the land office to open so they could file claims on farms and mineral rights.

Some waited for spring to sneak into the Black Hills.

Some waited to earn, or steal, enough money to go back downriver to St. Louis.

Some waited for news, money, or friends from home.

Brazos Fortune was not one who waited well.

Captain Mallory at the army encampment assured Brazos that no one, in any size group, had left Fort Pierre for the Black Hills. He had a patrol on the road east every day. His words had been quite direct: "General Crook has eliminated the settlements in the hills,

135

and I can assure you there are not any people other than Sioux or Cheyenne within one hundred miles of the Black Hills."

But the Captain had talked to Sergeant Robert Fortune, who had stopped by two days earlier in search of his sister. He had told Robert the same thing he told Brazos, and no, he did not know where Sergeant Fortune was at the time.

Brazos hiked down the muddy ruts of Fort Pierre that served as both street and sidewalk. His coat was buttoned high on his neck, his gloved hands shoved deep in the pockets of his canvas coat.

Grass Edwards met him next to a small log cabin that had been turned into a boardinghouse, sleeping eight to a room. "You find out anything, Brazos?"

"They claim there's no one in the Black Hills at all and that none have been allowed to leave here on that journey." Fortune's breath fogged at every word. "Which is all a crock, because they're sneakin' into the hills by the dozens any way they can. How about you, Grass? You find anyone?"

"No Dacee June, no Robert . . . and no Jamie Sue. No one in any saloon knew anything. This is the dumbest bunch of people I ever met in my life. Ever'one's makin' their own plans, not carin' about the next guy. It's gold fever, ain't it?"

"I suppose."

"Good thing we don't got it," Grass said.

"Did you mention to the rushers about the big band of Lakota out west of here?"

"Yeah, but they said that was impossible. Said the

army was makin' up stories like that to scare them from headin' to the hills."

"Well, it must have worked. I haven't seen anyone leave town to the west since we pulled in."

"Looks like a storm's rollin' in. No one likes to leave on a trip during a storm. What are you going to do now, Brazos?"

"I'm goin' to eat some supper and do some contemplatin'. I'm thinkin' about goin' on downstream . . . maybe that's what Robert's doin'. I wish I knew where he was lookin'. Grass, you about ready to eat?"

"I was thinkin' of checkin' the dance halls . . . you know, maybe someone there's heard of Jamie Sue . . . not that she's the type to frequent dance halls."

"Of course not."

"Where will you be eatin'?" Grass said.

Brazos looked up the street at an unpainted cedar building with a faded sign that jutted out into the street. "Reckon that one is as good as the next."

The Wild Goose Cafe was crowded. Brazos found a spot at a table built for six, that, counting him now, held ten men. None had seen a little girl, knew a Sergeant Fortune, or had any intention of passing the biscuits or gravy.

A short serving girl, with bright yellow hair stacked up on her head and wearing a long apron that at one time had been white, buzzed by him.

Her face was round, plain.

Her expression exhausted, pained.

Her shoulders sagged.

But her necklace was stunning.

When Brazos spotted it, he leaped out of his chair. His carbine tumbled to the floor. He blocked her retreat to the kitchen. He felt a lump in his throat and his heart raced.

"Excuse me, ma'am, where did you get that beautiful necklace?"

"It's a winner, ain't it? My Eddie got it for me."

"Your boyfriend?"

She stared around the room. The noise of the patrons isolated them. "Well," she shrugged, "with a hundred men to every girl, I ain't exactly limitin' myself to one boyfriend, if you know what I mean."

"Where did Eddie get the necklace?" Brazos probed.

"Now, ain't you the one, demandin' this and that? There ain't no more like it, if that's what you is searchin' for. It's custom-made."

"I know. It was made by Enrique Cordova-Sanchez in Brownsville, Texas, in 1866. That's why it has a CS66 on the clasp."

"I think I need to get back to work." The woman brushed past him.

Brazos reached out and grabbed her arm.

"Get your hand off me, mister!"

Brazos let go. "I'm sorry. Hear me out. This is critical. The reason I know about that necklace is that I had it specially made for my wife. My wife died a few years back, and I gave it to my daughter. Now, my daughter's run away from home, and I'm looking for her."

"Did you beat her?"

"What?"

"Is that why your girl ran away from home? My daddy beat me all the time. One day I just took his best gelding and rode off and ain't seen him since."

"My daughter ran away to find me. Where did your Eddie get the necklace?"

"He traded for it fair and square. You cain't have it back."

"No, ma'am, that's all right. It looks very lovely on you, and I hope you have as much enjoyment with it as my wife did."

"Thank ya, but I've really got to get back to work."

"Did your Eddie get the necklace here in Fort Pierre? Please, I really want to find my daughter."

"He got it on the boat."

"Which boat?"

"The *Far West*, when it was comin' upstream. He came back from St. Joseph a couple of days ago and said he traded a short, double-barreled Greener shotgun and two boxes of shells for this necklace."

"Who did he trade it with?"

"A little girl."

"Brown hair, big blue eyes, and a sweet Texas drawl?"

"Yeah, is that your daughter that ran away?"

"Yes! Did your Eddie say where she got off the boat?"

"Right here in Fort Pierre," she reported.

"When?"

"Day before yesterday."

"Dacee June was here two days ago!" Brazos

exclaimed.

"Is that her name?"

"Have you seen her around town?"

"I ain't seen her at all, mister."

"Where's Eddie?"

"He might be out huntin'. If so, he won't be back 'til next week."

"You don't know where he's at?"

"Mister, I told you I ain't limitin' my possibilities to just one man. I don't know where he is, and I've really got to get to work. Hope you find your girl." The waitress waltzed into the kitchen.

When he turned, someone was sitting in his chair and eating his supper. He retrieved his carbine and pushed his way to the front door.

A cold evening breeze hit his face as he walked out into the shadowy street. He stared to the west, where the heavy clouds hung low, darkening the sky, making it seem even later than it was. *Oh, Lord . . . she bought herself a shotgun and she's going to the Black Hills!*

Brazos covered every square inch of town twice before he finally retired to the boardinghouse room where he found a floor littered with men in bedrolls. He didn't bother to pull his boots off, but flopped down on top of the canvas bedding.

"Any luck?" Grass Edwards whispered.

The room was stuffy and reeked of sweat and alcohol. "Well, she's not in Fort Pierre, and she's not downriver. I've learned that much."

"What are you goin' to do now?" Grass whispered.

Across the room, Brazos heard a man snore as if

gasping his last breath. "I'm going to find my baby girl."

"How?"

"At daylight, I'm goin' to ride out on the prairie to the west to make sure she's not gone off with any group headin' into the hills."

"But they wouldn't take a little girl . . ."

"I hope not," Brazos sighed. "I'll cut a twenty-mile circle to the west to see just how many did head for the hills."

"Ever'one of them will run into the Sioux."

"I know." Brazos reached down on his bedroll to make sure his carbine was stretched out beside him.

"I'll go with you."

"I need you to stay here, Grass, in case I'm wrong. Robert or Dacee June may show up in Fort Pierre. Can you do that for me?"

"Yep, I'll do it. I ain't found no trace of my Jamie Sue either. What direction are you headed?"

"I'll be somewhere between the Cheyenne and the Wapka Shicha Rivers. South of there would be in the heart of Sioux country."

"And north would be in the badlands. No fool in his right mind would ride through that," Grass added. "If you ain't back in three days, I'm comin' after you. Don't go out there and get yourself killed, Brazos. That Dacee June is goin' to need her daddy."

"Grass, there's nothin' worse than havin' your baby lost."

By nine o'clock the next morning, Brazos could no

longer see Fort Pierre or the Missouri River. By noon, the clouds hung so low, he could see no more than a mile ahead of him. By five o'clock, he could see nothing at all.

With clouds hanging only a few feet above his head, darkness fell quickly and completely. Brazos camped in a shallow draw that housed a clump of six-foot-tall sagebrush. He built a small, smoky sage fire and hunkered inside his bedroll next to the flames, his carbine inside the blankets.

Lord, it just seems like yesterday that we lost Veronica and Patricia. They kept crying, begging me to make 'em feel better. Frail little things with their mother's eyes. Sarah Ruth, I will always feel like a failure. They needed me, and I couldn't do a thing. A grown man just sitting there on the bed pattin' their hands and tellin' them it was goin' to be all right.

We knew they were dyin', didn't we? We were just kiddin' ourselves and them, until they went home with Jesus. But they had each other. It wasn't like they had to go it alone. Within hours they were up there side by side.

But Dacee June's by herself.

And she doesn't have her daddy by her side.

Oh, Lord . . . maybe it would have been better for me to die on the prairie in an Indian fight.

He took a corner of the cold, rough wool blanket and wiped the corner of his eyes.

But it wouldn't have been better for Dacee June, would it?

After a near sleepless night, Brazos had coffee boiling before daylight and was already mounted and circling the rolling prairie before it began to rain. It was a light rain, but a cold one that blew west to east, pelting his face and soaking his coat. With the visibility no more than a hundred feet, it was impossible to spot any movement at all on the prairie.

Needing to pull his hat low to protect his face, Brazos found he was unable to scout much more than the path immediately in front of Coco. The rain brought with it the cold smell of doom.

No one could be out in this. Even the Indians are smart enough to stay in their lodges. If I turn back now, I could make it back to Fort Pierre a little after dark. This isn't smart. People get into trouble out on the prairie because they do dumb things.

This is extremely dumb.

The clouds were so thick he could not tell the position of the sun. *If that wind ever changes direction, I won't know north from south. Maybe the wind has changed in the night. Perhaps I'm going the wrong direction now. There aren't any landmarks.*

There's nothin'.

Lord, you said you had thoughts of peace and not of evil towards me . . . well, this is not a peaceful situation.

Actually, this is peaceful country. The only turmoil at the moment is in my head . . . and heart.

Maybe I took a wrong turn somewhere.

Like Fort Worth . . . or Waco . . . or back in Coryell County.

The next rise led him to another . . . then another . . . and another.

His clothes were soaked with rain and rubbed raw

against his skin.

The cold seemed to be concentrated in his bones and radiated outward.

Rain ran off his beard, but his mouth was dry, his lips chapped.

He could smell a wet prairie, a wet horse, a wet, wool saddle blanket, and a dirty, wet canvas coat.

There was no movement that he didn't make.

No sound other than his own and Coco's.

At a clump of sage, much similar to the one where he spent the night, he cut the trail of a single rider. It had traveled perpendicular to the direction he was going.

It's been plastered down, and the low spots are holdin' puddles of water . . . maybe today . . . maybe several days old . . . rain makes it impossible to tell. But it's the freshest trail I've seen. 'Course, it could be Indian tracks. The horse was shoed. They could have stole him. He's headed south. That would be Sioux country. Could be one of their scouts.

But the Sioux aren't south of here . . . they're west of here. Any brave would know that. It could be someone who thinks he's headed towards the Sioux. Who in his right mind would do that?

Or her *right mind.*

I refuse to believe my Dacee June would ride off into a storm, across Indian land, on her own. No sir, I don't believe that.

Brazos turned southwest and followed the tracks until he came to an outcropping of limestone rocks no bigger than a shed. In the midst of the boulders was a small circle of wet, black ashes.

No tellin' how long ago that fire was lit. Probably isn't Sioux. They wouldn't feel the need to hide in these rocks.

Brazos climbed down to the muddy prairie, reins in his left hand, carbine in his right. He approached the fire circle. He dug the toe of his boot deep into the soaked ashes, then dragged the boot a second time, plowing a little furrow in the muddy prairie beneath where the fire had been.

The furrow began to seep full of water, and he squatted down, tugging off the leather glove on his right hand. He reached deep into the muddy furrow with his fingers, then stood straight up.

That ground is still warm! All this rain is from this morning. Someone camped here last night!

One man out on the prairie?

Or one little girl?

She knows how to camp. I took her to round up wild cattle on Cowhorse Creek that time, and she insisted on doin' all the camp chores. Only nine, and she built the fire and baked me a Dutch oven peach cobbler. Then she sat around the fire singing church songs. Remember that, Lord? The sweetest little voice in Texas. I know you remember. "And can it be that I should gain an interest in the Savior's blood? . . ." Charles Wesley, you never sounded better than that night.

Brazos allowed the tears to mingle with the rain on his bearded cheeks and searched the ground trying to find boot prints, but could locate no identifiable ones. Even the horse prints were beginning to fade in the water and mud.

Someone's a few hours ahead of me riding south. Sooner

145

or later they'll run into the Bad River, then they'll have to go east or west.

Lord, if it's Dacee June, may she turn east.

If it's anyone other than a Lakota Sioux, may they turn east!

Brazos followed the muddy track to the next rise, then dropped off the shelf of the prairie. The clouds remained at the higher elevation, and his vision improved to several hundred yards. There was still no one in sight, and the horse prints were blending into the muddy ground. He thought he spotted a reflection of a ribbon of water stretching south. He rode Coco east about thirty feet, then stood in the stirrups. He pulled out his spectacles and jammed them on his cold, rain-drenched nose.

By studying the ground directly in front of him and tracing it due south, he began to connect the reflections.

It's a wagon track! A light wagon. A carriage . . . no one in their right mind would bring a carriage this far from Fort Pierre!

Brazos could feel his head begin to throb. He pushed his hat back a little.

But someone did come out here.

And someone else is following the carriage.

Brazos rode south following the carriage tracks marked by standing water. Both knees stiffened in the cold and began to ache. He kicked his feet out of the stirrups and tried to ride with his legs stretched.

I'm too old for this land.

It's a young man's world up here. Wild. Primitive.

146

Unspoiled. Harsh. Dangerous.

I'll be fifty in the spring.

A sharp pain settled in his lower back, and he tried to straighten up, even with the storm in his face.

Good heavens, Sarah Ruth, you always were the only one with common sense. Sometimes life is like a dream. This is not real. I'm not soaking wet on the prairie searching for my little girl. Dacee June is home on the ranch . . . in the kitchen learning how to cook with you, darlin'. Veronica and Patricia are on the porch sewing. Todd, Samuel and Robert are branding down at the corral, and I'm trying to put hobbles on a rank mustang that I captured down at Black Butte.

There's a warm gulf breeze rustling the leaves of the pecan tree near the barn. The dog is barkin' at the big, gray cat that's sittin' on a fence post, ignorin' the entire world. The branch water is runnin' clear, and corn and peas in the garden is head high.

Now, that's real life.

The way it's supposed to be.

This is just a dream.

He felt an uneasiness in the pit of his stomach. Almost like a cramp. Almost like needing to vomit.

It's a lousy, cold, painful, confusing dream.

It's like I'm up there with you just lookin' down at all of this.

Brazos cocked the hammer back on the Sharps carbine that lay across his lap. For a moment he thought about squeezing off a round, just to hear the sound.

Sarah Ruth . . . I'm either freezin' to death or startin' to lose my mind. And I don't know which would be worse.

147

Something's wrong here, Lord. I'm gettin' disoriented.

Brazos pushed his hat back and wiped his bandanna across his forehead which was covered with cold rain and hot sweat.

This is not good, Lord. I'm not findin' my baby girl. I've got to get back to town.

I've got to stop and build a fire.

I'm gettin' dizzy. I should've eaten something besides coffee and jerked meat.

He slumped forward and felt the saddle horn brush across his stomach.

I've got to keep from fallin' off my saddle.

Lord Jesus . . . it's all up to you now.

A sharp pain hit Brazos in the right shoulder when he rubbed it to loosen the muscles, and then his entire right side cramped up with a sharp pain.

I've got to lay down. I've got to rest. I could sleep in the mud. It doesn't matter . . . nothin' seems to matter.

In the distance to the south of him he heard a rain-muffled report of a rifle, followed by four or five more shots. The cramp in his side started to fade as he stood in the stirrups and tried to peer across the cloudy prairie.

That's a gunfight!

Brazos spurred Coco's flanks and began to trot south. He counted five more shots fired. By the time he reached the top of the next rise in the rolling prairie, the pain in his knees had melted away. He wiped the rain off his spectacles and replaced them on his nose. He rode Coco over to a patch of sage and peered down as the prairie sloped to a narrow river, lined with leaf-

148

less cottonwoods and brush.

Must be the Wapka Shicha . . . the Bad River. I'm that far south? Even in the dampness of the day, he could spot the gunsmoke from a rifle a split second before the report reached him.

I don't know whether the rider has pinned the people in the carriage, or the carriage has pinned the rider.

Maybe this has nothing to do with either!

Following a row of sage, Brazos rode closer to the river and continued to listen to the sporadic gunfire.

Scattered shots . . . no one's getting a look at the enemy . . . repeaters . . . lever action guns . . . but that's a single shot returning fire.

.45-70.

Trapdoor.

That's an army man.

At least, an army gun.

Brazos leaped to the ground when he spotted the five ponies, the carbine at his shoulder. Three of the horses were covered with Indian saddles. The .50-caliber bullet shattered the sapling that the horses were tied to, and all five mounts stampeded towards the east. He squeezed off another shot at the hooves of the lead horse and the cavvy galloped out on the prairie. A buckskin-clad Indian darted out from behind a cottonwood stump and sprinted in the direction of the horses.

Brazos followed him with the metal sights of the Sharps carbine.

Mister Indian, I squeeze off this trigger and you're dead.

Brazos raised his head up off the carbine. *Lord, I*

can't shoot someone without knowin' why. I reckon I'm not too good at killin'.

An explosion rang out, and the bark flew on the tree next to his right shoulder.

Now his single shot cannoned from his shoulder.

Boom!

He shoved another bullet into the chamber.

Boom!

And another.

Boom!

The report from the .50 Sharps was deep, loud, and bounced off the low clouds as Brazos threw the three shots in rapid succession into the clump of cotton-woods.

Several shots were randomly fired his way, then two more buckskin clad Indians dashed toward the direc-tion of the fleeing horses. The horses bolted out of sight, with three fleeing Indians in dogged pursuit. Brazos led Coco closer to the river. He stopped behind the safety of a large, leafless cottonwood.

"Mister? Are you all right in there? Did you take any lead?" Brazos shouted.

There was a pause. Then a deep, crisp reply. "No, sir! Did any of you get shot?"

When Brazos heard the voice, it was like a warm sip of hot coffee after a long, cold night. It gave him the same rush of warmth that he had felt sitting in the audience when a thirteen-year-old boy won the blue ribbon for steer raising at the Coryell County Fair.

"No one shot out here," Brazos replied. "You're alone, aren't you?"

"Yes, sir," the man shouted back. "How many's out there with you?"

"It's just me."

"All those shots from one gun?"

"I got a little excited with my ol' Sharps, Sergeant."

"I can't see you, mister. Can you see me? How did you know I was a sergeant? Did you say . . . a Sharps?"

The cloud cover was still thick, but Brazos thought for a minute it felt like spring. He thought about singing.

"Say," the man yelled out. "You wouldn't happen to be a decrepit old man from Coryell County, Texas, who totes a Sharps carbine and refuses to wear a sidearm, would you?"

"Keep yourself hidden, Robert, I'm not sure when those Sioux will be back . . ."

"They're Sahiyela and Lakota. But I haven't seen you in over a year. I don't plan on hidin' in the brush now."

"Is your pony OK?"

"I got him here with me," Robert said.

"Ride through the brush down the river. I'll watch from here to see that they don't back-trail you. I'll catch up a few miles west of here," Brazos instructed.

"I presume you are out here lookin' for Dacee June?" Robert shouted.

"I'm out here lookin' for two of my children. I found one."

Brazos waited almost five minutes. The Indian braves didn't return, so he mounted and rode east along the Bad River. He spotted the dark blue raincoat

151

of a tall, thin young man standing beside a long-legged, yellow-maned, light sorrel gelding wearing a McClellan saddle.

Brazos dismounted.

Robert pushed his hat back and gave him a brief salute. "I'm glad to see you, Father."

"You salute officers, young man. But you hug your daddy, you understand that?"

"Yes, sir!" Robert was the same height as Brazos, and the two men found themselves hugging dripping wet coats. Brazos thought it might have been one of the best hugs he had received in his life.

"You're an answer to my prayers, Son."

"I was doin' a lot of prayin' holdin' off those Indians by myself. I didn't know the Lord would use one old man to deliver me. They're supposed to be way south of here. I didn't expect them this far north, or east."

"There are several hundred lodges of Sioux and Cheyenne between here and the Black Hills."

Robert stepped back in surprise. "That's just an army bluff, to keep people out of the hills."

"I'm afraid not. I skirted their camp comin' out."

"I don't think the army knows about that," Robert said.

"I presume Sergeant Fortune will inform them. Let's build a fire, Son."

"What if the Indians sneak back here and attack us?"

"Then I'll die warm. My bones are freezin', Son."

He looked Robert over from head to toe. Clean shaven. Neatly trimmed mustache. Steel-gray eyes. Square chin. Broad shoulders. The kind that won't back down when he's right. The kind that's right most of the time. "Son, findin' you out here is one of my life's most cherished blessings."

"Well, you're going to be double-blessed when we find Dacee June."

Both men scouted the brush along the river for anything that would burn on a wet day.

"Did you get a telegram from your Uncle Milton?" Brazos asked.

"Yes, sir. I didn't know how to reach you. I figured you went out of the Black Hills with General Crook, but I hadn't heard from you in months. I sent a telegram down to a friend at Fort Russell who was goin' to try to find you in Cheyenne City. I thought maybe you'd be headin' home for Christmas."

"I sent a letter out to you about a month ago. Looks like it didn't get to you. I wish it wouldn't have gotten to Dacee June. I can't believe she took off like that. Aunt Barbara must be worried sick. At least Dacee June made it to Fort Pierre. That much I know. I presume you spotted your mamma's jewelry?"

"Mamma's jewelry?" Robert carved deep into a wet stick with his hunting knife before he found some dry shavings. Both men squatted around as the sergeant sparked his flint in order to start the fire.

"A lady at the Wild Goose Cafe said her boyfriend traded a shotgun and two boxes of shells to a little brown-haired girl on the boat with a sweet Texas accent. Dacee June had a gun," Brazos said.

"That's not all she has," Robert reported.

Brazos squatted next to the deep, white smoke,

153

holding his hand over nonexistent flames. "What do you mean?"

"A woman at the trading post said a girl came in and traded them to her for a tent and a bedroll . . . a little girl with a sweet Texas accent."

"She's goin' to the hills, Robert. She's set on goin' to the Black Hills."

"She's goin' to find her daddy, that's where she's going. She'd march into Hades to find you if she had to."

Brazos retrieved his canteen, two tin cups, and a handful of damp coffee from the saddlebags on the back of his saddle. Then he squatted back down next to the fire. "I should have never left her, Son. God knows, I shouldn't have done it. At the time, it actually sounded like the Lord's leadin'. What would get into a girl to do such a thing?"

"She's just like you, Daddy. You know that. Mamma knew that. That's why she prayed so much for Dacee June."

"And Samuel."

"Sam can take care of himself," Robert said.

"I know . . . I know . . . all you boys can. It's li'l sis that I'm frettin'. What's this carriage you're followin'? Surely no one would rent a carriage to a little girl alone. I didn't pick up the track until today."

Robert's wet leather gloves were steaming as he propped his coffee cup on the flaming sticks. "Well, I left Fort Pierre before this storm hit," Robert reported. "The army is patrolling the trail west. But I couldn't see where anyone had left Fort Pierre. I rode north thinkin' maybe they skirted around up there. I was hopin' she got in with some others going west, so I was looking for several horses, or a wagon, or something. I finally found these carriage tracks up along the Cheyenne River."

Brazos swirled the coffee grounds in his cup with a small stick. "You can't take a carriage all the way to the Black Hills."

"I know, but I was curious what they were doin' out here. It was the only decent trail I could find."

"Dacee June might have bought that stuff in Fort Pierre but taken the boat on upriver," Brazos suggested.

"Yep, that nags on me, too. But she's a bulldog, and if you mentioned comin' to Fort Pierre, she might have decided to ride out and meet you comin' in. Anyway, yesterday afternoon the carriage made a turn to the south and came straight down here. I camped up in some rocks, and by daylight the trail was about washed clean. Anyway, I followed the trail down here to the Bad River, and it suddenly turns back to the east."

"East? They're goin' back to Fort Pierre! You figure it's someone out from Fort Pierre on a drive or a hunt?"

"Or someone lost . . . confused . . . cold . . . or all three," Robert said.

"Someone who's twelve and has a sweet Texas accent?"

"I was hopin' it was her. Anyway, just as I picked up the trail back east the warriors showed up demanding my horse and gun."

"And you declined the offer."

"Yeah, well, they got persistent. So I holed up behind some logs, and we traded shots for a while until you showed up."

"Were there just three Indians?" Brazos said.

"That's all I saw," Robert replied.

"They have five horses."

Robert stared into his cup. "I didn't see their horses."

Brazos took a swig of coffee and felt the tin cup burn his lips, the liquid burn his throat. "Two of the horses weren't saddled."

"You think . . ."

Brazos nodded. "They could be carriage horses."

Both men stood up and began kicking out the fire.

Chapter Six

The cold rain drifted to snow before they reached the curve in the river. Brazos knew they couldn't keep the horses galloping much longer so he slowed down to a canter as they followed a muddy carriage track up a grade, away from the Bad River. At the crest, he reined up.

"Do you see anything?" Robert called out.

"Nothin', yet . . . and this snow will blanket their tracks. If we don't locate that carriage soon, we won't be able to trail it at all."

"I've been thinkin' about the shotgun you said Dacee June traded for," Robert pondered.

"What about it?"

"Those Indians didn't have a shotgun. At least, they didn't employ it. And you know they wouldn't hesitate to filch it, if they could have. So those Indians stole the horses and not the shotgun . . ."

"Then Dacee June still has that shotgun!" Brazos blurted out.

"I do believe li'l sis would pull the trigger if she had to."

"You're right about that." Brazos thought back on how many times he had taken Dacee June bird hunting, much to her mother's dismay. *Sarah Ruth, you always said a young lady shouldn't be shooting a gun, especially one that leaves her shoulder black and blue. But my, how that girl loves to hunt.*

Both men trotted east, their backs now to the squall. Each snowflake seemed to whistle as it sailed past.

"But if she's stuck out in this storm, she'll freeze to death before mornin'," Robert said.

Brazos brushed the snow off his shoulders. "I reckon she'll huddle near that carriage, wherever it is."

"What's over by those boulders?" Robert pointed across a horizon of rolling prairie, dead grass, sage, snow, and mud.

Brazos stood in his stirrups and scanned the horizon. "In this storm, a person can't tell between sky and ground . . . just a blanket of white . . ."

"Over there! I think it's a buckboard or a surrey!" Robert broke into a gallop.

Brazos pursued. *Lord, how come I didn't see that? Maybe I need some new spectacles. Maybe I need the eyes of some twenty-two-year-old kid to locate things for me.*

As he advanced, he could not observe anyone around the old, wet buckboard with three wooden bench seats and a tattered top of oilcloth and snow. Robert reached the wagon first and slid down from the saddle.

"Dacee June!" Brazos shouted. He circled his horse through the brush next to the rig. "You find any sign, Robert?"

"There's nothing in the wagon. Nothing at all!"

"Dacee June!" Brazos called again.

Robert mounted his horse and looped around behind him. "Dad, we don't know for sure that Dacee June was in this rig. It could have been anyone. We don't . . ."

"I know . . . I've been arguin' with myself about it. I want to believe she's back in Fort Pierre . . . or Bismarck . . . in some warm hotel room. But I wanted to believe she was sitting here at this wagon, waitin' for us . . . but she's not. She could be anywhere. She could be injured. She could be lost. She could be . . ." Brazos couldn't make himself conclude the sentence.

"Do you see any tracks leadin' away from the wagon?" Robert asked. "This snow is coverin' up everythin'. Whoever was in this wagon could have headed in any direction. There's no way of knowin'."

Brazos studied the backboard. "If Dacee June was here, I know which way she went."

"How's that?"

"The wagon is pointed east. This wagon was headed back to Fort Pierre when it was stopped and the horses stolen. Dacee June has been with me enough to know that she should follow the way the wagon's pointed. Like the time you, Sam, and those Devore girls broke an axle out west of the Leon River and Dacee June and I had to come find you. We just kept goin' straight to where the wagon was pointin'."

"That only works until you lose sight of the wagon . . ." Robert pointed to a ridge straight ahead of them a couple hundred yards. "After that she could wander in any direction."

Snowflakes were the size of two-bit pieces by the time they reached the ridge. A fresh, white quilt covered the ground, erasing all tracks. Both halted and gaped into the storm.

"Now where?" Robert inquired.

Brazos stood in the stirrups, whisking the snow off his jeans. He tried to study the eastern horizon. He removed his spectacles, folded them, and jammed them into the leather case. "Don't need those in this storm." He kneaded the bridge of his nose and squinted as the snowflakes blasted his face. His heart throbbed through his temples.

Lord, at some point Robert and me will have to think about gettin' out of this storm and savin' our own lives. At least, savin' Robert's life. I am so tired, Sarah Ruth. If I find our girl dead in the snow, I'll just lay down next to her and die. He tried to summon enough energy to talk. "Draw us a straight line in the snow from here, back to the wagon . . . maybe we can project it on up ahead."

Lord, I know that it ain't right to only be concerned if it's my Dacee June. Whoever was in that wagon is some other father's son or daughter. I'd like to help them, no matter who

159

it is. But I can't rescue what I can't find, and I can't track what I can't see.

With Robert digging a line with his boot heel, Brazos squinted both eyes almost closed and traced the direction of the line into the snowy horizon. "Is that some rocks up there?" he called out. He began to feel a surge of heat in his bones.

"What?" Robert replied, remounting his sorrel horse. "Where? I don't see anything."

"Follow the horizon about thirty degrees south of that line you made. See them up there?"

"There's nothin' there."

"Sure there is . . . look again. If Dacee spied out those rocks, she'd head for them to get out of this storm."

"Daddy, I don't see anything. I think you're just being wishful. You don't even have on your spectacles."

"I don't need them for that," Brazos insisted.

"Our best bet is ridin' this straight line." Robert offered. "It will at least get us towards Fort Pierre. If we veer off to the south again, we'll hit the Bad River . . . or Indians . . . or both."

"I'm sorry your sight is playin' out on you, Son, but we're going this way." Brazos booted his heels into Coco and trotted off into the storm.

The shout, "Daddy!" faded behind him.

Visibility was not much more than twenty feet.

And everything that was visible was white.

Robert rode alongside Brazos, and after a romp into the storm that featured horses slipping and stumbling, he reached over, seized Coco's chin strap, and yanked both horses to a halt.

Brazos slid forward in the saddle and clutched the horn with his left hand.

"What did you do that for?" Brazos shouted.

"We're goin' the wrong way!" Robert hollered.

"Turn loose of my horse!"

"Daddy, come on. You're gettin' snow blind!"

The once heavy snowflakes ceased as if on cue.

"I know what I'm doin', son."

"And I know what I'm doin'. We've got to get you back to Fort Pierre before you freeze to death. We're going too far south, and you know it," Robert argued.

Brazos extended the barrel of his carbine and cuffed Robert's hand away from the bridle. "I'm goin' after my baby girl."

Robert stretched over with a gauntlet-covered hand and jostled his father's shoulder. "Your mind's playin' tricks on you. Come on, I'm takin' you to town!"

A Chinook wind wafted from the south, slowly lifting the clouds off the horizon.

"I'm not goin' back without my Dacee June!" Brazos thundered, and he slapped Robert's hand off his shoulder.

"Dad, we don't know where she is! Come on, let's go warm up and then figure this out!"

"Not unless you plan to whip me and hog-tie me to the saddle."

"If that's what it takes to save your life, I'll do it!"

Robert's eyes flared. For a brief second Brazos thought he was looking straight at Sarah Ruth. Then he gazed off to the east. *Have I been starin' at a mirage? Is he right? Is this storm whippin' me and I'm seein' things? Freezing . . . exhausted . . . losing hope. What's happening to me? Has it gotten so bad my children have to take care of me?*

"My word, you were right!" Robert suddenly shouted.

Brazos peered straight over Coco's ears. "I was? Those rocks . . . do you see them, too?"

"There's no way you could have seen those from back there," Robert protested. "The snow on top of them makes them almost invisible from here, even with the storm subsiding." He jolted his horse's flanks and loped towards the outcrop of brush and rock on the top of a rise about a half-mile away.

Brazos trailed him, and by the time they reached the bottom of the incline, he observed a sliver of blue sky behind the heavy, gray clouds. *Just like that, the storm is liftin'? Maybe the storm was all in my mind.*

Robert slowed to push his horse through the thick, leafless brush that surrounded the jagged, snow-covered rocks. Robert's horse faltered, regained its foot, then lunged through the branches.

At that moment a limb the size of a hitching post came swinging out from behind the rock, catching a startled Robert Fortune in the stomach. He plunged off the horse, but managed to seize the branch and hold on, wrenching the assailant to the snow.

Brazos, his carbine at his shoulder, surveyed the two people rolling in the snow. *A woman? Who is she?* The lady's cape hood plummeted off her head, exposing coal-black hair that was halfway unfastened and

162

draped across her face. Robert straddled her, pinning her arms to the snow.

"Who are you?" he shouted.

"Who are you?" she yelled back, her round, smooth face, blushed red from the raw storm, or embarrassment, or both.

"I'm Sergeant Robert Fortune . . ."

"Robert!" a young girl's voice wailed from somewhere behind the rocks.

One time, several years earlier, Brazos and Sarah Ruth had driven to Dallas with Milt and Barbara Ferrar and listened to a visiting orchestra from New York City perform select works of Beethoven and Bach. Until this very moment, he always figured those were the most beautiful sounds he would ever hear in his life.

But a young girl's scream in the Dakota storm far exceeded the melodies of the orchestra. In the background he was sure he could hear choirs of angels.

Brazos vaulted from his horse and plummeted through the thicket of brush. "Dacee June!" he yelled.

"Daddy!" the voice cried.

By the rocks, the hood of her cape buttoned under her chin, thick, wool gloves wrapped around a short-barreled shotgun, red-cheeked, blue-lipped, and eyes dancing, posed the most beautiful girl he had ever seen in his life.

"Dacee June!" The carbine tumbled into the snow.

Dacee June discarded her shotgun and sprinted towards him. She was over a foot off the ground when they met. Her enthusiastic arms knocked his hat off and

163

encompassed his neck with a breath-stopping clutch.

Their tears mingled as he held her freezing cheek against his.

"Your face and lips are cold," she informed him.

"But my heart is very warm," he said.

"I just knew I'd find you," she sobbed. "I knew I could. No one thought I could, but I found you, didn't I? I came to Dakota and found my daddy!"

"You found me, darlin' . . ."

"Actually," a woman's voice skimmed through the cold air from the midst of the outcropping, "both Thelma and I were quite confident we would locate you."

Two caped and blanketed women strolled closer. "Yes, we didn't really start to lose hope until this morning when the hostiles pilfered our horses. I tried to convince the others to burn the wagon for a signal fire, but Louise felt that would attract the wrong element."

"The March sisters?" Brazos gulped. "What . . . why . . . how . . . ?"

"Would you please let me up!" the dark-haired woman shouted as Robert rolled off her and struggled to his feet.

"Hi, Robert!" Dacee June called out, but didn't liberate her father's neck.

"Li'l sis, I'm surely glad to see you." He reached back to offer the woman on the ground a hand. She refused, struggled to her feet, then slipped and fell. This time she held out her hand as Robert assisted her.

"I can't believe you sisters are out here in the middle

of a Dakota storm!" Brazos muttered.

"It's been quite an adventure!" Louise Driver declared.

"Especially the past forty-eight hours!" Thelma Speaker said as she sauntered straight up to young Fortune. "Hello, Robert, it's so nice you could meet us with your father. I'm sorry we can't offer you a cup of chocolate and a cookie."

"Mrs. Speaker," he said as he tipped his hat, "Mrs. Driver, nice to see . . . I mean, I'm amazed to see you. I trust all of you are well," Robert stammered.

The young lady with the long, wavy black hair whisked snow off her cape and dress.

"I don't believe I know the young woman who tackled Robert," Brazos inquired.

"Tackled him? I tackled him?" the lady huffed. "I thumped him from his saddle. He's the one who shamelessly threw me to the ground and rolled over on me like I was some dance hall darling. I've never been so . . . ."

"Actually," Louise announced, "after what we've been through in the last two days it's amazing we didn't shoot you two on sight."

"Let me introduce you," Thelma moved over next to the woman, using the same tone and expression as if she were at a ballroom in Austin. "Mr. Brazos Fortune, and his youngest son, Robert . . . I'd like for you to meet Miss Jamie Sue Milan from Des Moines, Iowa. She has been our companion the past two days and is a delightful and talented young woman."

"Yes," Louise concurred. "She reminds me so much

of my daughter, Julie."

"*The* Jamie Sue?" Brazos choked. "You are the famous Jamie Sue?"

A slight smile burst across the woman's smooth face for the first time. "Yes, how have you heard of me?"

"There's notices posted all over the Black Hills about you lookin' for your brother."

The woman's brown eyes sparkled. "Do you know Vincent?"

"Actually . . . Miss . . . I don't know him . . . but, I, eh, well," Brazos stammered. "A friend of mine had some dealin's with your brother."

"Really! Oh, that's wonderful! Is he in good health?"

"I understand he's in better shape than . . . eh, than he looked at first glance. Anyway, this friend of mine is in Fort Pierre and will tell you all about your brother," Brazos mumbled.

"Oh, this is so wonderful! I have an estate settlement I must discuss with my brother. He's never been interested in money, but I, at least, need his advice," she gushed.

"Well, a fella like your brother . . . just might, you know, change over the years," Brazos mumbled. "Could be that money means more to him nowadays."

Dacee June slackened her grip on his neck as he let her feet slip down to the ground. "Daddy, I'm cold."

He retrieved his hat and shoved it on his head. "I think there's enough brush around here for a fire. We'll get one going, then Robert and I will ride back for the wagon. I reckon these two saddle ponies can do a little drivin', if need be."

"You aren't leaving me," Dacee June insisted. "I'm going wherever you go."

Robert fetched the guns, then secured the horses to some brush. "Dad, you guard the ladies and I'll go get the buckboard."

"You'll need help. These two ponies won't be too anxious to be rigged."

"I'll go with him," Jamie Sue offered, still shaking snow out of her hair. "I've been around horses and jackasses all my life. Both the four-legged and two-legged varieties."

"I would rather do it on my own," Robert insisted.

Miss Milan tried to repin her hair. "You think I can't hitch a team?"

"I didn't say that." Robert shook snow off some dead branches. "I think you should stay with the women and warm up by the . . ."

Jamie Sue marched straight at him, like a bulldog on the attack. "I'm perfectly capable of takin' care of myself without your advice."

"Since you two seem to rile each other," Brazos began, "maybe you should . . ."

"Rile each other? Rile would be considered a positive term compared to what I feel at the moment!" she huffed. "And I'm going to go help bring that wagon—that's settled. May I borrow your shotgun, Dacee June?"

"Oh, yes! My daddy will protect me now." She handed the weapon to Miss Milan. "Are you scared the Indians will return?"

"No," Jamie Sue said. "I want protection for the next

time the sergeant decides he wants to throw me to the ground and wrestle."

"Me? This is absurd. I am not taking her." Robert stomped off to look for more firewood.

"You might need help," Brazos called out. "Take her with you, but promise you won't shoot each other."

"I'll make no such promise," she raged.

"Well, you better both warm up . . . on the outside . . . before you ride off," Brazos lectured. "We'll all need to dry off a little before we make a run for Fort Pierre. Where's your satchel, li'l sis? You didn't run away from home without some belongin's, did you?"

"I didn't run away from home." When she looked up at him her nose was turned up even more than usual. "My home is with you, Daddy."

The fire was hot, explosive, and smoky. But no one complained. The March sisters sipped on hot water from a common shared cup, while Brazos drank boiled coffee and filtered the grounds with his teeth. Robert and Jamie Sue rode off on the two horses, squabbling over the merits of McClellan saddles. Above them, the storm clouds loitered but were now spaced by cold, blue sky.

Dacee June perched beside him, hanging on his arm, and mauling a piece of tough jerky. Brazos's carbine was propped up against his right leg. The March sisters sat on their duffles on the far side of the campfire.

"I want to hear this whole story, Dacee June," he insisted.

"You mean, how I got clear up here to Dakota?"

168

"That's right."

"It all started when I got the letter that you weren't coming home for Christmas. That's when it dawned on me that you could never come 'home,' because we don't have a home anymore."

"I meant that I wouldn't be coming to your Aunt Barbara's."

"Yes, but that's not our home. Anyway, I cried myself to sleep for a couple nights and then that sheriff showed up looking for you."

"What sheriff?"

"The Tarrant County sheriff," Dacee June said.

"What did he want?"

"To apprehend you for resisting arrest in Fort Worth."

"That's preposterous."

"That's when I realized that my only home is with you, and you couldn't come back to Texas, so I should go to you, and since you thought I was all content at Aunt Barbara's you would never, ever ask me to come live with you. So I just up and decided on my own." Dacee June sucked in a big, deep breath.

Brazos glanced across at the two middle-aged ladies. "And just where do the March sisters come into this picture?"

"I assure you, Brazos, we had nothing to do with her decision to leave Texas," Louise informed him.

"Heavens no!" Thelma added. "We were in Kansas City at the time, on our way home from visiting our children, and we knew nothing about this. But when we saw Dacee June at the railroad station there . . ."

"Let the young lady tell the story," Louise insisted.

"Yes, you're right." Thelma folded her hands in her lap. "Go right ahead, dear."

"I sold some of Mamma's jewelry and rode the stage to Dallas, then bought a train ticket to Kansas City," she explained.

"They let you ride on a train by yourself?" Brazos searched for a pleasant way to spit the coffee grounds out of his mouth.

Dacee June rolled her round eyes, then stared at the lingering clouds. "I told them my daddy had died in Dakota Territory, and I was going north to bring the body home."

"You told them what?" Brazos coughed the grounds into his gloved hand, then brushed them into the mud at his feet.

"Well, it worked."

Brazos snatched the coffeepot off the flames and poured himself another cup. "It was a lie."

"The Lord will forgive me. My heart was right," she explained.

"You can imagine how surprised we were to find Dacee June at the train depot in Kansas City," Louise broke in.

"Let Dacee June finish her story," Thelma insisted.

Dacee June took a small stick and poked at the flames. "When I got to Kansas there was Mrs. Speaker and Mrs. Driver at the depot."

"We were very glad to see her," Louise interrupted. "There was this simply wretched banker from Baltimore who kept following Thelma all around the terminal!"

"He wasn't completely wretched . . ." Thelma mused.

"But he was annoying."

"That's true. And I rather pity his two valets who had to tote all that baggage," Thelma added.

Brazos felt his daughter's thin, warm hand brush his arm. He yanked off his glove and slipped his fingers into hers. "Now, young lady, just exactly what did you tell the March sisters when they asked where you were going?"

"I told them the truth."

"Oh?"

"Mostly the truth," Dacee June conceded. "I told them I had gotten a letter from you and that you were settled into the Black Hills and I was going up to be with you."

"Settled?"

"Well, you said you wouldn't be back to Texas until next summer. That sounds like you settled in to me."

"She has a point there, Brazos Fortune," Louise lectured. "Heaven knows we didn't have any intention of telling someone else how to run his family. But after all, Sarah Ruth was our very dear friend . . ."

Thelma broke in at Louise's first breath, "So we decided that a young lady shouldn't have to travel alone . . ."

"And since we had no immediate plans . . ."

"We might as well take the stage with her to St. Joseph, and ride the steamboat up the river." Thelma Speaker took a deep breath when she concluded.

"I thought you would be in Fort Pierre," Dacee June added.

Louise Driver fiddled with the high lace collar on her heavy, dark dress. "We decided to just come up to Dakota, have a nice little supper with you and your daughter, then return downriver. It seemed like quite an adventure."

"Which it certainly has been. My goodness," Thelma continued, "I never dreamed that there were fifty men for every woman in Fort Pierre."

"One hundred to one . . ." Louise corrected.

"We certainly would have visited here sooner!" Thelma chuckled, then turned to Dacee June. "I was just kidding, dear."

"When I got to Fort Pierre and couldn't find you," Dacee June continued, "we thought we'd ride out and meet you coming in."

Brazos stretched out his long legs, to work off a cramp. "But what if I wasn't on the trail?"

"Then I just thought I'd join up with some others going to the Black Hills and surprise you," she announced.

"You certainly surprised me, all right. You just rented a buckboard and took off across the prairie?"

"Heavens no!" Thelma gasped. "It's much more complicated than that."

Louise reached over and patted her sister's knee. "Now, dear, let Dacee June continue."

"Well, Daddy, I thought the March sisters were going back to Texas when we got to Fort Pierre, so I . . ."

"So you bought a shotgun and camping gear." Brazos tossed a couple more wet branches onto the fire.

Dacee June dropped her chin to her chest. "You aren't mad at me for trading away the jewelry, are you?"

He reached over and hugged her. "At the moment, I'm extremely happy . . . but I reserve the right to give you a whippin' after it all sinks in."

"Oh, my . . . I do trust you'll be gentle with her!" Thelma gasped.

"Daddy doesn't ever whip me!" Dacee June grinned.

"Well, this might be the first!" he warned.

She hugged his neck, kissed him on the lips, then sat back down, wrinkling her nose. "He threatens a lot, but he's pretty easy to see through. My mamma taught me that."

He waved an ungloved finger at her. "You still haven't explained how you got out on the prairie."

"I asked at the livery stable if they rented rigs that go to the Black Hills."

"What did they say?" he quizzed.

"They laughed and said no one could take a rig to the Black Hills, and they weren't about to rent one to some fool kid."

"Good for them."

"Daddy!" Dacee June groaned.

"Go on, then what happened?"

"The lady I bought the bedroll and tent from knew of a group of men who were going into the hills and said I should talk to them about traveling with them.

173

But by the time I found someone who knew them, they had already left. That's when I ran across Mr. Jamison."

"Who?" he asked.

"Luke John Jamison," Dacee June said.

"Who's he?"

"A scoundrel, that's who he is!" Thelma retorted.

"Now, dear, he did leave us the rig and the shotgun," Louise reminded her.

Brazos sat straight up, his hand reaching for his carbine. "He did what?"

"Well," Dacee June said, "Mr. Luke John Jamison, which is probably not his real name at all, overheard me ask about a carriage and said he would drive me out on the prairie to catch up with that party going to the Black Hills."

"For a price, no doubt," Brazos mused.

"Ten dollars," she reported.

"Ten dollars! Where did you get ten dollars?"

"The ruby brooch," Dacee June said.

Brazos glanced over at the thoughtful-looking Louise Driver and a pensive Thelma Speaker. "That doesn't account for the March sisters."

"When we heard that Dacee June was coming out on the prairie with some man, we decided to ride along," Thelma explained. "We didn't think it right for her to be alone."

Brazos gazed through the thick, white smoke drifting from the fire. "I owe you ladies thanks for looking after my girl."

"Actually," Louise shrugged, "she sort of looked

after us."

"What?"

"First . . ." Dacee June said, "let me catch up. Mr. Jamison seemed happy that the March sisters were going along, and when Miss Milan heard that we were going, she insisted on coming too, because she's looking for her brother."

"So this man Jamison had a wagonload of ladies for ten dollars apiece?" he probed.

"Yes. We went north to the Cheyenne River to avoid the troops patrolling the main trail, so he said, and then turned south. He said we'd cut their trail that way, and if we didn't, it meant we were ahead of them. Anyway, we pulled into an outcrop of rocks . . ."

"About like this one," Louise broke in.

" . . . late in the afternoon," Dacee June continued.

Thelma tried to brush her mostly blonde, curly hair out of her eyes. "And you'll never guess who was waiting for us in the rocks."

"A gang of holdup men?" Brazos offered.

"My, how did you know?"

"It's an old trick," Brazos said.

"So they robbed us of all our valuables," Dacee June reported.

"Not exactly all our valuables!" Thelma raised her eyebrows. "A woman has a few places to hide most of her wealth."

"And some have more hiding places than others," Louise chided.

"Anyway, they took Mamma's rings, Daddy." Dacee began to sniffle.

"It's all right, darlin'," Brazos comforted her. "They left you alone, right?"

Dacee June nodded her head in his chest.

"They took two gold eagles from me and the same from Thelma," Louise reported. "But I think Miss Milan lost almost one hundred dollars."

"Then they told us to go back to Fort Pierre and be happy *they* robbed us, instead of the Sioux. Then they rode off."

"Which direction?" he asked.

"To the west, I think," Dacee June informed.

"What about the Indians?"

Dacee June stood and turned her back to the fire. "That was this morning," she reported. "It was so late by the time they rode out of sight, we camped at some rocks for the night and slept under the buckboard."

"Some slept," Louise reported. "I didn't."

Dacee June waltzed around the fire as she talked. "Miss Milan knows a lot about horses, and she hitched the team the next morning and volunteered to drive us back."

"But it was extremely cold and raining this morning," Thelma added, "and we were disoriented."

"So I said we should just keep on a straight course until we hit a river, then follow it downstream to the Missouri," Dacee June explained.

"Which we did. But by then it was raining hard so we stopped and built a fire." Louise let the cape hood drop off her straight, black hair. "That's when the Indians rode up."

"They wanted us to feed them," Dacee June

declared. "But we didn't have anything to eat."

"They became quite indignant," Louise added. "They said they would take us back to their camp peacefully or they would scalp us."

"But they were easy to read," Dacee June replied. "They weren't going to scalp us."

"I must honestly report that only Dacee June believed that," Thelma declared.

"Yes," Louise bubbled, "then your dear Dacee June showed her true colors and saved us all."

"What did she do?" Brazos challenged.

"She threatened to shoot us," Thelma announced.

"What?" he gasped.

"She grabbed her shotgun and said if the Indians came any closer she would shoot Jamie Sue, Thelma, and myself," Louise explained. "She was quite convincing."

"You were going to shoot them?"

"I hoped I didn't have to do it. Anyway, they took our horses and rode off mumbling about a bunch of crazy women."

"Is it true they leave crazy women alone?" Thelma asked.

"Doesn't everyone?" Brazos countered.

"Yes, quite right," Louise nodded.

"So we picked up our satchels and decided to hike back to Fort Pierre."

"But," Louise continued, "when it started to snow we sought some protection in a shallow cave back in these rocks."

"And that's when you came along!" Dacee June

triumphed.

"Except we thought it might be that rascal, Luke John Jamison," Thelma said.

"So, Jamie Sue clobbered the first rider?"

Louise's smile was wide and easy. "Precisely."

Brazos pulled off his hat and shook the melted snow out of his hair. "Well, the Lord's been mighty good to you gals."

"Good?" Louise choked. "We've been robbed twice and left to die on the prairie!"

"But you weren't beaten, shot, stabbed, assaulted, raped, scalped, or killed," he reminded them.

"Yes, that does give it some perspective," Thelma mused.

Brazos and the ladies spent the next half hour rotating their position around the fire, drying out their clothing. Then Dacee June climbed the highest rock and shouted. "Here comes the buckboard."

"Are they both in it?" Brazos called.

"Yes."

"Good. That means one of 'em didn't kill the other."

"They are sitting on the same seat," Dacee June called out.

Brazos hiked over to where she was perched. "That's good."

"Close together."

"How close?" Thelma questioned.

"Real close," Dacee June exclaimed, jumping down from the rock into her father's arms.

That's not good. Brazos's mind flashed to Grass Edwards and his folded handbill written by his 'sweet'

Jamie Sue. *That's not good at all.*

When the excitement of the reunion on the prairie finally subsided, it was determined since everyone was tired, cold, grouchy, and hungry, they would head back toward Fort Pierre and keep going no matter how late it was when they arrived.

Because neither saddle horse enjoyed being under a harness, Robert volunteered to straddle the lead horse and keep him honest. Brazos drove the rig, Dacee June hovered at his side, Jamie Sue Milan next to her. In the middle seat, under every available blanket and bedroll, were the March sisters.

The sky never cleared completely, but the scattered clouds sailed across without losing any precipitation. About dark, the sky cleared and the air cooled. Brazos drove on a northeast angle until they cut across the main trail east out of Fort Pierre. It was the route patrolled by the army, the one they all had avoided when they left town. But the troops were not about to halt people coming into Fort Pierre from the west, only those who tried to exit that way.

The muddy road was frozen by the time they reached it. The wagon rolled along without nearly as much effort as earlier in the day. Sometime before midnight, Brazos stopped the buckboard in a rocky campsite, and they built a fire.

Brazos, Dacee June, Robert, and Jamie Sue huddled around the billowing white smoke and blazing red flames.

The March sisters refused to leave their wool blanket

cocoon in the wagon.

"The horses are mindin' better now that we're on the road to town. You better come back and crawl under some blankets so you don't up and freeze," Brazos cautioned his youngest son.

"Yes," Jamie Sue encouraged, "we have plenty of blankets."

"I don't want to disturb the sisters," Robert shrugged.

"No," Jamie Sue continued, "I mean in the front seat. We can make room for another, can't we, Dacee June?"

Dacee June leaned on her father's shoulder, his arm around her. "Sure, but it will be kind of crowded," she said.

"That's how we can warm up . . . sitting close like that." Jamie Sue scooted over to Robert and flopped a corner of her blanket around his shoulders.

Brazos sipped his coffee and studied the slightly embarrassed grin on young Fortune's face, then glanced at Jamie Sue. She said something to Robert that Brazos couldn't hear over the crackling of the campfire.

That Jamie Sue is not exactly a shy girl. Robert's always been hesitant around the women. Not like Samuel. He's not even like Todd. Robert's been too busy. There was studies, and training horses, and then the cavalry. I always figured him to marry some general's daughter.

She's a cute girl. Black hair, brown eyes, full eyebrows, large, almost pouting lips. She'll turn heads in any western town. In Deadwood, she'd be elected queen!

180

But I don't know anything about her.

What's her background? What's her family like? Her brother is a scoundrel . . . what about her? Where's her faith?

The boys know what my standards are.

And Robert's the one who wouldn't vary from those standards, no matter what.

I think.

She is awful cute.

They make a handsome couple. With his discipline, her outgoing nature . . . he could be Governor some day. The Honorable Robert S. Fortune, Governor of Dakota, and his lovely wife Jamie Sue.

Talk about handsome grandchildren. If they looked like mamma and daddy, they'd be stunning.

Of course, they could always turn out to look like their grandpa. Poor things. Lord, it might be better if they didn't look like me.

Brazos realized that he had been staring into an empty coffee cup.

Sarah Ruth, look at me. I've only known this girl for a few hours, and I'm marrying them off already. I sound just like you. When Robert was six years old you had him paired up with that neighbor girl . . . what was her name? Natalie . . . or Naomi . . . or was it Odelia? You know, the one with bright red hair who punched Robert in the nose and made it bleed when he was too embarrassed to dance with her?

I remember you said that some day, he would regret . . .

Brazos set his coffee cup down and gave the dozing Dacee June another hug. He could feel tears flood the corners of his eyes.

Lord, how I miss you Sarah Ruth.

But I've got my girl back. I thought I might have lost her.
For a while this morning, I thought I was losing every-
thing.

They arrived in Fort Pierre just before daylight and
convinced the owner of the Wild Goose Cafe to open
a little early for breakfast. The conversation around the
table started lively as they repeated to each other the
exploits and adventure of the previous day.

Brazos gave them all a report from Deadwood City.

By the time they had stuffed themselves on sausage,
ham, biscuits, grits, bacon, eggs, coffee, hot chocolate,
and dried figs, and allowed the heat of the cafe to warm
their bones, the entire gang looked drowsy.

A party of about a dozen men vacated their rooms at
the Muddy River Hotel about daylight to take a small
boat upstream. That allowed them to find two hotel
rooms at 8:00 A.M. in a crowded town. Brazos, Robert,
and Dacee June shared one room. The March sisters
and Jamie Sue took the other.

Lying three to a bed, with Dacee June in the middle,
Brazos did not intend to sleep. He lay down on top of
the comforter just to rest.

The sun was low on the cold, western Dakota
horizon, and Brazos was alone on the bed when he
finally opened his eyes. He was surprised that his back
did not ache. Nor did his legs cramp. Nor did his neck
stiffen. Only his wrists throbbed a little.

He searched the room with his eyes to locate his
Sharps carbine. He tried to remember where he was.

He suddenly found himself staring into two blue eyes and a soft, wide smile from a young girl sitting on a chair next to the bed.

"Hi, Daddy! You've been sleeping!"

He swung his legs out of bed, his socked feet hitting the hardwood floor with a thud. "Darlin', I reckon that was the best night's sleep I've had since I left Texas."

"Day," she corrected. "It's daytime, remember?"

He opened his arms and she hopped into his lap, giving him a hug. "You mean to tell me all of that out on the frozen prairie was true? I was hopin' it was just a bad dream."

"The March sisters said it was the most exciting adventure of their entire lives."

"Have you seen Mrs. Speaker and Mrs. Driver since we came to the hotel?"

"Oh, yes, we all had lunch together."

"When?"

"About two hours ago."

"Two hours? What time is it?"

"Almost 4:00 P.M."

"In the afternoon?"

Dacee June pushed away and strolled around the room, her long, yellow dress only inches above the floor. Her neatly combed light brown hair flowed out behind her and halfway down her back. "Daddy, how many 4:00 P.M.'s are there?" she giggled.

"Who had lunch?"

"Me, the March sisters, Robert, and Miss Milan."

"And you left me here to sleep?"

"Robert tried to wake you up, but he couldn't. Is it

true that you need more sleep when you get old?"

"Who told you that?" he quizzed.

"Louise Driver."

"I wouldn't have any idea," he huffed. "I'll tell you in twenty years." Brazos strolled over to a small basin of mostly clean water and splashed some on his face. "Did you see Mr. Edwards?"

"No, but Robert and Jamie Sue went looking for him."

Brazos spun around, water dripping from his beard. "They did? Why?"

"Because you said Mr. Edwards had some information about Jamie Sue's brother."

"Oh, yes . . . but I . . . well, I needed to talk to Grass before they . . . I mean, maybe I should go for a little hike and see if I can find them." Brazos sat on the edge of the bed and tugged on his boots. "You wait here, darlin', and I'll go see if I can . . ."

"I'm coming with you," Dacee June announced.

"This is a busy place, and you ought to . . ."

"Daddy, I'm not letting you out of my sight."

"Now, li'l sis, I want you to . . ."

"Daddy, I just spent the past three weeks thinking I might never see you again in my whole life. Please, Daddy, I don't want to sit in this room alone."

Brazos jammed his hat on his head. "You're right. Come on." He snatched up his carbine, propped against the head of the bed. "From now on, it's you and me."

Dacee June sprinted across the room and grabbed her cloak.

"Now, girl, you know it's sort of a man's world up here in Dakota. In order for you to make it, you'll have to pack a gun and shoot straight. I expect you'll be wantin' to chew tobacco. Make sure you hit the spittoon and not the floor."

"Daddy!" she squealed, then slipped her warm hand in his. "I'll do none of that and you know it!" They strolled out of the room into the hotel hallway. "But I did learn some very interesting words on the riverboat!"

"Dacee June!" he scolded.

"Mother was right," she announced.

"How's that?"

"She said you were very easy to tease."

"She did, did she? What other things about me did she tell you?"

"She said if I ever found a boy who was like you, I should marry him on the spot, no matter how old I was."

"Your mother said that?"

"Yes, she did."

"Well, she was wrong."

"She was?"

"Yep. I won't let you get married until you're at least . . . thirteen."

"Daddy! I'll be thirteen in eleven months!"

"Good. That gives you almost a year to find someone just like me."

"I don't know if I'll find anyone like you if I search my whole life!"

Brazos held the front door of the hotel open for her.

Oh, sweet Dacee June . . . you'll find him. And whenever it is, it will be way too soon.

As they walked in front of the Lakota Trading Post, Brazos spotted the March sisters inside. He and Dacee June slipped through the front door of the crowded store.

"Well, Miss Dacee June," Louise called out. "I see you're taking your father for a stroll. That's very considerate of you."

"Yes," Dacee June giggled, "a gentlemen his age does need his daily constitutional."

"I don't want to hear any more old man jokes," Brazos cautioned. "Especially from two girls who attended Coryell County School at the same time I did."

"Oh, my," Thelma smiled, "but we were several grades behind you."

"Not that many," he reminded them.

"Yes," Louise sighed, "our ages do seem to be getting closer over the years, don't they?"

Brazos ran his calloused finger along the new wool blankets stacked on the shelf in front of him. "What are you two doing in here? I thought you'd be booking passage on the steamboat."

"We've already done that," Louise told him.

"Are you going back down to St. Joe or all the way to St. Louis?" he asked.

Louise tugged on her tiny, single pearl earring. "We bought tickets for Bismarck."

"Bismarck?" Brazos felt his chin drop. "You two are going north? What on earth for?"

186

"We understand it's a better place for a Black Hills departure." Thelma's smile revealed a glimmer of why she had been selected Queen of the Coryell County Fair of 1849.

"Black Hills? You don't want to go to the hills!"

"Louise and I talked it over and decided that Deadwood City sounds like just the kind of place that needs a woman's influence," Thelma announced.

"But there aren't any women in there!"

"Precisely. There will be plenty of work for us," Louise concurred. "We can form a reading society, teach music, recite poetry, prepare Bible lessons for the children."

"There aren't any children in Deadwood."

"There will be at least one," Dacee June reminded him.

"Well . . . well . . . it's just too dangerous . . . you two can't go into the hills. I won't allow it!" he puffed.

Louise looked over at Thelma with a sly grin. "Oh my . . . he won't allow it!" she snickered. "What shall we do about that?"

Thelma stared right at him. "Brazos Fortune, do you intend to marry either one of us before next Monday?"

"Do what?" he shouted, silencing most of the conversations in the store. "Eh . . . eh . . . of course not!"

"Well," Thelma continued, "unless you happen to be a husband, I don't believe you have any say in where we go, or where we live."

"No disrespect to your father intended," Louise nodded at Dacee June.

"I think it would be great to have you live in Deadwood!" Dacee June bubbled. "Then I could come visit you when it was too cold for me to help Daddy dig for gold!"

"That settles it," Thelma announced. "We're going to Deadwood City."

"But you can't. How will you get there?"

"How is Dacee June going to get there?" Louise questioned.

"She's riding one of the freight wagons . . . at least, most of the way."

"That will be nice. We'll ride on one, too," Louise insisted.

"But it's too dangerous. You could get scalped," Brazos said.

"So could Dacee June," Thelma added.

"But you don't know how violent some men can be!"

"Yesterday was not exactly a church social."

"But . . . but . . ."

"Oh, Father, you just can't control everyone's life," Dacee June said. "I am lookin' forward to having the March sisters with us. They said they would teach me how to quilt, and make truffles, and help me memorize the works of Shakespeare."

"I do believe you three are gangin' up on me," Brazos complained.

Dacee June raised her thin eyebrows. "Did it work?"

"What choice do I have?"

"Smart man," Louise said.

"Sarah Ruth always said Brazos was a very perceptive man," Thelma quipped. "Of course, she did have him tied around her little finger."

Brazos pulled off his hat and ran his fingers through his hair. *I'm going back to the gulch with Dacee June and the March sisters? We'll have to build another cabin. What will Big River and the Jims say to that? What will Grass say . . . Grass!* "I need to find Grass Edwards. Have you ladies seen him?"

Louise ran her finger along the shelf in front of her and examined the dust she collected. "Robert and that charming Miss Milan looked all over for him. Someone told them they thought Mr. Edwards returned to Bismarck."

"Where is Robert?"

"He's with Miss Milan, of course. Don't they make a delightful couple?" Thelma gushed.

I'm not sure Grass Edwards will think so. "Just where is the delightful, charming couple?"

Louise brushed the shelf dust off her glove. "On their way to Bismarck, of course."

"Why?"

"To find Mr. Edwards and learn about Miss Milan's brother," Dacee June explained. "Haven't you been listening? Robert said he would see us in Bismarck before we left for the Black Hills."

I was only asleep a few hours. How did all this happen in so short of a time? "When does the next boat leave for Bismarck?" he asked.

"Not until morning," Louise informed.

"Tell us, Brazos, should we purchase supplies here or in Bismarck for the trip to the Black Hills?" Thelma pressed.

"You'll find more supplies at better prices in Bismarck," he mumbled.

"In that case, we'll go see if we can find a decent cup of tea in this town," she announced.

"Yes, indeed. Put that on our list," Louise instructed her sister. "We should buy several pounds of tea in Bismarck."

The two ladies strolled toward the front door of the store.

"I wonder if we'll be able to buy any orange pekoe?"

"Black Chinese tea," Thelma added, "you know how I love black Chinese tea."

"You didn't like it before you read that article about . . ." Their voices faded with the closing of the door.

"What are we going to do until morning?" Dacee June asked him.

"Right now we have to find Grass Edwards."

"They said he went to Bismarck."

"I know better than that. He has two very good reasons for waiting in Fort Pierre."

"What are those?"

"He promised me he would, and Grass keeps his word. And second, because he thinks his sweet Jamie Sue is in Fort Pierre."

"His sweet Jamie Sue? I didn't think they had ever met."

"They haven't," Brazos sighed.

Chapter Seven

Grass Edwards hovered at a round oak table at the back of the Heart of Dakota General Store and Grocery, studying a large sketchbook alongside a round-faced, sandy-haired man who wore a tattered suit and tie and gold-framed spectacles.

Both men looked up at the sound of Brazos's spurred boot heels striking the floor. When Grass spotted the young lady at his side, he stood up, as did the man next to him. His smile widened from ear to ear.

"Miss Dacee June! The pride of Coryell County!" Grass called out. "You cain't believe how relieved I am to see that you found your old decrepit Daddy. I was beginnin' to think he was lost on the prairie and I'd have to go find him."

"Hi, Mr. Edwards. You look very handsome today. My daddy found me, actually!" she said. "He and Robert found us. But I was doing OK. I had a shotgun and six shells left."

Grass stared at her from head to toe, shaking his head. "You look like you've grown a foot since I saw you last."

Dacee June curtsied, then spun around slowly. "I am twelve years old now."

"Are you married?" Grass quizzed with a grin.

"No . . . " Dacee June tilted her chin slightly towards the ceiling. "But a boy on the boat was very

191

interested in me."

"He was?" Brazos expelled the words as if they had been caught in his throat.

Dacee June winked at Grass Edwards. "He's very protective, you know. I tease him like that just to keep his heartbeat at a healthy level."

"He always was easy for you women to manipulate."

Dacee June glanced down at the papers on the table. "Mr. Edwards, I haven't seen you for over three years. You were on your way to California, if I remember."

Her presence seemed to put instant color in Grass Edwards's face and sparkle in his eyes, like an elixir to the spirit. "I went to see the elephant, Miss Dacee June. But your daddy couldn't get along without me, so I chucked it all and came back."

She wrinkled her smooth, round nose. "Did you like California, Mr. Edwards?"

"Nope, Dacee June. It was horrible. Why, the weather was like springtime all year round, and all them ladies wanted to do was dance, and the fruit trees is so plentiful they jist beg you to eat some of it. I spent most of the time sittin' in the shade and sippin' on hot chocolate. It's horrible livin' like that all the time. I'm like your daddy. I figure a man needs to work himself sick, suffer a lot, and live in poverty if he really wants to be happy."

She looked up at Brazos and back at Grass. "Mr. Edwards is taunting me."

Brazos slipped his arm around her shoulder. "He's just a little touched, honey. That's what happens when you wade around in the Black Hills gulches too long."

"Can we buy my new clothes now?" she asked.

Brazos released her shoulder. "Eh, I need to talk to Mr. Edwards a few minutes."

"May I look for some on my own?"

"Yes, but don't leave the store."

"May I buy a dress with short sleeves?"

"No, you certainly may not."

She rocked forward on the toes of her lace-up shoes. "What kind of clothes can I buy?"

"Warm ones. It's going to be mighty cold in Deadwood."

"Deadwood?" Grass choked out the word.

Dacee June skipped down the aisle of the store.

Brazos pushed his hat back. "Dacee June's coming with us."

"Well, don't that beat all?" Grass brushed down the sides of his drooping mustache. "I know it's dangerous, but it surely will brighten up the place. I'm mighty glad you found her safe. You found Robert, too?"

"Yeah, we teamed up about a half a day west of here." Brazos paused and looked away from Edwards's eyes. "In fact, Robert wanted to talk to you."

"Well, send him over. I've been back here studying these illustrations most all the time you were gone."

Brazos glanced down at a large, watercolor painting of a yellow flower. "That's a nice picture, mister." He addressed the round-faced man with spectacles who had silently witnessed their conversation. "Did you paint it?"

"That ain't no anonymous flower," Grass instructed. "That there's a *Viola nuttallii*."

"It's a very good likeness. We saw a few of those on the prairie last spring. Grass, you'll never guess who else I met up with out on the prairie."

"And you'll never in a thousand years guess who this here artist is!" Grass nodded to the sheepish young man who looked about twenty-five.

"Well," Brazos mused, "you aren't nearly old enough to be the original Thomas Nuttall." He reached out his hand to the man, "Howdy, I'm Brazos Fortune."

The man enthusiastically shook Brazos's hand. "I'm glad to meet you. Mr. Edwards has told me quite a lot about you. I appreciate your letting me go back with you to Deadwood."

"Go with us?"

"Yes, I want to work with Mr. Edwards to sketch all the plants of the Black Hills. I find it a unique opportunity to work with someone who has such great knowledge as he has."

"Yep, that's Grass, all right." Brazos glanced over at Edwards, who beamed with the pride of a father of a newborn child. "He's just a bundle of intellectual surprises. Why, you hang around with Grass long enough, and he's liable to name a weed after you."

The young man's eyes widened. "Really?"

"By the way," Brazos pressed, "I didn't catch your name."

There was a wide, toothy grin. "Milan. I'm Vincent Milan."

Brazos felt his carbine grow heavy in his left hand as his shoulders slumped.

"Yep, he's my sweet Jamie Sue's brother." Grass

tapped his fingers on the stack of illustrations. "He's a naturalist out here studying the prairie after finishing his schoolin' back east. Ain't that something?"

"But . . . but . . . what about . . . ?" Brazos stammered.

"That guy we met who claimed to be Vincent Milan? I reckon he was just an imposter, using Vince's name to set up an ambush. Probably stole the name off the handbill."

The young man pulled off his spectacles and held them in front of his face. "I can assure you, Mr. Fortune, I have no connection to such blackguards."

"Don't that beat all?" Grass grinned. "And him a naturalist? Why, Jamie Sue and me is just destined to be together. Vince and me teamed up, but couldn't find her in town."

"She was with Dacee June. I brought her back with me," Brazos announced. "Someone told her that Grass went back to Bismarck, so she took off to find him there." He glanced over at Vincent Milan. "She had no idea that you were here."

"She's actually lookin' for me?" Edwards pressed.

"I told her you could tell her about her brother, thinkin' that bushwacker was Vincent Milan. I didn't want to break that kind of news. Good thing I didn't."

"Wait until she finds out I located Vince. This is even better than I planned," Grass beamed. "Just like that there Bible verse of yours. The Lord has 'thoughts of peace, and not of evil, to give you an expected end.' That's the way I've been expectin' it to end up ever since I plucked up that notice along Lightnin' Creek." He danced around the table. "Vince showed me a pho-

195

tograph of sweet Jamie Sue. Is she as purdy as her picture?"

"She's a very attractive young woman," Brazos said.

"What did I tell you? I knew that from her notice. Yes, sir . . . I told ol' man Fortune, this is a beautiful woman. But he jist scoffed." Grass stopped his prancing and spun around to face Brazos. "But I cain't believe you'd let her go north all by herself."

"She didn't go by herself," Brazos assured. "Robert escorted her."

"Robert's your son?" Vincent Milan asked.

"My youngest boy. He's a sergeant in the cavalry." Brazos could feel the penetrating stare of Grass Edwards's eyes, so he talked to Grass without looking at him. "And not only that—this will knock your hat off—the March sisters were with Dacee June, too, and they want to go to Deadwood, too!"

"What do you mean, Robert went with her?" Grass questioned.

"He needs to get back to Fort Abe Lincoln. You didn't want me to send her up there by herself, did you?"

"You knew I was in town," Grass growled.

"No one could find you, partner. Don't worry, they're just pals. You know how young people are." Brazos finally looked up at Edwards's eyes. "Now, what do you think Big River Frank and the Jims are going to say when we show up with Louise Driver and Thelma Speaker?"

Grass Edwards leaned forward and grabbed the canvas collar of Brazos's coat. "What do you mean,

196

they're pals? He ain't known her for twenty-four hours, and I've been pining for her for months."

Brazos shrugged. "You figure on shootin' me in town . . . or waitin' until we're out on the prairie?"

Vincent Milan's eyes widened and he stepped back from the table.

"If this turns out the way I fear," Grass growled, "I'll probably do both."

It snowed on Christmas Day in Deadwood.

Not a heavy, wet snow that sticks to your boots and soaks your clothes. It was light, dry, small-flaked snow that whipped down the gulch like driven sand and swirled like frigid dust devils. The silver bulb of mercury shivered on zero.

Brazos Fortune stood near the front door of the rough, wooden building at daylight and stared out the ice-fogged glass window along Main Street. The Ponderosa pine wood window casing still emitted an aroma of forest freshness. A lone figure appeared on the uncovered wooden sidewalk next door. A bundled man held his hat on his head and scurried to the next building. Brazos swung the door open for him.

Big River Frank slapped the snow off his coat and shivered his way over to the cast-iron stove in the far corner of the room. In his hand he carried a small package wrapped in brown paper that sported a tattered red ribbon.

"Mornin', Brazos. Merry Christmas."

"Merry Christmas, Big River. Help yourself to some coffee. That's a genuine expensive blend all the way from Costa Rica."

"Where's that?"

"Somewhere south of Mexico. I ordered it out of Chicago. Figured we needed something special for Christmas."

Big River grasped the cup of coffee and plopped down on a crude chair that had been made from an empty nail barrel and slats. He gently set the package at his feet. "You ain't openin' the hardware store today, are you?"

"It's always open for you and the boys, you know that."

"Ain't for me. I ran across them fellas who bought No. 29 Above Discovery, and they figure they can keep diggin' on the tunnel that French Albert and them others started. I think they wanted some bull steel and eight-pound sledges. I told them you wouldn't open on Christmas, but they might be by anyway."

Brazos paced through the roomful of disorganized crates, barrels, half-empty gunny sacks, scattered tools, and parts. There were no shelves in the store. "You know, Big River, never in my life did I think I'd be a shopkeeper."

Big River Frank sipped his coffee from a thick pottery mug. "It just kind of snuck up on ya."

"When me and Grass and the ladies came back with that first load of freight, we needed a building to store it in while we peddled it off. I was figurin' just a cabin for me and Dacee June, but by the time the Jims got through carpenterin', I had this two-story building."

Big River unbuttoned his wool coat and loosened the

brand-new black silk bandanna around his neck. "Upstairs makes a good place for you and Miss Dacee June. She deserves the nicest place in town. Ever'one here knows that."

"Well, we can't do placer work in the winter when the creek is frozen. So maybe being shopkeeper is as good as any way to winter."

"Gives us a warm spot to sit, anyway," Big River nodded. "And we ain't goin' broke."

"We got us a budding boomtown, Big River. I've never been around anything like this. I'll probably sell out in the spring before it all goes bust. I've got to find me a better place than this dreary gulch to raise my girl."

"It will be a whole bunch drearier if you cart off our Dacee June." Big River ran his hand through his thick beard, which made his narrow face seem wider and took the emphasis off his soft, kind eyes. "You still searching for that special place the Lord's called you to? You still figure it's under that Dakota cross on Hook Reed's map?"

"It's for sure not here. I figure somewhere there'll be this big, old, tall mountain with a snow cross stretched down its flanks. There'll be a wide grass meadow flopped out in front of it with a nice stream of clear water. Not a gold creek that every bummer will tear up, no sir. It will be a beautiful place for a secluded ranch. I'll know it when I see it. And when I find it, I'll buy a patent deed and settle down."

"It's a purdy dream. You reckon that's your dream . . . or the Lord's dream?"

"It's goin' to happen, Big River."

Big River finished his coffee but continued to hold the cup. "In the meantime, we keep making more money than we can spend. You don't reckon it's sinful, do you? I've been poor all my life, but happy. I always told myself rich people ain't happy. You suppose we'll lose our happiness over a few ounces of gold?"

"Big River," Brazos laughed, "with any luck we'll both be broke by next summer."

"Might be the best thing. I been thinkin' there's a lot more important things than gettin' rich. Don't that beat all? You and me's been tryin' to scratch out a livin' for years. Now we sit here on the verge of somethin' big, and I'm worried about it. You reckon we're scared of gettin' rich?"

"It can ruin a man, sure enough. But I figure as long as we have more important things in life than wealth, we'll probably do all right. Big River, you're gettin' mighty philosophical this early in the mornin'," Brazos said.

"Christmas Day kind of puts a man to meditatin'."

Brazos nodded. "You know what I was thinkin' about when you came in?"

"Mincemeat pie?"

Brazos laughed. "Nope, but my-oh-my how my Sarah Ruth could make a mincemeat pie. She marinated that meat for several days, then she'd use butter, lard, and flour and whomp up the flakiest tender crust you ever tasted. She wouldn't tell nobody, but she'd put just a little taste of rum in there and then whip up some fresh cream. I'd tell her it's the sweetest thing I ever tasted in my life, and she'd say, 'Why, Henry Fortune, you told me my lips were the sweetest thing you ever tasted!'" He stared across the store. He rubbed the bridge of his nose, then fingered the neatly trimmed beard on his chin. Finally, he mumbled, "I'll never taste those sweets again."

"Now before you get mopin' too much, you need to count your blessin's," Big River encouraged as he looked upstairs. "And you got a lot more to count than me. How's our Dacee June?"

"Sleepin'."

Big River glanced down at the package near his feet. "Now, what was it you were ponderin' when I came through the door?"

"I was thinkin' about how we need a church in town."

"We don't have a preacher."

"I know, but it does seem strange to celebrate Christmas, and not have a church to go sing hymns in," Brazos said.

"We could still sing hymns," Big River Frank suggested. "I don't have many learned by rote, but I can hum along. Quiet Jim must know a hundred hymns, if we could get him to sing them out loud. Remember that time last October when we was sluicing out color left and right and we worked all day Sunday listenin' to Quiet Jim sing? That was the most peaceful worship I think I ever had." Big River Frank looked away and brushed the corners of his eyes.

Brazos poured himself a cup of coffee and sat at the fireside end of a long, wooden bench. His clean, white shirt was buttoned at the wrists, his black silk tie tucked neatly into his wool vest. "You're right, Big River. We could sing. If the weather lets up at all, we'll let it be known up and down the gulch that we're singing hymns right here at the store tonight. Might be a few other men who would like to join in."

"Plus a young lady and probably the March sisters."

The door opened, and a man with a long, black overcoat entered. He closed the door quickly and tugged at black leather dress gloves. He hung his coat on a hook and strolled towards them. A small package wrapped in wrinkled, gold-colored paper was in his hand.

"Wheweee!" Big River hooted. "Would you look at that new Christmas suit! Don't he look swell today!"

Grass Edwards looked flushed. Brazos didn't know if it was from the compliment or the cold. "Merry Christmas, Brazos," he offered. "I already greeted Big River when he was stompin' around our place awhile ago."

"Merry Christmas, Grass," Brazos replied.

"That Louise Driver is one good seamstress! Look at this." Grass Edwards waltzed to the cast-iron stove and held out the hem of the jacket. "This is fine material imported from England. I tell you, boys, I've never had a custom suit before. I'm beginning to enjoy Deadwood more and more." Grass grabbed a cup of coffee and plopped down on the bench next to Brazos. He set the package next to him. "Of course, I could enjoy it more if a certain individual wouldn't have backstabbed me and gave away my sweet Jamie Sue. I ain't one to name names, but his initials are B. F."

"I told you a hundred times, Grass, they rode off threatenin' to kill each other and came back all scrunched up together," Brazos explained. "I don't know what happened. Prairie fever, maybe."

"Fever in a snowstorm?"

"What can I say?"

Grass Edwards slapped Brazos on the back. "Shoot, it ain't a total loss. Me and Vince Milan is busy writin' our book on the flora and fauna of Dakota. He figures with my text and his illustrations it will be a classic. Can you imagine that? I can see it in the papers now: 'Wealthy Dakota businessman and mine owner, Grass Edwards, has once again demonstrated his true genius in writing this here definitive work on plant life of the Black Hills.'"

Big River grumbled as he swished his coffee around in the thick, porcelain mug. "Ain't no one goin' to buy a book about weeds, no matter who wrote it."

"Now there's a man with narrow vision. I believe he's the same man who wanted to sell those two Above Discovery lots for five thousand dollars. What was our latest offer?"

"Hearst said he'd give us twenty-five thousand dollars for them," Brazos said. "'Course, by next summer they might not be worth a plug of tobacco."

"If we got folks movin' in even durin' the winter, they're for sure goin' to move in come spring and summer," Grass added. "And most figure all the claims will be gone in another month. That means they have to buy existing ones."

Big River rolled his eyes. "We'll see . . ."

Yapper Jim burst through the door, waving his arms. "Hey, how about a little help with this," he called out. "Me and Quiet Jim is about to break our backs!"

Brazos, Big River, and Grass scurried across the bare wooden floor of the hardware store. "What have you got in that big crate?" Brazos quizzed.

"Never you mind. We jist need a little he'p, that's all," Yapper Jim informed. "It ain't for you, so keep your shirt on."

The heavy, wooden crate was four feet high, five feet wide, and two feet deep. A trail in the snow on the wooden sidewalk showed where it slid all the way up from the Double J Lumber Yard. They shoved it over to the center of the room. Quiet Jim laid a large, brown envelope on top of the crate.

Brazos scratched the back of his neck and circled the crate. "Is that the grindin' wheel I freighted in for you?"

"Grindin' wheel?" Yapper Jim hooted. "That's what we wanted you to think. That there is somethin' special."

"All the way from Philadelphia, Pennsylvania," Quiet Jim added.

"But you aren't goin' to tell me what it is?" Brazos insisted.

Yapper Jim tossed his arm around Brazos's shoulder. "Sorry, partner, it just ain't for you!"

Fortune surveyed the four men who migrated towards the woodstove and the coffeepot, each wearing new, Sunday-best outfits. "I figured you'd all be sleepin' in today. I can't believe all of you are up so early on Christmas."

"And I cain't believe a certain young lady isn't stirrin' around at the break of day. Why, when I was a shirt-tail lad, we used to be up before light on Christmas," Yapper Jim blurted out.

"That's who this crate is for," Brazos triumphed. "It's for Dacee June. Well, she had quite an evenin' last night at the community dance. 'Course, she did say that most of the younger men were scared to death to talk to her, since you four threatened to hang any man that looked at her twice."

"There ain't a boy in this camp good enough for her," Yapper insisted. A chorus of "Amens" followed.

"She's only twelve," Brazos laughed. "It's not like she's lookin' for a husband."

"You cain't be too careful. My baby sister got married when she was fourteen," Grass added.

Quiet Jim warmed his thin hands in front of him. "You don't reckon that your freight wagons will come in today, do you, Brazos?"

"I told the crew to lay over in Bismarck for Christmas. But I do feel funny not being with 'em. This is the first trip I haven't made myself. I hate sendin' them on a freezin', dangerous trip without me goin' along."

"You've got to stay and run the store," Grass reminded him.

"Store? Look at this place!" Brazos moaned. "Just a big room with no shelves or counters and crates and goods scattered all over the floor in no apparent order."

"That's what's so great about it," Big River

explained. "It's comfortable and informal lookin'."

Brazos glanced back at Quiet Jim. "You gettin' anxious for that steam mill?"

Quiet Jim flashed his shy, wide smile. "You boys know it's been my dream to own my own sawmill someday. I never thought I'd actually have the money to buy my own mill."

"There's a lot of things happenin' for the first time in this town," Grass exclaimed. "All five of us dressed up like bankers, for one."

"Brazos and Dacee June have a hardware store on the side. The Jims got their lumber mill . . ." Big River shook his head. "Me and Grass been talkin' about buildin' a hotel."

"You know anything about runnin' a hotel?" Yapper asked.

"We can hire someone who knows how to run a hotel. All we want is a good clean, dry room with a nice view of the gulch," Grass Edwards whooped.

"I know where you can get a good deal on sawed boards," Quiet Jim added. "I'd donate a few boards in trade for a good room with nobody snorin'."

"I ain't never heard myself snore," Yapper insisted.

A woman's voice startled all five men. "I do hope we aren't interrupting anything!"

Louise Driver and Thelma Speaker swished into the store. The men stood, each one removing his hat.

"Merry Christmas, gentlemen," Thelma called out.

"Same to you, ma'am," Quiet Jim offered. The others chorused their greetings.

Louise carried two large, flat, neatly wrapped boxes.

"We don't want to disturb you. We'll just slip upstairs and visit with Dacee June."

"Actually," Big River Frank admitted, "we was all just sort of waitin' for Miss Dacee June to come down here."

"Yes, I see. Why don't Thelma and I go up and help her get ready?"

"That would be quite nice," Edwards nodded.

"It surely is a beautiful suit you sewed for Grass," Brazos called out, as the ladies scurried to the stairway at the back of the store.

Louise Driver turned at the bottom of the stairs. Her straight, dark hair was neatly pinned up in her small felt and feathers hat. "Yes. Lawrence does look quite fetching in it."

The two women scampered up the stairs.

"Lawrence?" Yapper Jim hooted. "Your Christian name is Lawrence?"

"Yeah," Big River teased, "his real name is Lawrence Fetching!"

"Now, boys, I never figured you all would resort to this type of petty jealousy," Grass said.

"You going to start courtin' a woman older than you?" Yapper pressed.

"Actually, Louise is only two years and forty-one days older."

"I'm glad to see you're gettin' over you-know-who," Brazos teased.

"I will live with the pain of your treachery, Fortune, until my dying day," Grass insisted.

"We could speed that up, if you like," Big River

Frank suggested.

"Speed up what?"

"Your dyin' day."

"Let him with a lady friend of his own cast the first stone," Grass goaded. "Besides, a mature woman has a lot more skills than some young girl."

"Oh?" Yapper Jim raised his thick, bushy eyebrows. "What kind of skills did you have in mind?"

"Cookin' for one. There ain't no one who can make better sausage gravy than Louise Driver."

They had finished their second cups of coffee when the March sisters descended the stairs, followed by Dacee June Fortune. She wore a green-and-white silk dress and white lace-up boots.

A choir of "Merry Christmas, Miss Dacee June" greeted her.

She ran over to Big River, threw her arms around him and kissed his cheek. "Merry Christmas, Big River Frank."

Then she hugged and kissed the next man. "Merry Christmas, Mr. Edwards!"

Yapper Jim was next to receive a hug, a kiss, and a greeting.

Then it was Quiet Jim's turn. His face turned deep red, but he hugged her tight.

"We figured it was time for you to open presents," Big River announced.

She held up her necklace. "Did you see the gold locket Daddy gave me? It has a picture inside of it of him and Mamma on their wedding day. He was quite handsome back then."

"I wonder whatever happened to him," Yapper teased.

Thelma Speaker tilted her chin higher. "Many discerning women consider him handsome still."

The March sisters and the five men sat in a circle while Dacee June sat on top of the big crate to open her presents.

There was an ornate silver clock from Big River. A china rose vase from Grass Edwards. A throw quilt, a dress, and a hand-embroidered apron from the March sisters.

Quiet Jim wouldn't let her open the plain, big brown envelope until after she opened the large crate.

"It's so big!" Dacee June squealed. "I don't know how to open it."

"I reckon your daddy has a crowbar around here," Yapper instructed.

Brazos worked for a moment to pull the nails out of the top, then lifted the lid.

Dacee June yanked back a packing quilt and shouted, "It's . . . it's a pump organ. Daddy, look, it's my very own pump organ. It's what I always, always wanted!"

"All four of us chipped in to buy it." Yapper's tone was unusually soft and gentle. "It was Quiet Jim's idea."

"This is the very best present in the whole world!" Dacee June exclaimed. "I think I'm goin' to cry."

Brazos looked away and wiped back tears from his own eyes. "You boys did yourself proud. I can't believe you snuck that to town without me knowin'. Maybe I'd better inspect all the crates that come in."

"Oh, Daddy, open it all the way. I want to play it. My very own organ! It's the only one in town. I think I'm the luckiest girl in the entire world."

Brazos pulled the sides off the crate.

Quiet Jim handed the big, brown envelope to her. "Now, you can open this, Dacee June."

She ripped into the envelope and yanked out the contents. "It's a hymnbook and sheet music . . . lots of sheet music!"

"I been sort of savin' that up for years, waitin' for a special event."

"Quiet Jim, that's your music collection, you don't have to . . ." Brazos tried to protest.

Quiet Jim sounded almost forceful. "Ever'body knows it's Dacee June who makes these Black Hills joyful. Now she'll be able to add music to her smile."

"We'll begin lessons immediately," Thelma announced.

"Do you know how to teach organ?"

Thelma browsed through the sheet music. "Certainly. I didn't spend two years at the conservatory in Memphis learning to sew."

Louise sashayed towards the organ. "Now, dear sister, you're sewing isn't all that bad . . ."

Brazos finished opening the crate. "It even has its own stool, Dacee June."

"We wanted the best," Quiet Jim added.

Brazos shook his head. "You boys shouldn't have spent so much money on her. I don't know what to say."

"We didn't give it to you, Fortune," Grass instructed. "So you really can't say nothin' at all."

"Dacee June is about all the family I've got left . . ." Quiet Jim rubbed his rough, calloused hand across the top of the polished, cherry-wood pump organ.

An icy blast of air roared through the front door as a short man bundled in a blanket coat stumbled into the store, his beard and eyebrows covered with frost.

"Partner, come over by the fire. You look like you're frozen," Brazos called out. The man gave a stiff nod and shuffled toward the stove. Quiet Jim had a cup of coffee poured for him by the time he reached the others.

"The hardware isn't open today," Brazos said, "but you're mighty welcome to warm up by the fire."

For a moment he just let the steam of the coffee melt the frost off his face. Then he backed away. "I could be a little frostbit," he mumbled. "Better not get too close."

"You just come to town? I don't believe we've met," Big River Frank announced.

Quiet Jim tossed a wool blanket over the man's shoulders.

"This ain't a good storm to be out in. It can kill you if you don't be real careful," Grass said.

The man took a small sip of coffee and glanced at each face. "One of you named Fortune?"

"That's me," Brazos admitted.

"I came across the prairie with your freight wagons."

"But they were supposed to wait this storm out," Brazos said.

211

"They didn't make it to town. They broke down yesterday at Cherry Creek Crossing, up by Owl Butte. They sent me on ahead to get help."

Brazos shot a glance at the other men in the room. "I can't believe Gustin tried to make it in this storm."

"This Gustin fella wasn't with them. It's them boys of yours that was drivin' the wagons," the man announced.

"Boys of mine?" Brazos choked.

"Robert and that tall one . . . Todd," the man replied.

"Todd?" Dacee June shouted. "Todd came to Dakota?"

The man nodded and took another sip. "You got anything stronger than this?"

"There's nothin' in the world stronger than Brazos's coffee," Yapper Jim declared.

"I don't have any liquor, if that's your bent," Brazos added. "If my boys were driving the wagons, why didn't one of them come in to get me? It's not like them to send someone else to do the work."

"Todd said he wouldn't leave the freight, and Robert said he wouldn't leave that Jamie Sue."

"Jamie Sue? That kid of yours brought my Jamie Sue out in a storm like this?" Grass protested.

"Your Jamie Sue?" Louise countered.

"I mean, Robert's Jamie Sue," Grass corrected.

"A Chinook blew in last week," the man continued. "It was almost springlike. I reckon they decided to make a run for it while the weather was good. But the Chinook didn't last two days before it cooled off."

"They should have gone back to Bismarck," Brazos asserted.

"Them boys of yours were dead set on havin' Christmas in Deadwood." The man surveyed the room. "Is there a saloon open in this town?"

Big River Frank pointed towards the door. "Ever'thing's open on the lower side of town."

He turned towards the door. "Well, I'm going to find the nearest one. I don't intend to spend Christmas Day sober." He pushed his way back out into the storm.

"What are we going to do?" Big River asked.

"I'm going to bring my boys in," Brazos announced. "Even if we abandon the freight, we've got to save some lives."

"Count me in," Big River declared. "I ain't no good at sendin' a friend out on his own."

"We all have to change clothes," Quiet Jim reminded them.

"I ain't got no big plans. I might as well tag along," Yapper offered.

"Let's take a wagon," Grass suggested. "Might be we have to transfer a load."

"Let's take it full of firewood," Quiet Jim suggested. "We might need to thaw them out before we make a run back for the hills. There's never enough wood out on that prairie."

"Quiet Jim's right. We'll meet at the livery in fifteen minutes," Brazos ordered. "Bring ever' buffalo robe and wool blanket you can round up." The four men grabbed their coats and scurried towards the door. Brazos turned to the March sisters. "If you gals would look after Dacee June, I'd appreciate . . ."

"I'm going with you," Dacee June insisted.

"Not in this kind of storm, darlin'."

"You promised!"

"I didn't promise to kill you in a storm."

Louise slipped her arm around Dacee June's shoulder. "Your daddy's right. You can't go out in this."

Dacee June pushed her way free and scampered to her father's side. "Daddy, I'm going with you!"

"I said, it's a killin' storm, darlin'."

"That's exactly why I have to go. What if something happens to you? What if something happens to Robert or Todd . . . or all three of you? Don't you see?"

Brazos stooped over and hugged the tear-streaked girl. "She's right. Live or die, we're doin' it together. Go put on two sets of long johns and ever' wool garment you can find," he instructed.

"Brazos Fortune, we simply cannot let you . . ." Louise Driver began to lecture, but stopped when Brazos raised his hand.

"Did you and me get married sometime in the past couple of weeks?" he asked her.

"Of course not!" she snapped.

"Then it looks like you got no say in this matter."

"Dear," Thelma said, "I believe that is the same argument we used on him last fall."

By the time they pulled out of the livery on the lower side of Deadwood, all the passengers were burrowed into the pile of firewood that covered the back of the freight wagon. The wood was covered with a tarp, and the combination took the passengers out of the wind and the snow, if not the bitter cold. The road, hastily built only six weeks prior, was lined with tree stumps. Now the ground was frozen solid, but come the spring thaw and mud season, there would be no way to get a wagon into Deadwood.

At the moment, Brazos's only concern was a party of pilgrims trapped in the arctic storm.

The five men took turns driving the rig pulled by four blanketed draft horses who seemed neither to be bothered by the grade nor the cold. Dacee June kept several blankets pulled over her head in her woodpile cave.

With Big River Frank at the reins, Brazos crawled in beside her.

Her round face peeked out from under the covers. "I got so many clothes on, I can't move. If I don't let a little air in here I'll break out in a sweat and catch pneumonia."

The canvas tarp that stretched over them shadowed an already dark day. It seemed like sunset, even though it was not yet noon.

"You boys all right?" Brazos called out, as the wagon jostled along.

"It's like spendin' the winter livin' with beavers, that's what it's like," Yapper Jim hollered.

"I'll take the next shift," Grass shouted. "I'm gettin cramps in my legs back here."

"Quiet Jim? Are you all right?" Brazos called.

"He's asleep," Yapper shouted back.

"A man who can sleep anywhere, anytime—that's a

gift," Brazos sighed.

"Daddy, I'm really excited about seeing Robert and Todd. It's like having the whole family together on Christmas. Except for Samuel, of course."

"Well, I hope they found some shelter and built a fire. If you don't have a fire, this kind of storm can deceive you."

"What happens?" she said.

"It can make you so cold you fall asleep and never wake up."

Her drooping eyes popped open wide. "I'm not going to sleep."

"Oh, I didn't mean in here. Bundled up in here there's no worry. In fact, I think I'll rest my eyes."

"I'm going to keep mine open." She whispered, "Daddy . . . I sure do like my pump organ. But it must have been expensive. Why did they buy me such a wonderful gift?"

Brazos leaned his face near her bundled ear and whispered back, "Darlin', these men think of you as their own daughter. You're the only family they have this Christmas. They have more money than they've seen in a while and no children to spend it on. Enjoy it, darlin', because they certainly enjoyed buyin' you things."

"I just might be the luckiest girl in all the world. I can't imagine a better Christmas!"

Brazos huddled down next to Dacee June. *I can, sweet darlin'.* He closed his eyes. *She's happy, Sarah Ruth. I'm truly glad she's happy.*

It was on Brazos's third turn to drive when Owl

Butte came into view. He searched for a plume of smoke. He spotted one to the east of the butte. Cherry Creek was frozen solid and was no obstacle to cross. Just past the creek he spied the two freight wagons. They were lined up in a steep draw, hidden from the horizon and protected from the wind. The fire was tiny and only two men huddled near it.

"There they are," he called out.

"Can I see, Daddy? Can I come see, please?"

"Keep that blanket around your shoulders and come on up." He glanced back at the tarp-covered load. "Big River, you and the boys might as well wait 'til this wagon stops rollin'."

Dacee June snaked out from under the canvas and onto the cold, wooden bench next to Brazos. He tossed the buffalo robe that he used for a lap blanket over her legs.

"It's Todd and Robert by the fire!" Dacee June yelped.

"You can see that far?"

"Sure. Can't you?"

"I can't make out who it is . . . my specs are in my pocket." *In fact, I can't tell if it's two women or two men.*

"I wonder where Jamie Sue is? Maybe she's in one of the wagons. Look, Todd's wearing Robert's army hat."

Brazos reined up and stopped the wagon.

"Time to get out?" Big River Frank called out.

"No!" Brazos barked. He spoke softly to Dacee June. "Are you sure that's Todd wearing Robert's hat?"

"Of course, I'm sure, Daddy. I know my own brothers."

Brazos rubbed his mouth with his gloved hand. "Get your guns cocked, boys, something's wrong here." He started the team forward. "Stay under the tarp until the shootin' starts, or I say 'Now!'"

"Shooting? Daddy, it's Todd and Robert."

"Dacee June, you get back under . . ." He put his hand on her shoulder. "No, that would signal them that we're suspicious."

"Who?"

"I don't know. But Robert never, ever would let his brother wear his army hat. It's against regulation. Somethin's wrong. Darlin', without showing your hand to the freight wagons, reach down and pull up your shotgun. Keep it under the buffalo robe. If shootin' starts, dive back into the woodpile and only use the shotgun if it's an emergency."

With his right thumb, Brazos cocked the huge hammer on the Sharps carbine that lay in his lap.

"I've got the gun. Now what?"

"Do you see any guns next to Robert and Todd?"

"No."

"Neither do I. I taught them better than that. Somethin's very wrong here. I need you to make believe everthing's OK and wave and greet your brothers."

"Really?"

"Don't let them know we're on to it. Pretend like it's a school play."

The wagon was now within fifty feet of the column of smoke. He could see the raw, red faces of his sons.

"Hi, Todd!" Dacee June yelled. "Hi, Robert! Merry Christmas! You'll never guess what I got for Christmas.

Daddy got me this wonderful locket with his and Mamma's picture. The Jims, Big River, and Mr. Edwards got me a pump organ. My very own pump organ! Mrs. Speaker is going to teach me how to play and everything."

That-a-girl. I do believe you could talk a mamma bear out of her cub, young lady.

"Merry Christmas, li'l sis," Robert called back in what struck Brazos as a flat monotone. *You're coverin' somethin', boy. You never could keep things from me.*

Todd tipped the army hat, then placed it back on his head.

I see the hat. It is strange.

"Got word you boys needed a little help." Brazos could feel the frigid air burn his mouth and throat.

Neither son left their stance to come to the wagon. Todd stood an inch or two taller than Robert. His broad shoulders, square, whisker-covered chin, and blue-gray eyes always brought comparison to his father, but Brazos knew that never in his life had he been as handsome as Todd.

"Hi, li'l sis. Didn't know Daddy would be bringin' you out," Todd called out. His voice sounded nervous, flat.

Brazos parked the wagon twenty feet short of the fire, so he could study both freight wagons. The way the rigs were parked he couldn't tell if anyone, or anything, was on the far side of the wagons or not.

"Dacee June's just like a wart." There was no humor in the tone of Brazos's words. "No matter how hard I try, I can't get rid of her."

"Daddy!"

Robert rubbed his mustache with the palm of his hand, holding out all four fingers and his thumb.

Five of them? Or maybe four . . . should I count the thumb?

"Robert, where's Jamie Sue?" Dacee June blurted out. "We thought she came out with you."

Two gun-toting men burst out from between the wagons, with two hostages in front of them. A small, middle-aged man with a woolly, flapped bill cap pulled down over his ears . . . and Jamie Sue Milan. "She's right here with us, Fortune," the man with the shotgun said. His black and purple wool muffler was wrapped around his neck and up over his mouth, his hat pulled low.

Two other men with Winchester '73 carbines posed at each end of the freight wagons.

That only makes four. Robert signaled five, I think. I wonder if they meant that the fifth one was the one who came to town. "Do I know you?"

"You do now. What do you have under that canvas?"

"Firewood," Brazos reported. "I didn't know you had anything to burn out here."

"Well, that sure is nice of you. That way it will take the corpses longer to freeze."

"Who did you kill?"

"No one, yet," the man sneered. "Toss that Sharps to the snow."

"I'd like to keep it," Brazos insisted. "It's sort of a family heirloom."

"Throw it to the ground, Fortune, or Jamie Sue here

takes a bullet in the brain."

Brazos let the hammer down to safety, then tossed the carbine into the snow. "What's this all about?"

The man scooted to the fire circle, yanking Jamie Sue in front of him as a shield. "I'll tell you what it's about. We rode out here just to rob your freight. Figured it would be winter wages if we took it to Montana and sold it. But Jamie Sue happened to mention that the boy's name was Fortune. I just couldn't resist callin' you out. I'm mighty glad C. W. could ride into town and convince you to come out here on Christmas Day. Yes, sir, it just warms a heart to see such family dedication. Or maybe you came out just so you wouldn't lose money on freight."

"Mister, I still don't know who you are," Brazos reiterated. *The fifth must be good old C. W.* "Have we met?"

"Oh, we met . . . we just ain't been introduced. Most folks call me Doc. Doc Kabyo."

Brazos felt his neck burn. "You killed a good friend of mine down on Lightning Creek."

"He shot at Doc first. Two times," the man next to Kabyo reported. "I ought to know. I was there."

"He isn't a real doctor," the small man in the heavy wool topcoat standing next to Jamie Sue reported.

"Shut up," Kabyo growled at the man.

Brazos pointed at the man in the woolly hat. "Who's this?"

"He's a dentist," Robert reported.

The man's expression was somewhere between terror and pride. "Dr. Nash is the name. Most just call me Tooth Nash. I'm goin' to begin a practice in Dead-

221

wood City."

"That remains to be seen, Mr. Nash." Brazos glanced at the nervous little man, then back at Kabyo. *From this distance I can't read his eyes. It's hard to size a man if you can't read his eyes.* "Kabyo, you hold the guns. So it's your play. What's this all about, besides a little revenge?"

"Don't sell revenge short," Kabyo asserted. "It's settled many a conflict. But I don't need to do any more killin'. I plan on lettin' you walk back to Deadwood. But I will shoot you right here, if you don't tell me what I want to know."

"What is that?"

"I want Hook Reed's map, the one he won in a poker game in Tucson, Arizona. The one that showed the location of the Dakota cross. You chased us off, just when we located Hook. That's not happening this time."

"It's a worthless map," Brazos reported. "We searched the hills for months and didn't find its location."

"Good. Then you wouldn't mind givin' it up," Kabyo said.

"I didn't bring the map out here."

"Maybe you can just draw it on the ground for me."

"I don't know what's on it."

"That's a lie. Nobody totes a treasure map without studying it over and over. You said you searched for months. You got it memorized and you know it."

"I forget easy."

Kabyo grabbed Jamie Sue's black hair. Her hood

tumbled to her back. He shoved the barrel of his revolver into her cheek. Robert rushed towards him, and the man next to Kabyo slammed the barrel of his carbine over Robert's head.

He crumpled to the ground. Then the assailant shoved the barrel of the gun into Todd's stomach. "That ain't smart, brother," he warned.

"Now maybe your memory has improved," Kabyo called out. "I'm cold, hungry, and tired of this blasted snow. I'm tellin' you the truth, I'll kill them if you don't tell me what was on that map."

Brazos stared down at his carbine in the snow. "I'm tryin' to remember . . ."

"Try harder," Kabyo hollered.

Jamie Sue whimpered as he yanked on her hair.

"What are you going to do with a gold claim, Kabyo? You boys aren't exactly the types to do hard labor in the stream."

"Gold claim? Oh, it's a gold mine, all right," Kabyo laughed. "Sixty thousand dollars in twenty-dollar gold pieces."

"Gold coins?" Brazos said.

"The Union Pacific robbery, a year ago September. The old boys who stole the funds near Cheyenne headed north to the Missouri River. But they got trapped by Sioux and had to stash the gold in the Black Hills. Only one made it out, and he only brought enough money to reoutfit and go back after it. But he lost the map in a poker game down in Tucson to Hook Reed. He unfortunately had a memory lapse in the alley and died."

223

"So you couldn't beat it out of him?"

"He was a dumb, stubborn man. I trust you aren't that dumb, nor stubborn. Now, here's what I'm going to do. I'm going to shoot a person every sixty seconds until you tell me the contents of that map."

"How do you know I didn't already dig up those gold coins?" Brazos challenged.

"Because you were surprised when I told you it was coins. You thought it was a mining claim. Are you going to tell me? Or do I send Miss Jamie Sue to her heavenly reward?"

"I'll tell you. What choice do I have?" Brazos spoke much louder than was necessary. "You've got one man at the head of the wagons, another at the foot, both holding .44-40 carbines. Then you two have guns pointed at my friends and family. That makes four of you against me, and my gun's in the snow."

"You're smarter than you look, Fortune. What about that map?"

"Maybe I could get down and draw it in the snow."

"Get down slow," Kabyo barked.

Brazos tucked the buffalo robe around the wide-eyed Dacee June.

He stood up on the wagon.

"Keep your hands away from your vest," Kabyo called out.

Brazos raised his hands, then climbed off the wagon.

"Come over here and draw us the map," Kabyo ordered.

"Over here next to the wagon is smoother snow," Brazos reported. "The snow's melted around that campfire."

Kabyo shoved Jamie Sue and the dentist in front of him. "Go on over there," he growled. "You men keep the two sons covered."

Brazos glanced at Todd, who stooped down to help Robert struggle to sit up, his head in his hands. Then he looked straight at the other outlaws. "You fellas wonder why Kabyo doesn't want you to see this map I'm goin' to draw?"

"Shut up," Kabyo yelled.

"Might be he doesn't plan on dividin' up that railroad gold, after all." Brazos stooped down by the wagon. "Could be he don't want you to know."

Kabyo's face grew beet red. His words fogged the air in front of him. "I told you to shut up!" He pointed his revolver at Brazos's head.

"Don't that beat all, boys? He's ready to shoot me, and I'm the only one on earth who knows what that map says."

"Don't shoot him, Doc," the man near the front wagon called out. "At least, not yet."

"Come on over, boys," Brazos called out. "You might as well all take a look."

"Stay there and cover the sons," Kabyo hollered.

"Shoot, Doc, we can cover them from over there. I'm half froze waitin' for Fortune to show. Figure I'd like to see that there map myself," the man at the front end of the freight wagons called out.

Brazos began to draw in the snow with a gloved finger. The outlaws quickly huddled around him. "Now here's what's on that map. On the right is a big river."

225

"A what?" one of the men asked.

"A BIG RIVER!"

"There ain't no big river in the Black Hills."

"Boys, if it was easy to find, I would have found it by now. I'm just tellin' you about the map. In the middle was a wide stretch of grass."

"You mean a meadow?" Kabyo pressed.

"I mean GRASS!" Brazos shouted.

"What is those two triangles over on the left?" Kabyo pointed to the snow with his revolver.

"Those aren't triangles. Those are mountain peaks."

"They don't look like mountain peaks."

"I'm not a very good artist," Brazos explained. "This one on the end is QUIET Mountain and the one next to it is TALKING Mountain."

"That's funny names for mountains."

"You know how them Indians are with their names," Brazos explained.

"And where's them gold eagles buried?"

"NOW, that's what I'm gettin' at."

"Well," Kabyo insisted.

"I said, NOW . . . that's what I'm gettin' at . . . right NOW!" Brazos hollered.

At the final "now," Big River Frank, Grass Edwards, and the Jims threw back the tarp, each of them pointing a gun at a different outlaw.

"Drop the guns, boys!" Brazos commanded.

Kabyo raised his hands but held on to his revolver. The others dropped their guns in the snow.

Brazos scooped up his Sharps carbine and cocked the hammer. "You're lookin' at Hook Reed's friends,

Kabyo. Ever'one of us would love for you to give us a reason for shootin' you. I said, drop it!"

"Dad," Todd hollered, "there's five of them!"

"The other one's still in Deadwood," Brazos replied.

A short man with a dark, wool coat slipped out from behind a freight wagon and pointed a battered Henry rifle at Dacee June. "The sixth man went to town," he growled. "Drop all them guns or this little darlin' gets plugged."

Todd took two steps towards the wagon and lunged at the fifth outlaw. The man swung around to shoot, and when he did Dacee June pulled the trigger on the shotgun under the buffalo robe. The blast sent buckshot over the man's head, knocking his hat to the ground. He pulled the trigger of his own gun as he spun. His bullet hit Doc Kabyo in the left kneecap. Brazos could hear the bone shatter as Kabyo toppled to the snow, screaming in pain.

Like a wounded dog lashing out when cornered, Kabyo raised his gun and shot his own man in the stomach. At the same moment, Brazos slammed the barrel of his carbine into Kabyo's skull. The outlaw leader crumpled in the blood-splattered snow.

The gut-wounded man cried out in pain.

Jamie Sue got hysterical.

The dentist fainted.

Dacee June sat with her mouth wide open but didn't scream or cry.

Brazos quickly gave orders. "Todd, take care of your li'l sis. Robert, if you're up to it, help Jamie Sue calm down. Big River, you and Grass get these three tied up

227

by the fire. Jims, drag the two wounded over by the flames. Don't put them too close. We're going to toss on some of this firewood."

"You goin' to leave them warm?" Yapper protested.

"We'll build a fire so big, maybe some Indian braves might see it," Brazos announced.

Brazos waved his arms. "Let's get going. We can make Deadwood sometime this evening, if there's enough light to see."

"Just leave 'em?" Grass Edwards protested. "Hook was our friend. It don't seem fair to leave Kabyo alive."

"Soon as a Chinook blows in, he'll die of gangrene," Big River suggested.

Within minutes, the fire was roaring, and everyone was ready to load up. Brazos gave the final instructions. "Jims, you drive that rear wagon. Big River and Grass, take the middle one. Stay under those buffalo robes if you can and don't take chances with frostbite. We've got enough wood left in the lead wagon for some protection from the cold, so we'll have Dacee June, Robert, Jamie Sue, and the dentist hunker down there. Todd and I'll drive it."

"What about them? We really going to leave them like that?" Big River pointed to the bound men.

Brazos nodded. "They've got a fire. And we left them their horses."

"My horse's lamed up," one of the men complained.

"That's the least of your worries," Brazos counseled. "But I am neither a killer nor a horse thief."

"You're taking our guns," the man whined.

"I'm leaving you one revolver with five bullets, right

228

over there on that chunk of firewood. Whoever gets untied first can claim the gun."

"What if the Indians show up? We need more bullets than five."

"Why? There's only five of you," Big River snarled. "If you use 'em right, you'll all be dead before they scalp you."

"Chances are the gut-shot man won't last 'til mornin', and Kabyo . . ." Brazos swung up into the lead wagon. "Well, I reckon one of you better grab that gun before he wakes up. He's the type to shoot the rest of you, for sure."

The wind died down about sunset. The storm lifted, and a few stars could be seen in the night sky. A bit of light reflected a glowing trail off the snow. Brazos and Todd sat close together, a buffalo robe stretched across their laps, a wool blanket across their shoulders.

"I'm mighty glad you came to visit, Son. I was kind of hopin' you'd come up, but didn't have the right to ask you."

"Spending Christmas in Texas with my whole family gone didn't sound too joyous," Todd replied.

"Things are changin'. My future's up here, somewhere. You're twenty-seven years old . . ."

"Twenty-eight, Dad."

"No, I was twenty-one when you were born, and I'm . . ."

"You'll be fifty next month."

A sharp pain cramped his right shoulder blade. Brazos tried to stretch it out. "The point is, you've got to make your own decisions. But if you had a hankerin' to move to the Black Hills, we've got a couple of claims to work, plus it looks like we're going to be in the hardware business for a while. You and Robert have seen what this trail's like. Not many will chance freighting it, until the Indian land opens up. In the meantime, it's a mighty good but dangerous business. You could make yourself a sizable stake."

"You going to keep running freight all winter?" Todd asked.

"Whenever there's a break in the weather. It's actually easier to get a wagon into town when the roads are frozen."

Todd folded his arms across his chest. "I don't have any permanent plans this winter. Maybe I should stick around and help out . . . at least 'til spring."

The pain in Brazos's back lessened. He allowed himself a small smile. "'Fortune & Son, Hardware and Mining Supplies'. That's got a nice sound to it."

"I didn't say I'd stay more than a season," Todd cautioned.

"Neither did I, Son. Neither did I." Brazos slapped the reins on the rump of the draft horse. "Wait until I tell li'l sis."

"I heard everything," a small voice filtered up from the back of the wagon.

"Won't it be nice to have big brother around for a while?"

"If he promises not to tease me."

"No such promise, Dacee June," Todd laughed. "It's my God-given duty as the firstborn to make sure all the others are properly harassed."

"And it's my God-given duty as the baby of the family to be spoiled. You remember that," she lectured.

"None of us will have trouble remembering that," Brazos added.

"What do you mean?"

"Never mind. Did Robert hear this conversation, too?"

"I don't think so," Dacee June reported. "He and Jamie Sue are busy."

"Busy with what?" Brazos blurted out.

"How would I know? They're way at the back of the wagon, behind some logs, hiding under a blanket."

"Doin' what?" Brazos pressed.

"Relax, Dad," Todd cautioned. "Little brother is twenty-two. I can assure you he knows exactly what he's doing."

Brazos glanced back at the wagon. "How about you, Mr. Dentist? Are you survivin' this cold?"

"I think he went to sleep," Dacee June called out.

"You ought to hear him talk," Todd laughed. "He's got this scheme for getting rich by inventing a new tooth powder."

"Tooth powder?" Brazos chuckled. "What's wrong with plain old bakin' soda?"

"Oh, he says he's about to come up with a product that will eliminate bad teeth within our lifetime."

"A good pair of pliers and a few yanks can do that."

"He knows a lot about teeth," Todd responded.

"He should have a lot of business in Deadwood."

"Who's singing back there?" Todd asked.

"Quiet Jim," Brazos replied.

Todd's breath fogged in front of him. "It's a peaceful song."

"If we weren't freezing to death, it would be a mighty peaceful evening." The lunge of the wagon rolling over a boulder caused Brazos to reseat himself.

Todd reached over with a strong, gloved hand and squeezed Brazos's shoulder. "Merry Christmas, Daddy."

Brazos pulled off his spectacles, roughly rubbed his eyes and nodded. "Merry Christmas, Todd." He reset his spectacles, then squinted at the snowy, nighttime trail. *Sarah Ruth, I've got three out of four with me tonight. That's a lot better than I figured when the day began. Lord, look after Samuel. May he remember whose birthday this is, no matter where he might be tonight.*

As they started the incline into the Black Hills at the northern slope of Crook's Mountain, the wind drift carried Quiet Jim's voice to the first wagon with increased clarity. Brazos found himself humming along.

How silently, how silently the wondrous gift is given.
So God imparts to human hearts the blessing of His
heaven.
No ear may hear His coming, but in this world of sin,
Where meek souls will receive Him still, the dear Christ
enters in.

Chapter Eight

"How do I look, Daddy? Isn't my hair beautiful? I like having flowers in my hair. Do you think I'm pretty? Jamie Sue is so beautiful. Someday, perhaps I'll be quite fetching. I'm sort of fetching now. But I'd like to be quite fetching. Maybe I should put flowers in my hair every day. My new shoes hurt my feet, but they make me look taller. I wish I'd grow more. Do you think I'll be taller when I get older? I certainly hope so. I think perhaps I'd look more mature if I wore lip rouge. I don't know why you won't let me wear any. Columbia Torington said she wore lip rouge when she was only eleven. Of course I won't really look mature until I . . . eh, you know . . . fill out more.

"I hope I remember what I'm supposed to do. Do you think lots of people will be there? This just might be the most exciting day of my entire life. Daddy, I'm so glad you let me come to Deadwood and live with you. Every day is an adventure! Someday I'm going to have a great big wedding, just like Jamie Sue. Except I want it to be in a church. We will have a church in Deadwood someday, won't we? And I want Todd and Robert and Samuel to be groomsmen, and you will walk me down the aisle. Maybe you could wear a top hat. Would you wear a top hat for me? Please! And everyone in town will be there.

"Everyone I know is going to be at the wedding today. I certainly hope Carty Toluca isn't there! I'll punch him in the nose if he is. Are you nervous, Daddy? I think, maybe, I'm a little nervous."

Brazos held on to Dacee June's shoulders and slowly turned her around. The lavender dress with white lace at the collar, cuffs, and hem seemed to bring out the smoothness of her complexion and the sparkle in her blue eyes. Her long, light brown hair was neatly pinned to the back of her head, her round, straw hat cocked slightly to the back, a white lace ribbon trailed down her back.

Sarah Ruth, our baby is growin' up, darlin'. She's right. Someday she will get married. It will certainly be a bittersweet day.

"Daddy, did you hear me? I asked if you were nervous."

"Darlin', there's only one thing that I'm nervous about."

"What? It's the shoes, isn't it? I knew I shouldn't have bought these shoes. I know I'm awkward, aren't I? Jamie Sue was going to show me how to walk in them, but she's sort of busy. Do my shoes make you nervous? They certainly make me nervous."

"No, it's not the shoes," Brazos insisted.

"What is it?"

"I'm afraid you are just going to confuse a lot of the young men at the wedding. You look so pretty, they are all going to think you're the bride."

"Oh, Daddy!" Dacee June raised her chin, strutted across the room, then twirled back towards him. "I won't be getting married for four or five years."

"I'm certainly relieved to hear that."

234

"Daddy, can I go over to the hotel and see Robert? I want to see if he's nervous."

"Go on, darlin'. But don't get dirty crossin' the street. It's dusty today."

"Oh, I won't. Jamie Sue taught me how proper ladies cross the street. I'm supposed to keep shoulders back, head level with the ground, parasol slowly twirling, and smile, and stroll with my hips sort of leading the way."

"She told you all that?"

"Some of it I just learned on my own."

As far as I'm concerned, you can put on your old shoes and run across the street like a little girl. "I need you back here by 11:30."

"What time is it, now?"

Brazos pulled the gold-chained pocket watch from his vest pocket. "Almost 10:30."

"'Bye!" She strutted out of the room and down the hall.

Brazos strode to the street-side window, the leather heels of his new boots striking the wooden floor with authority.

No spurs. I don't know if I'll get used to boots without spurs. Brazos Fortune, what are you doin' here?

He stopped in front of a full-length mirror, tilted it a little higher, then stepped back.

The man in the mirror frowned.

Hair's cut. Half-gray beard's trimmed. New spectacles sit high on that crooked nose. Eyes surrounded by crow's feet and look tired . . . as always.

You got a new wool suit.

Silver-buttoned vest.

Stylish tie.

You're a mine owner. A businessman. A community leader.

My word, Sarah Ruth, I can't even see me anymore. Whatever happened to your Texas drover?

A wide smile broke across his narrow, chapped lips.

You'd love this. You were always tryin' to get me to dress up. You were forever buyin' me ties that I never wore, pointing out suits that I would never buy. Well, here I am, darlin', just as handsome as ever.

That's what you always used to say. "Henry, you're just as handsome as ever." Which, I always recklessly assumed, was a compliment. You brought out the best in me, darlin'. Dacee June has taken on that role, and by the looks of the man in the mirror, she's doin' fairly good . . . at least on the outside.

The frown returned, and Brazos abandoned the silver-plated reflection. He sauntered towards the window facing Main Street.

How I miss you, Sarah Ruth. I've been dreadin' this day for a month. A weddin' is supposed to be a joyous, happy time. Ever'one smilin', jokin', laughin'. There are no failures on a weddin' day. Potential is overflowin'. Plans abound. Possibilities are unlimited. You ought to be here.

I need you, Sarah Ruth.

I just want to sit in the corner and watch as you waltz around through the crowd as the queen mother.

Brazos brushed the tears from his eyes.

It don't seem right that you didn't get to see a one of them married. Now, I know you can probably see things from up there, but what with all that praise and them choirs of

236

angels, I reckon you get distracted.

Well, darlin', they make a handsome couple.

The truth is, they're a solid gold couple. That Jamie Sue can make most men's hearts stop still with just a glance. And Robert? He takes after his mamma, of course. He walks into a room, and all the ladies find an excuse to flitter his way.

They're a lot alike, Sarah Ruth.

Decisive, principled, thoughtful, and strong-willed.

Maybe just a little too alike.

In the street below the window he watched as a string of freight wagons plodded past the store. Diagonally across the street, he surveyed the front of the Central Hotel, which advertised "French Restaurant: Meals at All Hours, Day and Night." Several drifters in ill-fitting suits lounged on a bench in front of the hotel. The balcony of the hotel was draped in red, white, and blue bunting.

There's a celebration going on today, Sarah Ruth. And I'm not going to be melancholy anymore. At least, not until the service and I start rememberin' our weddin' day.

Brazos plucked up the black, wide-brimmed hat and carefully set it on his head.

I know, Sarah Ruth, you're thinkin' that I should be wearin' a silk top hat. Dacee June tried her best. I just couldn't . . . I tried one on. Made me look more like a cast-iron stove with a short stack than the father of the groom. 'Course you would've told me it made your heart flutter, and I would have bought the fool thing, no matter how silly it looked.

It's been a long, long time since I made a woman's

heart flutter.

"Daddy . . . Daddy!" A breathless Dacee June scooted into the room, her straw hat now tilted to the side. "There's a preacher downstairs who wants to talk with you about the wedding."

Brazos glanced at his gold pocket watch. "Wouldn't he rather talk to Robert?"

"Yes, but I can't find Robert or Todd anywhere! Where did they go?"

"Probably for a walk." Brazos strolled towards the door. "I'll see the chaplain."

"He's not the chaplain." Dacee June slid to his side. "What do you mean for a walk? Why did they go for a walk?"

"To sort things out." Brazos glanced down at the Sharps carbine leaning against the doorjamb. "What do you mean, he's not a chaplain?"

"Mr. Edwards said Robert got word that the chaplain from Fort Lincoln couldn't make it. I think Robert was kind of upset. But then, the Lord brought this preacher to town. Robert asked him to do the service, but now Robert's gone. Preacher Smith came up from Custer City with Captain Garner's freight train." She slipped her arm into his. "What are Robert and Todd talking about?"

Brazos gently rubbed the small of her back. "Robert's trying to get up the courage to go ahead with the wedding." *Do I need to take my carbine? Will it seem strange to take it . . . or reckless to leave it?* "This Preacher Smith . . . what kind of preacher is he?"

"I don't know. He's kind of old, though." She slipped

her soft, warm fingers into his large, calloused ones. "What do you mean, Robert's getting the courage to go ahead with the wedding? This is his wedding day. He has to go ahead with the wedding!"

"Right about now, Robert's havin' a tough time keepin' his knees from shakin'. It's finally dawned on him that he doesn't have any idea what he's gettin' into." Brazos squeezed her hand. "How old is this Preacher Smith?"

With the tall shoes, Dacee June came up to Brazos's chin. "He looks about as old as you, Daddy. Did you go for a long walk before you and Mamma got married?"

"I went for a long horseback ride." Brazos could smell the sweet aroma of her lilac perfume. "Old as me? Well, I better hobble down and say hello. Perhaps he'd like to borrow one of my canes!"

"Daddy, that's not what I meant. You are very distinguished looking all dressed up and don't look a day over forty-five. The March sisters told me so." She dropped her hand out of his. "How old are the March sisters?"

"That, young lady, is none of your business."

"Daddy, when did you decide to ride back to the church and marry Mamma?"

"When her father and brother rode out after me with shotguns."

Dacee June's eyes grew wide. "Really?"

Brazos gave her a hug and laughed. "No, I'm teasin'. But not about the ride. Sometimes a man needs to take some quiet and think through what he's about to commit himself to. That's all. Let's go meet this decrepit old preacher and see if he can do the wedding. If you'll just give me your arm and help me shuffle down the stairs."

Her eyes sparkled. "I'll race you down the stairs!"

Thank you, Lord. She hasn't lost all of the little girl yet.

Main Street in Deadwood City, Dakota Territory, was a wide avenue of mud or swirling dust, depending on the season. A mild, mostly sunny spring had brought the dust season early.

It had also brought thousands of gold seekers.

Most every mining claim along Whitewood, Deadwood, and adjoining creeks had been taken by February. By June, most had been sold a time or two, or more. The street was lined with log cabins, a few clapboard-sided houses, a half-dozen two-story buildings, and a good number of tent-walled establishments.

That was the substantial side of town.

On the outskirts were tents, lean-tos, brush shelters, and any other domicile that would house a disillusioned gold seeker.

With a long, dark beard covering the lower portion of his middle-aged face, Preacher Smith had the look of a seasoned Methodist circuit rider. He stood at the front of a packed ballroom at the Central Hotel. Of the three hundred plus in attendance, only thirty were females, most of whom lived on the respectable side of town.

Jamie Sue was ushered down the aisle by her brother, Vincent Milan. Todd Fortune served as best man for his youngest brother. An exuberant Dacee June Fortune, balanced precariously on her tiptoes, stood up as maid of honor.

Thelma Speaker played the little pump organ.

Quiet Jim sang "The Lord's Prayer" and "Love Divine, All Loves Excelling," mostly *a cappella*.

Preacher Smith prayed.

Jamie Sue and Robert vowed.

The March sisters cried.

Brazos loomed in the front row of the congregation, his hands folded in front of him, hat in hand, head bowed. His Sharps carbine lay on the polished wooden floor at his feet.

No one sat down. They couldn't. There were no chairs in the room. There weren't enough chairs in all of Deadwood City for the crowd.

Then the new bride and groom kissed.

Dacee June giggled.

Thelma March Speaker played a semblance of the "Doxology."

Then everyone gave their shout of approval.

After the wedding, the crowd drifted back and forth between the street and the ballroom. It was nearly dark when Brazos got an opportunity to talk to Robert. "I wish you didn't have to leave tomorrow."

"Army rules, Daddy. She surely is beautiful, isn't she?"

"I've only known one bride who was more beautiful."

"Mamma?"

"Yep. You promise you'll send her back with Vince

next week?"

"If they give me a few days, we might go down to Cheyenne. But either way, she's coming back here. I'd rather she stayed here with you and li'l sis while we're on the summer campaign," Robert insisted. "Word came down from Colonel Custer that we'll have the Sioux rounded up by the Fourth of July. He's got some speaking engagements back East he doesn't want to miss. So maybe I'll be back here to help you celebrate the Centennial."

"I'll look forward to that. But don't underestimate the Sioux," Brazos cautioned. "And don't take chances."

"Come on, Dad, we've been though this before. I'll be all right," Robert assured. "This is my job."

"Now that you're married, if you'd like a different career, your brother and I could use a partner."

The grin on Robert's face was identical to his mother's. "You keep saying the Lord is leading you to a special place under a Dakota cross. In a few months, you might not even be here."

"I guess what I'm sayin' is, no matter where I end up, I'd surely like to have you nearby."

"Somehow, I can't imagine stayin' away very long. Fortunes seem to like comin' home."

Brazos hooked his thumbs in his vest pockets and stared down at his now dusty boots. "Except for one."

Robert threw his arm around his father's shoulder. "Sam will come home someday, Daddy. Mamma always said he would."

"That she did." Brazos bit his lip. "Now go on, grab

that bride of yours. You're surrounded by several thousand jealous men, some of 'em won't stay sober or sane a whole lot longer."

Brazos worked his way through the crowd to the punch bowl. He noticed Yapper Jim, Big River Frank, and Quiet Jim leaning against the far wall. Grass Edwards and Louise March Driver were busy serving refreshments. Thelma Speaker flitted between the hotel kitchen and the ballroom.

"Well, Grandpa, how do you feel?" Big River teased.

"Grandpa? I'm not a grandpa yet."

"That's what comes next, don't it?"

Quiet Jim glanced across the ballroom floor. "They will have handsome children."

"I don't know why you are in such a hurry to get me to be a grandpa."

"Grandpa Brazos," Yapper Jim chided. "Somehow I just can't picture that."

"I can," Quiet Jim added. "Don't reckon a man minds being called that. I wouldn't mind being called Daddy, neither."

"Wheweee," Yapper exclaimed, "a weddin' sure brings out the worst in a man, don't it?"

"Well, Quiet Jim, you aren't going to have any luck at snaggin' a wife if you don't get out there and visit with the ladies," Brazos challenged.

Quiet Jim tugged on his black tie and gazed across the room. "There's ten men for every woman out there."

Big River Frank brushed back his mustache. "Yeah, but there's thirty ladies for ever'one Quiet Jim."

A soft, easy smile broke across Quiet Jim's leather-tough face. "Yeah, I reckon you're right about that."

"You got one picked out?" Brazos questioned.

Quiet Jim blushed. "I was thinkin' about that dark-haired one."

"Miss Columbia Torington? She's twenty years younger than you. Why, shoot, Quiet Jim, with Jamie Sue married off, ever' man in town will be thinkin' about Miss Columbia," Yapper Jim said.

"It don't hurt to give her a choice." Quiet Jim plucked up two glasses of punch and scooted through the crowd.

Big River Frank stared up and down at Brazos. "You look about as comfortable in that outfit as a broomtail in a squeeze chute."

"And you?"

"I feel like a fat hog in a roastin' pan. Fortune, what in the world are we doin' pretendin' we're city folks?"

Brazos cocked his black felt hat to the side of his head. "Big River, I woke up this morning on a soft mattress with clean sheets. There was no rain drippin' through a tent roof, no snow coverin' my bedroll, no sand gnats swarmin' around my mouth, no dust in my eyes, and no varmints lurkin' in my boots. I didn't have a stubborn heifer or a balky calf to catch. I didn't have cold beans and hard biscuits for breakfast. I didn't have to rub down my legs so I could stand up straight. I didn't have to buck the kinks out of a thousand-pound sack of horseflesh. I really didn't care if it were sunny or rainin' . . ."

"Yeah, I know what you mean," Big River smiled. "I

244

woke up homesick, too."

"Maybe we're too old for that kind of life," Brazos said.

"We? Speak for yourself, Fortune. I'm still a young man."

"You won't see forty again . . ."

Big River Frank sighed. "You know, Brazos, I probably should have married that Carter girl down in Brownsville right after the war. We'd be livin' on some big old ranch down on the Rio Grande."

"What? And miss all this fun?"

Big River took a sip from a near empty, cut-glass punch cup. "There's probably a lot of truth in that. We've had some good times, partner. And we've seen a whole lot of God's creation. Reckon we've had more than most."

"You gettin' sentimental on me, Big River?"

"Must be the weddin'. When's Jamie Sue comin' back?"

"Next week."

"Did Todd move to his new house up on Forrest Hill?"

"Yep. But he's just kind of campin' up there. He's got a lot of buildin' to do yet."

"That's really somethin'. I ain't never heard of a single man buildin' himself such a fancy house."

"I don't think he plans on being single forever."

"Well, Quiet Jim's right about one thing. The choices aren't great around here. Maybe Todd ought to go back to Texas to find a wife."

"He's thought about it," Brazos said.

"Robert's still ridin' out with Custer, ain't he?"

"Yep. He wants to be wherever the action is."

"If they don't move the Sioux east, the action could be right here in Deadwood," Big River warned. "Several hundred warriors come ridin' up this gulch and most of these bummers would get so excited they'd shoot each other."

"The government seems to have conceded these hills to us. We just need the Sioux to do the same."

The first gunshot in the middle of the night caused Brazos to sit up in bed.

The second drew him to the window, wearing only his long johns.

From the lower end of town, no doubt. It's named correctly . . . the Badlands.

Lord, I've talked to you about that element before. But you keep sayin' those are the ones you came to save.

The flannel sheets felt stiff as Brazos slipped back into bed. His mind jumped from Dacee June . . . to Todd . . . to Samuel . . . to Robert and Jamie Sue . . . to Sarah Ruth.

It ain't fair, darlin', you interruptin' my night like this. Here I am worryin' all about the kids. When you were by my side, I could turn over and go to sleep knowin' that you would worry about them enough for both of us.

The banging noise sounded like a loose shutter during a windstorm.

But the wind wasn't blowing.

And they didn't have any shutters.

The squeaking of the bedroom door jolted him to

swing to the side of the bed.

"Daddy?" The word floated across the dark room.

"Darlin', can't you sleep?"

"Not with someone beatin' on the front door."

"Someone's downstairs? The front door of the store?"

"Can't you hear them?" she said.

I can hear a shot fired from the other side of town, but I can't hear someone at my door? "Probably a drunk trying to find his way home."

"Are you going to check it out?"

"I'm goin'. Light a lantern for me, Dacee June." Brazos yanked on his old denim trousers, then fumbled for his spectacles on the nightstand. But his fingers only found dust.

"Do you need your carbine?" she asked.

"To open the front door?" He crossed the room barefoot. She handed him the lit lantern . . . and the Sharps carbine.

The floor of the hardware and mining supply store was well polished by boot soles, and well swept by the clerks. The merchandise, under Todd's leadership, was now placed in neatly stacked aisles and shelves, stretched like shadowy hedgerows across the room. Brazos followed the sound of the banging on the ten-foot-tall oak front doors.

He set the lantern on a barrel of miner's candle-holders, then lifted the iron bar with his left hand. His right hand cradled the carbine. Two men stood in the shadows of the open door.

"Big River? What on earth is goin' on?"

A tall, barrel-chested, dark-skinned man next to him sported a thick, black beard about a foot long. He had the smell, and the caked grime, of a prospector. His left arm was wrapped with a bloody flour sack. He toted a brown, burlap bag over his right shoulder.

"You carryin' a bullet there, amigo?" Brazos quizzed.

"I carry the wound," the man asserted. "The bullet passed through."

"We better go wake Louise Driver. She's a mighty good nurse and the closest thing we have to a doctor."

"I was shot last night, and I am not dead yet. It will wait," the man stoically replied.

Big River Frank and the man marched into the room. "Stir up the fire and put on a cup of coffee, Brazos. We got some visitin' to do."

"What happened?"

"Got a wild story you should hear," Big River reported.

Brazos lit several lanterns near the stove at the back of the room.

"Brazos, this here is Tiny Martinez."

Brazos nodded at the man, with dark, expressionless eyes. He stirred up the coals in the stove with a small piece of pine kindling.

Big River Frank and Tiny Martinez plopped down on a bench. The burlap bag hit the floor with a loud bang.

"I was standin' guard at the hotel when . . ." Big River began.

"Standin' guard?" Brazos challenged.

"The boys down in the Badlands was gettin' stewed

and plannin' a little shivaree for your Robert and Jamie Sue. Me and Grass decided to take shifts with the nightguard to make sure the couple weren't disturbed on their weddin' night."

"Why didn't you tell me? I would have spelled you."

"That's why we didn't ask. You never get any sleep as it is. Besides, it ain't your hotel. It's ours. We didn't want no windows broke or guests disturbed. Anyway, that ain't the point. I was sittin' on the porch a few minutes ago when Tiny comes gallopin' a mule right down Main Street in the dark of night. I could tell he was wounded."

"I rode all night," Martinez reported.

"Why?" Brazos quizzed, while scooping coffee into the pot and slapping it down on the cast-iron stove.

"Just wait . . ." Big River cautioned. "Tiny has been prospectin' with Juan Tejunga over in Spearfish Canyon."

Brazos realized his hair was wild and uncombed and tried to brush it down with his hand. "How is our friend Juan?"

"Dead."

"What?" Brazos found himself glancing back where he propped his carbine.

"Some claim jumpers bushwhacked them. Juan got killed," Big River announced.

"He got shot in the back," Tiny reported. "But I don't think they wanted our claim."

"Who did it?" Brazos pressed.

"That's the thing. Tiny said he hadn't seen them before. There were four of them led by a narrow-eyed man with one leg."

"One leg?" Brazos rubbed his eyes and wondered where he had left his spectacles. "I don't know any one-legged man in the Black Hills. Did you catch any of their names?"

Martinez nodded. "The man with the brown hat and narrow eyes was called Doc."

The hair on Brazos neck bristled. He stared into Big Frank's eyes. "Doc? Doc Kabyo?"

Big River nodded. "That's what I was thinkin'. I reckon the gangrene could have took Kabyo's leg last Christmas when they tried to ambush the freight wagons."

The aroma of burning pine filled the room. The heat warmed Brazos's bare feet. He stared across the shadowy storeroom. "Mr. Martinez, did they steal your pokes?"

"Our pokes? We didn't have ten dollars of gold dust between us. I think this is what they wanted," Martinez pointed to the sack. "But I don't know why."

"What's in there?"

"Juan called it our good luck charm, but it has only brought tragedy." Tiny Martinez reached into the burlap sack and pulled out an eighteen-by-thirty-inch thick, plain, tarnished silver cross.

Brazos stepped towards the man. "A cross? Where did you get that?" Brazos quizzed.

"It fell out of the sky," Martinez announced.

"It did what?"

There was a slight smile on the big man's brown, leathery face. "Juan liked to say it fell out of the sky.

When we decided to open a horizontal shaft into the cliff, we set off several loads of dynamite, and this cross tumbled right into camp, barely missing Juan by a foot or two."

"You figure it was lodged somewhere in the rocks up the side of the cliff?" Brazos quizzed.

"That's what we supposed. The explosion must have loosed some rocks and it plunged down."

"Did you ever climb up the cliff to see if you could spot where it was lodged?" Brazos asked.

"It's straight up from there. No one would want to climb that wall."

Brazos stared at the cross. "Someone did."

"Who?"

"The ones who put it there."

"Perhaps it was many years ago." Martinez fingered the worn cross. "I think it is very old. Perhaps it was Coronado. Or Juan de Onate and his men."

"I don't think any of them came this far north. But who knows?" Brazos plucked the cross from Martinez's hand. "Must weigh eight or nine pounds."

"Fifteen," Tiny reported.

Brazos turned it over in his hand. "This isn't solid silver."

"No, it's just iron, with some silver wash," Martinez admitted. "Much of it has been worn off."

"It's quite a find, anyway. I suppose any of the prospectors could have toted this into the hills from Mexico . . . or Arizona . . ."

"That might be where it came from, but it was found in Dakota," Big River challenged.

"A Dakota cross? Could it be?" Brazos stammered.
"It's not exactly what I was lookin' for . . . a real cross?
It never dawned on me to look for an actual cross!" He
handed the relic back to Martinez. "Tiny, you might
have a treasure there."

"I do not think it is worth much. Juan took it to
Sundance and offered to sell it for ten dollars. No one
was interested."

"I'll give you twice that," Brazos offered. "But the
treasure might not be in the cross, but under it."

"I will gladly sell it to you, but what do you mean?"
Martinez asked.

"Some people say there is sixty thousand dollars
worth of gold coins buried under a Dakota cross."

Martinez whistled through the wide gaps in his front
teeth.

"That's the rumor. The money was taken during a
train robbery three years ago near Cheyenne City."

"I lived in Cheyenne about then," Tiny said. "I don't
remember such a robbery."

Brazos paced in front of the stove. "Seems the Central Pacific didn't want to admit they were carrying
such funds, so they've kept it quiet."

"And if someone found the money, the railroad
would either deny it was theirs, or give you an awful big
reward to keep quiet," Big River suggested.

"I don't know where it was on the cliff. I doubt if
there was any gold buried under it," Tiny Martinez
remarked.

"It might be worth climbin'," Big River added.

"Not with four men waiting to shoot me. I do not

intend to be shot again," Tiny said.

Brazos leaned closer. "Just exactly how did you get away from them?"

"I hid back in the mine shaft we were diggin'. They are waiting at the mouth until daylight, I suppose."

"How did you get out?"

"I crawled out an air vent we had dug. We kept our mules in the brush and saddled for such emergencies. There are rumors that the Sioux will try to clean out the canyon any day now."

"So, when daylight breaks and they find you're not there, they'll be headin' this way?"

"Perhaps. But if, as you say, they are looking for stolen money, they might stay and search."

"If they find it, they'll ride on. If they don't, they might come lookin' for you," Brazos suggested.

"I could wait several days to go back, but I would rather not leave Juan's body unburied."

"Big River, maybe it's time to saddle up and pay an early morning visit to Spearfish Canyon," Brazos announced.

"That's what I was thinkin'."

"They are violent and dangerous men," Martinez warned.

Brazos nodded. "We've run across them before."

"You want me to round up Grass and the Jims?" Big River asked.

"Yeah, I'll pack some grub, in case we're out longer than we plan."

Martinez stood. "I will need a fresh horse. I ran the mule down."

"You'll need to get that arm doctored. We'll get Louise to look at it."

"I will survive."

"You'll be the one-armed man if you don't get it taken care of. You stay here in town, and we'll check out Spearfish Canyon."

"Would you allow evil men to kill your friend, then run away and leave his body for the buzzards?" Martinez challenged.

Brazos glanced over at Big River, then back at Martinez. "No, I wouldn't."

"Neither will I."

Brazos leaned over and stared into a bushel basket of short, white miner's candles. Then he lifted a pair of gold-rimmed spectacles off the candles and shoved them on his nose.

Brazos stuffed his saddlebags with dried meat and .50-caliber bullets. His canvas coat was rolled up and crammed into his bedroll, which lay by the open front door of the hardware store, next to the Sharps carbine. He stood in the doorway and stared out into the black night. He could hear music, shouts, and laughter from the lower end of town. The upper end was quiet. Several lights flickered from the hotel across the street.

His spurs lay silent on the heel ledge of his worn, brown boots. A slight drift down the gulch cooled the night air. When a small, soft, warm hand touched his arm he almost jumped out into the sidewalk.

"Daddy?"

"Darlin', what are you doin' up? You should be in bed."

"What are you doing? Where are you going?"

"Me and the boys need to ride out to Spearfish Canyon."

"In the middle of the night?" she probed.

"There's been a little trouble, and we need to help a friend."

"What kind of trouble?"

"A man was shot."

"Is he dead?"

"Yes, he is," Brazos said.

"Are you going after the wicked men who did it?"

"Yes, with the help of Big River, Grass, and the Jims."

"Why do you have to go?"

"Mr. Tejunga was our friend. There's no law out here. The government doesn't recognize us, so our only law is mining camp law and we have to enforce it ourselves."

"Is it that awful man, Doc Kabyo?"

"Why do you say that?"

"It is, isn't it?"

"We think so."

"Sometimes I have nightmares about him."

"I want you to go back to bed and have some pleasant dreams."

"I will get dressed and come with you," Dacee June announced.

"That's out of the question. This could be dangerous."

"You promised you'd never leave me again."

"We've been all through that. I am not going to leave you. This is our home. I'm not moving. But you can't just go everywhere I need to go."

"Why not?"

"I told you, young lady, it's too dangerous."

"You mean, you might get shot?"

"That's a possibility," he admitted.

"That's why I must go. If you die in some canyon, then you'll have left me alone in Deadwood. You promised not to leave me alone."

"You're not alone!" His voice grew to almost a shout. "Todd is here in town. Besides, I'm not going to get shot."

Dacee June hollered back. "Then I shall go with you."

"You will not!"

"You promised," she wailed, tears tumbling down her cheeks.

"Young lady, you are going to stay upstairs until your brother opens the store. Then you will help him and the clerks until I return, which will probably be before supper tonight."

"You're not going to stay overnight?"

"Probably not," he snapped.

"Then why are you taking your bedroll?"

"In case of emergency."

"I don't see why I can't go," she pouted.

"Look, here come the boys." Brazos plucked up his bedroll, carbine, and saddlebags. "You lock the door behind me, then go back to sleep."

"I will not sleep."

"We'll talk about it when I return. My promise does not mean what you think it means."

"That's obvious," she pouted, then stormed back inside and slammed the door.

"Lock the door, Dacee June!"

As the five men rode up in front of the store, Brazos heard the iron bar slide into the braces inside the building.

Lord . . . why am I snapping at her? She's my whole life, and here I am yellin' at her. This is crazy. Sarah Ruth, you're supposed to be here and explain it to her. Daddies act. Mommies explain. That's the way it is.

Isn't it?

It took two-and-a half-hours of rough riding to reach the east rim of Spearfish Canyon. By then the sky had gone from black to charcoal gray to pale blue. Brazos had led all the way from Deadwood, but now waited for Martinez riding a short-legged white mare to catch up.

"Which way, Tiny?"

"North." He waved the barrel of his carbine at the cliffs. "Two miles up, on the east side of the creek."

Big River rode up beside them. "You think Kabyo and them will still be at the mine shaft?"

Brazos reached into his saddlebag and grabbed out a handful of .50-caliber bullets. "I reckon we'll find out."

"What will we do if we capture them?"

"Send them out to Yankton and put them on trial for Juan's murder." Brazos shoved the bullets into the pockets of his brown leather vest.

Quiet Jim rode up. "What's the plan?"

Brazos pointed up ahead. "How about me, Tiny, and Big River riding up the right side of the creek. You, Yapper, and Grass give us a three-minute lead. Then ride up the west bank. Whichever one finds trouble first, the others can come to the rescue."

"What will be the signal?" Yapper Jim asked.

"Gunfire," Brazos said.

Cottonwood, poplars, and willows lined the path of Spearfish Creek as it wound its way through the limestone walls of the canyon. Ponderosa pines huddled in bunches throughout the canyon, on rocky ledges, and on both rims.

With sunlight breaking up high on the western rim, and the dark green grass growing in the narrow canyon floor, the scene looked like an artist's painting.

Brazos's carbine balanced across his lap, hammer pulled back to the safety position. In the distance, two jagged, white limestone peaks lipped the eastern rim. "Your claim is on the canyon floor, just right of those peaks."

Martinez looked puzzled. "How did you know that?"

"A friend of mine had a map of this place once. He described it to me, only we figured the cross was a geological formation of some kind."

"Was he one of the train robbers?"

"No, he won the map in a poker game with the last surviving train robber."

"You really think there's treasure buried up there?"

"He did. And so did the ones who killed him."

"Who was that?"

"Doc Kabyo. The same one who killed Juan."

"I think the man is a demon."

"You might be close to right, Tiny. What do they know about the cross?"

"They knew that it fell off the mountain. Juan told that story to any who would listen. But they acted like we knew more than we were tellin'. Which we didn't. Juan died not knowin' a thing about those gold coins."

"I suppose they might be digging around on their own."

"That could be. But it would be extremely hard work to climb the cliff. You could not do that with one leg."

"Kabyo wouldn't do that with two legs. But he might have one of the others try. Is there any way to approach your claim undetected?"

"The best would be to ride straight down the creek. The brush could hide us for a while."

Big River Frank nodded agreement.

They walked the horses slowly down Spearfish Creek, pausing often in thickets, scouting the canyon ahead of them. The water gurgled and sprayed just loud enough to cover the splash of the hooves. Tiny Martinez pointed out a pile of rocks that signaled the beginning of his claim.

Big River Frank rode up beside Brazos.

"Looks like all four horses up there." He pointed his carbine towards the base of the cliff. "They must be in the shaft."

"Or in the brush near the base of the cliff," Tiny replied.

Brazos pulled out his spectacles and shoved them on his nose. "Where's Juan's mule?"

"I think he ran off when I rode away last night."

"If we start shootin' and they try to escape, which way will they go?" Brazos asked.

"If we come in from this direction, they'll cross the creek and ride north," Martinez suggested.

Brazos waved his hand to the south. "Big River, ride back and tell Grass and the Jims to circle around and cut off the trail north. We'll wait here and keep a eye on things. I'd rather wait until they come out of that shaft. If they're holed up back in there, it might take days to flush them out."

"Unless they crawl out the air vent like Tiny did," Big River Frank proposed.

Brazos turned to Martinez. "Can you sneak around and guard that air vent?"

"On foot, yes."

"I'll stay here until Big River returns, and we'll just wait them out."

Tiny Martinez tied off his horse in the brush and disappeared in the cluster of willows that lined the bank of the creek. Big River Frank rode back upstream as Brazos studied the opening of the five-by-five-foot shaft that disappeared into the darkness at the base of the limestone cliff. He aimed his carbine at the opening and gauged it to be two hundred yards away.

Lord, I've spent almost a year wanting Kabyo dead. He tests my theology. I do not know why people like him should still be alive. He's forfeited his right to exist. He is like Satan himself: a stealer, a destroyer, a killer . . . continuing to torment the innocent.

There was no movement and Brazos lowered his carbine.

A Dakota cross was up there? This isn't what I've been thinkin' it would be. There is no room against that cliff for a decent house, let alone a ranch. This can't be where you were leadin' me, can it?

Where was that cross before some train robbers used it for a marker? Maybe it was out on the plains. Maybe it was in some nice Black Hills meadow . . . maybe it was in Wyoming . . . or Colorado . . . or Arizona. Hook won that map in Arizona. If this is the right cross, how will I find the right place? This doesn't make things clearer. It's more complicated.

The blast of a rifle report echoed down the canyon wall. Brazos threw his carbine to his shoulder. A white puff of gunsmoke drifted from halfway up the cliff above the open mine shaft.

Big River Frank splashed his way up the creek. "Where did that shot come from?"

"On the cliff!"

"Who did he shoot at?"

"I can't tell."

Another shot blasted from the cliff, and two men sprinted out from the brush beside the mine opening towards the picketed horses.

"Where's Kabyo? I don't see a one-legged man," Big River hollered.

Several shots were fired from the brush across the creek. A man tumbled off the cliff and crashed into the

261

rocks a hundred feet below. Both men on the ground dashed inside the mine shaft.

"Who shot him?" Big River asked, as he and Brazos cautiously rode towards a cluster of twelve-foot cottonwood trees. "Grass and the Jims are still behind us. Someone else has ambushed Kabyo," Big River declared.

"I reckon he has plenty of enemies."

"That means someone else is in this canyon!"

Brazos kept his eyes on the mine. "Go signal Grass and the Jims to come back and wait here. I'll go get Tiny. Let's just wait it out and see who's shootin' who."

Several more shots were fired. The gunsmoke reply filtered out of the mine shaft. Brazos tied Coco next to Tiny Martinez's mare and crawled through the brush toward the canyon wall.

Gunshots continued sporadically until he reached a cluster of aspens and a crouching Martinez.

"Who's shooting?" Martinez quizzed.

"Don't know. What can you see from here?"

"The top of the air vent is right up there in that ledge of boulders."

"Have you seen any action?"

"Just the man falling off the cliff," Martinez reported.

"Is he one of the ones you saw with Kabyo?"

"Yes."

"Let's sit this out and see what we have when it's over. I've gathered the others down at the creek."

"Think I'll stay here," Tiny offered. "I don't want them coming up that air vent and escaping. I owe Juan that much."

"Keep yourself out of sight," Brazos cautioned, then pointed twenty feet up the side of the canyon wall. "Think I'll sneak up the cliff to those boulders and see if I can figure it out."

"The last man on the cliff didn't fare well."

"I'll stay behind those boulders. I don't reckon anyone will be lookin' over here in the shadows."

To keep hidden from the canyon floor, Brazos had to crawl hand over fist, lying flat against the rocks. Within minutes his hands and knees were raw, and his forehead was streaming with sweat. From his perch he peered downstream towards the north.

With his spectacles steamed, the trees seemed to dart to and fro. He wiped off the lenses and reset them on his nose.

The trees didn't dart any more.

But a number of men did.

Buckskin-dressed, dark-skinned men with long, black hair.

Sioux!

Dozens of 'em.

Maybe hundreds!

Lord, I believe that's a sign to get out of this canyon.

Quick.

Brazos slid on his rear end down the boulders and crashed into the brush next to a startled Tiny Martinez.

"Tiny, there's a hundred Sioux swarmin' up the canyon."

The Mexican's brown eyes widened. "They're really

doing it! They've been threatening to clean out this canyon all spring!"

"Maybe Kabyo and the others will get what they deserve. Come on."

"I want to make sure they don't escape."

"You don't want to be sittin' up here when the Sioux show up."

Tiny pointed to a narrow trail along the base of the cliff. "This foot trail joins the road about a half-mile south of here. We made it for an escape route. It's the one I used last night. Bring my horse there, and I'll meet you. That way I can make sure none escape."

"We'll wait for you there."

Tiny waved his bandaged arm. "If I'm not there, just tie up my horse and get yourselves on out."

Several shots rang out from the mouth of the mine shaft.

Brazos stooped and sprinted from bush to tree to boulder until he reached the others clustered in Spearfish Creek.

Yapper Jim rode straight up to him. "What's goin' on?"

"The Sioux are swarmin' up the canyon, ready for war," Brazos reported. "We've got to get out of here."

"Where's Martinez?"

"He's goin' to meet us down the road. Wants to make sure Kabyo and the others face the music right here."

"Under the Dakota cross?" Big River mused.

"How we goin' out?" Grass Edwards pressed.

"You and the Jims head up a hundred feet, then cover me and Big River. We'll leapfrog back and forth.

Try not to fire a shot. The longer we can go without them spotting us, the better."

Gunfire continued behind them as they retreated up the creek. No one spoke until they reached the foot trail and paused for Tiny.

"You think these Sioux will ride right into Deadwood?" Yapper Jim questioned.

"It's possible," Brazos mused. "Maybe this is what they've been plannin'. We always figured they would come in from the east."

"If they bring another war party from the Badlands, they could attack both ends of the gulch," Grass reported.

Quiet Jim stood in the stirrup and stared off in the direction of the sporadic gunfire. "We've got to get back and warn them."

"How long can we wait for Martinez?" Grass questioned.

"I'll go up and check on him," Brazos replied. "Keep yourselves out of sight."

Big River Frank pulled off his hat and wiped sweat from his forehead, then stared at the trail. "It looks like mule tracks."

"Tiny said this is the way he came out last night."

"Looks like two sets to me."

"He said Juan's mule ran off at the same time." Carrying the carbine, Brazos sprinted up the narrow, shady trail. Hugging the bottom of the cliff, the path was almost invisible from the creekbed and beyond. He leaped over the rocks that had toppled off the cliff.

His legs stiffened. His knees ached. Just ahead near

a fork in the trail, he spotted two crumbled bodies in the shadows. He ignored the stiff body of Juan Tejunga and searched for a pulse on Tiny Martinez.

Tiny's dead. Looks like he was tryin' to carry Juan out and got himself shot.

I didn't hear a shot. But then, there are lots of things I don't hear. Brazos leaned over the bodies. "Boys, I promise you I'll be back and see that you're buried proper."

Gunfire hailed from the creek behind him as he hunkered down and sprinted back up the trail. Still mounted, but hidden behind a stand of willows, Big River Frank waited for him, holding both Fortune's and Martinez's horses.

"Tiny's dead!" he called out as he swung into the saddle.

Big River's eyes tightened. His voice even lower than usual. "That's what we figured."

"Were they shootin' at you?" Brazos asked.

"Grass and the Jims surmised they could distract them enough for us to make a run for those boulders. Then we could do the same for them."

Brazos checked the lever of his Sharps and studied the casing of the .50-caliber bullet. "Did anyone get shot?"

"Oh . . . I got nicked, but it's . . ."

"Where?"

"My right leg," Big River said.

Brazos rode around to the right side of Big River Frank. "Whoa, partner, we've got to stop that bleeding."

"Later . . ." Big River leaned low in the saddle and spurred his horse to a gallop.

Brazos, leading Martinez's mare, raced along behind him amid several scattered gunshots. When they reached the boulders, both men leaped to the ground. Big River Frank took a step and tumbled to the dirt.

"Pull that belt off and tourniquet that leg!" Brazos demanded. With a handful of shells, he began to barrage the creekbed with the impact of .50-caliber bullets.

Big River began working the action on his '73 carbine. He emptied fourteen shots in the same time Brazos had shot six.

"Either bandage that leg now," Brazos yelled, "or I'll coldcock you and bandage it myself."

Big River Frank glared at Brazos and shoved the breech loading magazine full of .44-40 cartridges.

Brazos shook his head. "If I don't look after you, who will?"

Big River Frank sighed. "That's what life's all about, ain't it?"

"Lookin' after each other? I reckon so."

"You'll never hold them back with that single shot." He tossed Brazos his Winchester carbine.

As Big River Frank tied a tourniquet and then a flour sack bandage on his leg, Brazos emptied another fourteen shots into the Sioux stronghold at the creek. Yapper Jim led the way as he, Quiet Jim, and Grass Edwards charged up the trail to the safety of the boulders.

Within minutes they were deep down the trail

towards Deadwood. The gunfire ceased the minute they romped behind the boulders. After five minutes of hard riding, Brazos reined up and gathered the others. "Anyone take a bullet besides Big River?"

"We're clean," Grass reported.

"You think they'll follow us?" Yapper Jim quizzed.

"Can't say. It might depend on how many others they still have to clear out of Spearfish Canyon," Brazos mused.

"They could follow us right into Deadwood," Yapper groaned.

"That's a fact," Brazos concurred. "A couple of you need to race into town and sound a warning. Tell them to blockade both ends of Main Street and post guards. They should call ever'one out of the gulches and station them in town. The other three of us will drop back and slow them down."

"I'll stay back," Big River offered. "This leg don't feel like ridin' hard."

"That's exactly the reason you're goin' to town," Brazos demanded.

"He's right," Yapper Jim insisted. "The wounded are moved to the rear of the battle. That's common knowledge. That's one thing I did learn in the war."

"I think Brazos should go with Big River," Quiet Jim interrupted.

"That's out of the question. I got you boys into this, and I'll get you out. Besides, I can outshoot ever'one of you."

"When there's several hundred Sioux on the warpath, it don't matter how good a shot you are,"

Grass added. "I agree with Quiet Jim. You've got a family to look after. Go on."

"I'm not goin', and that's final!"

"Well, someone ought to go, or we'll all be ambushed while we argue," Yapper Jim insisted.

"You need to go, Brazos," Big River echoed. "You're the only one who might be able to rally the town."

"Besides," Quiet Jim added, "ever'one of us would rather die than have to ride back to town and tell Dacee June her daddy's dead."

Yapper Jim reached over and slapped Coco's rump just as Big River Frank spurred his own horse. Both men galloped up the trail.

Chapter Nine

The trail east to Deadwood was easier to traverse under the light of a bright June sun.

But not a lot easier.

Downed trees and rock slides from the previous winter lay where they fell. Everyone in the Black Hills seemed consumed with trying to find their bonanza. None had time to stop and clear the roadway. Big River Frank halted and waited for Brazos at a rock slide that blocked fifty feet of trail with a three-foot-deep blanket of fist-sized boulders.

"Is this where we walked the horses across last night?" Brazos asked.

Big River hesitated. "I reckon so. But it all looks different in daylight."

"How you doin', partner? You look pale."

"I, eh . . ." Big River took a deep breath and laid back against his cantle and bedroll. His hat slipped off his head and dangled by the stampede string. "Reckon I lost a little blood."

"Let's get you in the shade and give the horses a break," Brazos insisted.

"We've got to go warn them in town," Big River muttered. "I'll be all right . . ."

"I'm going to make sure of that." Brazos shoved his carbine into the scabbard, then slipped down to the rocky trail. Big River Frank sat back up but didn't protest when Brazos yanked the reins out of his hands. Brazos walked both horses slowly across the slippery rock slide. He was just leading them back down to the dirt trail when a blast from Big River's carbine caused him to drop the reins and dive for cover.

Coco bolted up the path. Big River Frank's horse reared, but the wounded cowboy spun him to the right and regained control. Brazos peered out from behind a pine stump.

"What in the world did you do that for?" Brazos hollered.

Big River's head and shoulders slumped as if he were about to nod off or fall off. He pointed the barrel of his carbine to a spot a few feet from where Brazos stood. The now headless rattlesnake looked to be about five feet long and as big around as a man's wrist.

"I decided one of us wounded was enough," Big River drawled. "Didn't want to see you snakebit."

"Where did he come from?"

"Didn't you hear him signal?"

"He rattled?" Brazos reached up and poked at his ears.

"Like a señorita's castanet in one of them border town cantinas."

"I seem to be missing some sounds."

"It's your advanced years. You'd better go catch your pony."

"I'm going to get you in the shade first."

"I'm fine right here."

"You're not even close to being fine, Big River. Now don't argue with your elder."

Brazos led Big River's horse down past several scrub willows to the creek no more than five feet across. The crystal-clear water gurgled over rocks and logs. He went around to help Big River.

"I ain't never had a day I needed help to dismount," he grumbled. He slid to the ground. His feet gave out, and he crumpled on his chest in the rocks beside the stream.

Brazos rushed to help him turn over and sit up.

"See," Big River announced, "I made it down, didn't I?"

"I've seen cleaner dismounts."

"But I made it. Think I'll lay a spell right here."

"Let me get you a canteen of fresh water," Brazos said.

"You don't need to fuss over me. You ride on and warn 'em in town. I'll ride in with Grass and the Jims. They should be along directly."

"That's the dumbest thing I ever heard of. No man

leaves a partner wounded. You'd do the very same thing if the roles were reversed."

"Yep. But you'd gripe and complain with me ever' inch of the way."

Brazos tied Big River's horse to a twelve-foot pine. Within a few minutes he had fetched a canteen of creek water, retied Big River's bandage and tourniquet, and retrieved his horse.

Big River Frank, his foot propped up on a rock, and his head resting on the leather-cased canteen, kept his eyes closed. "Time to get back on the trail?" he asked.

"If we give those horses five more minutes, we can sprint all the way to town. It's the quickest to Deadwood and you know it." Brazos stood up and surveyed the trail in both directions. He spotted no movement at all. *Don't know if Big River bought that, but he needs more rest or he won't make it to town at all.*

"We park here much longer, Grass and the Jims will catch up with us," Big River mumbled.

"That wouldn't hurt anything."

"Or maybe the Sioux will catch up."

Brazos let out a fairly flat, half-hearted laugh. "Now that could hurt a whole bunch."

A mule brayed. Big River Frank reared up on his elbow. Brazos snatched up his Sharps carbine.

"Whose mule is that?" Big River quizzed.

Brazos pointed to the northern ridge. "There he is. He looks lost. Probably the one that belonged to Juan Tejunga. Tiny figured the mule ran off when the gunfire began."

Big River closed one eye and squinted with the

other. "You reckon we ought to try to loop him?"

"I couldn't care two bits for a lost mule. Let the Sioux have him."

Big River laid back down. "They don't need any more animals. I think you better check it out."

Is this a way Big River can ask for a few more minutes' rest? I got to get to town . . . but I can't go any faster than Big River. "I reckon you ought to lay back down and rest a minute. I'll go get the mule," Brazos insisted. "There's never been a mule I couldn't rope by myself."

Big River Frank lay back down and pulled his hat over his eyes. "How about that one on the Trinity River?"

"OK . . . that's the only one."

"And that gray one down near Fort Phantom Hill?"

"Be quiet, Big River. I don't need a litany of my roping failures."

"Watch out for snakes," Big River Frank mumbled.

His carbine cocked back to safety and flopped over his shoulder, Brazos hiked up the hillside towards the stationary animal. *Watch out for snakes . . . joshin' about my ropin'. The tease is all a bluff. He's too proud to admit that he can't ride any further, and I'm stallin', just so I won't have to force his hand. Lord, I've got to get to town, and I can't leave him here.*

This is bad.

Real bad.

The climb was jagged. His boots slipped with each step. *This is too steep for a horse. Maybe a mule could make it, especially if he's scared. Obviously one mule made it.*

Brazos studied the mule who peered back down at

273

him from a wide, dirt shelf twenty feet higher. "What in the world are you doin' up there?" he mumbled mostly to himself. *Tiny said they kept the mules saddled in case they had to ride off in a hurry.* "Did your saddle fall off?"

Brazos carried his carbine in front of him as he slowly climbed the treeless stretch of the mountain. When he crested the plateau he could see the mule picketed near the rim of the mesa, a small fire circle of dead ashes a few feet behind it. Back near a cluster of small aspens a black horse was tethered.

This is someone's camp! What am I doin' up here?

The report of gunfire popped his ears. Granite splattered just right of his feet. He threw the carbine to his shoulder. Frantically, Brazos searched the rocks and trees for the assailant. There was nowhere to hide.

"Throw down your gun!" a scratchy voice shouted from large boulders near the aspens.

Finally, he spotted a rifle barrel but couldn't see who was holding it. Brazos left the Sharps at his shoulder, aimed at the protruding rifle barrel. "I hate to lower it until I know who's trying to kill me."

"Kill you? If I wanted to kill you, I wouldn't have shot at the rocks near your feet. Lay the Sharps down and step away from it."

"Afraid I can't do that. Look, I'm sorry about bustin' into your camp. I thought there was a stranded mule. There's Indians ridin' up the trail from the west, so I'll just back on out of here."

"Fortune, I could kill you."

"Mister, you already explained that you didn't want

me dead. Do I know you?" Brazos called out.

"Don't tell me you've forgotten about Doc Kabyo? Anyway, you ought to be worried about more than yourself."

"What are you talkin' about, Kabyo?"

"Lay the gun down."

Brazos tightened his finger against the smooth, cold trigger of the Sharps. "We've already gone around that bush. There is no way I'm lowerin' this gun. So make your play."

"Oh, I think you'll toss it down," the deep voice shouted. A girl's round straw hat with white lace ribbon sailed out from the cluster of stunted trees and landed halfway towards Brazos. "Does that look familiar?"

Brazos's gun dropped from his shoulder to his chest. A sharp pain hit both sides of his stomach at the same time. His shoulders sagged. "Where did you get that?" he yelled.

"I yanked it off a cute young lady's head. Put down the carbine!"

"Where is she?"

"She's safe, so far. Put down the carbine, and I'll tell you an interesting story."

"You're a dead man," Brazos screamed.

"I'm sorry, Daddy," an unseen Dacee June sobbed. "I'm sorry! I should have stayed at home. I just wanted to help you. I'm always getting in trouble. Don't let him shoot me!"

"Kabyo!" Brazos screamed.

"Drop it!"

"Dacee June!"

"She's chewing on a bandanna right at the moment, but she's not injured."

Brazos tossed the carbine to the dirt. He could feel his face and neck flaming like fire.

"Turn around and sit down," Kabyo instructed.

"If you're goin' to kill me," Brazos hollered, "you'll have to look me in the eye to do it."

"If I was going to shoot you, you'd be dead. Turn around and sit down."

Brazos turned his back to the aspens. He faced the edge of the cliff, then squatted down on his haunches. He heard noises in the grove behind him, then scuffling on the rocks. Glancing back, he saw Doc Kabyo limp his way forward with a crude crutch under one arm and a short-barreled rifle in his right hand. Protruding from his right pant leg was a wooden peg.

"Don't turn around!"

Brazos stared back out across the gulch to the mountain on the other side. From where he was squatting, he could not see Big River Frank or the horses tethered on the trail below.

"You did this to me. You took my leg, Fortune."

"You got accidently shot by your own man," Brazos retorted.

"It was your fault."

"Let Dacee June go, then you can deal with me. She has no part in this."

"That's where you're wrong. She has an important part."

"What do you mean?"

"There's sixty thousand dollars that I've laid claim to, and you repeatedly keep getting in my way."

"Kabyo, you're welcome to ride back into Spearfish Canyon and look for it. But I surmise your compadres are carrying Sioux bullets by now. So I imagine you'll be on your own."

"Fortune, some days turn out better than expected. Some worse. You'll have to admit this has turned into a lousy day for you. But it's ended up being a good one for me."

"How do you figure that?"

"I know where the sixty thousand is," Kabyo hollered.

"Where?"

"Halfway up the cliff behind the Mexicans' diggin's. Dell tossed me down a coin right before the Sioux showed up. We were just tryin' to figure how to get it down when the shootin' started."

"And you hopped on Juan's mule and ran away?"

Rocks flew to Brazos's right and shavings sprayed his arm like birdshot as Kabyo fired a bullet next to him. "I don't hop on any animal, thanks to you. I'm lucky to mount up at all. We were all tryin' to escape. It just so happens I made it, and they didn't."

"Did your escape include shootin' Tiny Martinez in the back?"

"He went for his gun. He was too slow."

"Undoubtedly carrying a dead friend over his shoulder slowed him down."

"The point is, one minute I'm tryin' to outdistance half the Sioux nation, and the next minute up rides a young girl all alone. I'll admit she wasn't too glad to see me, but I was certainly glad to see her." It was a sickening laugh. "I made her nightmares come true. You ought to teach your kid to stay at home, Fortune."

"So help me, Kabyo . . ."

A bullet ricocheted off the rocks to his left. Brazos shut up.

"I figured to just wait up here until sooner or later you came out from town lookin' for her. But she said you were already out this way. I thought it could take some time, but, what a pleasant surprise, here you are."

"What do you want from me, Kabyo?"

"Sixty thousand dollars."

"What?"

"Actually, I only want $59,980. I've got the one gold eagle. I want you to ride back into Spearfish Canyon, climb that cliff, and bring that money to me."

"I won't be of much help when the Sioux kill me."

"Oh, you're very resourceful. I think you can pull it off. Besides, your daughter told me a whole posse rode out with you. It's a simple trade. You bring me the money. I let your girl go unharmed."

"Why should I trust you?"

"Because you don't have any other choice."

"How much time do I have?"

"Oh, you take all the time you need. Your daughter is bound and gagged. I promise you I won't lay a hand on her or go near her until you return. I won't touch her, I won't feed her, and I won't give her any water. Now you can see how quickly you need to work."

Even if she's in the shade, that's not more than a couple of days.

"I'm not leavin' her here," Brazos said.

"Sure you are. You're no different than me, Fortune. You left several men back in the canyon to do your fightin'. And I saw you leave a dyin' man down there by the river, just for the money you'd make sellin' this mule. And you'd leave your daughter to go find those gold coins. My only concern is whether you'll even come back for her."

"I ain't exactly dead yet!" The deep voice of Big River Frank caused Brazos to spin around. Kabyo, only ten feet in front of him, kept his short rifle pointed at Fortune. Downhill to the left, Big River Frank leaned against a boulder about the size of a grizzly bear.

"You pull that trigger, cowboy, and this little Fortune girl loses her daddy," Kabyo screamed.

Brazos glanced over at his own carbine lying on the rock soil about eight feet to his right. "Shoot him, Big River . . ."

"You're a dead man, Fortune," Kabyo screamed.

Brazos perched on his toes, ready to leap for the Sharps. Big River suddenly took a couple steps towards Kabyo, then crumpled to his knees.

The outlaw spun around and fired at Big River Frank. At the same instance, Big River shot back.

Brazos dove for the Sharps.

Both the other men dropped to the dirt.

Fortune waited for Doc Kabyo to move.

He didn't.

Then Brazos sprinted toward Big River Frank.

"Dacee June, I'm OK. I'll be right there, darlin'!" He slowly turned Big River over. The .44-caliber bullet had hit him high in the right shoulder. Brazos jammed his hand against the blood flow that pumped out across Big River's shirt.

"Partner, you stepped forward and took that bullet on purpose."

Big River Frank didn't open his eyes. "Don't reckon I got enough blood for two wounds, do I?"

Tears flowed down Brazos's cheeks. He tried to rub them but only smeared bloody hands across his own face. "How'd you make it up this mountain?"

"By the grace of Jesus, Brazos. It ain't so steep back there against the mountain. I heard that first shot and figured you couldn't get along without me."

"You're right. I can't. So hang on, Big River. I'll get you to town. It ain't endin' like this. No, sir. We still got too many good times to celebrate."

"I reckon we do," Big River mumbled. "But that will have to wait until we're together on the streets of glory! Did I kill him?"

"He's dead."

"How's my Dacee June?"

"I haven't checked on her yet."

"Go on."

"I can't leave you."

"Please . . . Brazos . . . I've got to know she's OK! It's important to me."

"Big River, you promise you won't go dyin' on me?"

"I'll be here."

Brazos stood up and brushed his bloody hands on

his jeans, then stared down at Big River Frank.

"Don't let her see me like this," Big River groaned.

"That bullet was meant for me, partner, and you know it."

"Henry Fortune, I ain't never did much in my entire life that has any lastin' value. You know that. Well, I jist kept a little girl from becomin' an orphan . . . and an old man from losin' the light of his life. I figure that makes my life a success, don't you?"

Brazos tried to suck air and keep from sobbing. He watched Big River's chest stop heaving.

A night shower had settled the dust on Deadwood's Main Street and left the air clean.

"Did I tell you I've decided to name my first son Franklin?" Dacee June covered her eyes with the black ribbon that circled her straw hat.

"I don't believe you mentioned that." Brazos tugged at his bow tie as he paced the boardwalk in front of the Grand Hotel. "Have you got the husband picked out yet?"

"Daddy!" Dacee June rolled her eyes and sighed. "I meant when I'm old . . . you know, around twenty."

Brazos flopped down on the bench next to her. "Well, darlin', Franklin is a mighty fine name. I never had a better friend, nor known a braver man, than Big River Frank. And I probably never will again." He could feel the tears swell in his eyes.

Dacee June brushed down her skirt and folded her hands in her lap. "It was a nice service, wasn't it?"

"Yep. Preacher Smith does a good job of presentin'

the gospel. Big River would be proud of that roomful of people."

She waved her hand up the street. "Look, here they come!"

A rough, unpainted wagon draped in black bunting rolled up the street. Quiet Jim was driving. Yapper Jim sat next to him. Behind the wagon, Grass Edwards rode his horse and led Coco and Big River's black gelding.

"I don't know why you can't bury him in Ingleside," Dacee June quizzed. "Everyone could go over there."

"That graveyard is beyond the barricades. It could be dangerous out there."

"We haven't had a bit of Indian trouble since you all came back from Spearfish Canyon."

"Besides, we wanted somethin' special for Big River," Brazos tried to explain. "The graveyard at Ingleside can't be seen from Main Street."

"But it's a difficult hike up to White Rocks, let alone to tote a coffin."

"We'll pack him as far as we can. We surely won't go clean to the top . . . it's nothin' but rock up there."

"I think I'll stay down here with Todd. Carty Toluca said he saw a bobcat near White Rocks yesterday."

Brazos hugged her shoulders. "I told you that you could go if you wanted to."

"Jamie Sue is supposed to come in on the stage. Do you think the stage will get through?"

"They said the army would escort one in from Cheyenne City. But don't be surprised if it's runnin' late. They're takin' it real cautious these days. I'll be home as soon as we're through."

Brazos met the wagon, and Dacee June followed behind. "You boys ready for this?"

Grass Edwards handed Brazos the reins to Coco. "We're goin' to ruin our new suits climbin' this mountain with a casket."

"I certainly hope so," Yapper Jim blurted out.

"How come you have Big River's horse?" Dacee June asked.

"An empty saddle. It shows we lost a partner."

"Are you really going to put that cross on his grave?"

"Yep."

"Say good-bye to Big River for me, too," she called. "He's my hero."

"Ours, too, Dacee June," Quiet Jim added.

Brazos turned in the saddle and looked back at the young girl in the long, black dress and saw, instead, a young woman. "I will, darlin'."

"I love you, Daddy," she shouted.

"I love you, too, Dacee June!" *Sarah Ruth, what am I going to do? I don't know anything about raisin' a teenage daughter. I reckon the boys will start hangin' around the place. I suppose I could just shoot 'em all.*

Most of those in town had said their good-byes to Big River Frank at the service in the ballroom at the Grand Hotel. Many, though, came out to the slightly muddy street to watch the wagon and the horsemen ride by.

"We lost Hook last summer and Big River this summer. At this rate we'll all be gone in four more years," Grass Edwards announced as he turned south at the fork up Whitewood Creek.

"Boy, that Edwards is a cheery lot," Yapper Jim complained. "If we listened to him, we might as well dig five graves right now up on this mountain."

"Might not be a bad idea," Quiet Jim suggested. "I don't mean actually dig the holes, but we might reserve the ground. I ain't got no place I'd rather be buried . . . you know, when my time comes."

"I hear what you're sayin', partner," Brazos called out. "But who knows where we'll be when we lay it down?"

"There are worse things than being buried by your friends," Quiet Jim added.

"You reckon we'll all be right here next summer, Brazos?" Grass Edwards quizzed.

"Boys, by then this whole gulch might be a ghost town," Brazos cautioned.

"Or an Indian encampment," Yapper Jim added.

"Either way," Brazos declared, "there won't be a single structure left standin'."

"There'll be an iron cross up near White Rocks," Quiet Jim reminded them.

By evening the four dirt-caked, sweaty men shuffled down off the mountain. A half-moon peered through a twilight sky after they cleaned up, changed clothes, and gathered at the back of the Fortune and Son Hardware & Mining Supplies store. The March sisters bustled around the long, makeshift table that had been propped on barrels near the far wall.

"You shouldn't have gone to all this trouble, girls," Brazos insisted. He was dressed in old jeans, a leather vest, and even older boots. It was the first time he had been comfortable all day.

Thelma Speaker brushed sprigs of her blonde hair behind her dangling purple earrings. "We most certainly should have, isn't that right, Louise?"

"Yes, dear. We always fix a meal for the family after a funeral. And you four men and Dacee June are as close a family as Big River Frank could have." Louise's dark brown bangs flopped down to her thick, dark eyebrows as she pried under an enameled tin roasting pan lid poised on top of the wood stove.

Thelma Speaker rearranged the cut flowers in a green glass vase perched in the center of the table. "Louise is right," she added. "We must fix a funeral meal. Why, what would people think?"

Yapper Jim leaned against a barrel of black iron gate hinges. "What people?"

"Well . . . well . . . respectable people, that's who," Thelma said. She continued to fuss over the flowers. "I can't do a thing with these lilies."

"Actually, those are *Oenothera caespitosa* . . . tufted evening primroses," Grass Edwards corrected her as he rocked back on his boot heels, his hands dangling awkwardly at his side.

Thelma scooted over and latched onto his arm. "Oh, Lawrence, would you mind arranging these for me? You are so good with flowers. I have just never met a man like you before," she cooed.

The front door of the hardware store banged open

and Dacee June announced, "Here she is. Here's our Jamie Sue. She made it, even if the stage was four hours late."

A print carpetbag in each hand, a shawl over her shoulder, and a hat tied on with a blue ribbon around her chin, Jamie Sue Fortune burst through the doorway.

"Welcome back," Brazos offered. "We were afraid no one could make it to town. Let me carry those up to your room."

"Oh, no, please, Mr. Fortune, eh . . . I . . ."

"You got to do better than that. I'm either Brazos, or I'm Daddy," he insisted.

Jamie Sue's wide, full-lipped smile lit up the shadowy room. "I think I like Daddy Brazos."

"That's fine with me," he said.

"But it might take a little gettin' used to," she admitted.

"We'll all just call him Daddy Brazos," Yapper Jim hooted. "Just to help you out."

Jamie Sue stood open-mouthed, her eyes darting back and forth.

"Don't pay no mind to Yapper," Quiet Jim added. "No one else ever does."

"Well, no one is going upstairs for now," Louise Driver protested. "This food will get cold if we don't eat it. I want everyone to sit down. Those who are late will just have to take what's left."

"Yes," Thelma added, as she untied her full-length, lavender flowered apron and hung it on a peg next to several pitchforks. "I've made name cards for each of you. I thought we should sit boy-girl-boy-girl."

"I ain't been called a boy in thirty years," Grass noted.

"Don't care where I sit," Yapper Jim boomed, "jist so there's biscuits and gravy within reach."

Everyone circled the large, food-filled table to discover their place. One chair remained empty. After Brazos blessed the food, he turned to Dacee June. "Help yourself to the black-eyed peas, li'l sis, then pass them to Quiet Jim."

Dacee June wrinkled her nose. "Why do they call them peas? They look just like beans to me. Why don't they call them black-eyed beans?"

Brazos plopped a spoonful of black-eyes on her plate. "That's an intriguing question, but you still have to eat them." He then scooped a large spoon of scalloped potatoes onto his own white china plate.

"I have an intriguing question for Jamie Sue," Dacee June blurted out as she passed the vegetables to Quiet Jim and dug into the steaming bowl of scalloped potatoes.

Jamie Sue stopped buttering a biscuit. "What's that?"

"Are you goin' to have a baby now?" Dacee June stabbed a slice of ham as if it were about to attack her.

Jamie Sue blushed and dropped the biscuit in her plate. She carefully wiped her fingers on the white linen napkin. "Well . . . not . . . I mean . . . such things take time."

The men guffawed, then continued to heap steaming food on their plates.

Dacee June smeared an ear of white corn with pale yellow butter. "But you've been married over a week. Besides, a baby would be company while Robert is away."

"Looks like you got a little explainin' to do, Brazos," Yapper Jim laughed as he dissected a long, skinny sweet potato.

"Actually, dear," Louise Driver lectured, "as you undoubtedly know, there is a nine-month gestation period after conception takes place. So, assuming the marriage was consummated, as I suspect it was, it would still be completely undetectable for the first few weeks. Then the woman begins to . . . ."

Brazos waved his hands over the table. "Whoa, Louise, we're eatin' supper here."

This time the men blushed.

And the ladies snickered.

Brazos took a sip of coffee, harpooned a chop, then drowned it in white gravy. "You two gals didn't see Todd out there, did you?"

Jamie Sue wiped her mouth. "Oh . . . I forgot . . . I kind of committed him for the evening."

"Oh?" Brazos leaned forward to keep the forkful of meat and gravy from dripping on his shirt.

Dacee June's buttered corn dribbled down her chin. "Daddy, guess who came in on the stagecoach?" she interrupted.

"Someone selling napkins, I hope."

Dacee June wiped her mouth, then sat up straight. "No, it was James Butler Hickok!"

Yapper Jim whipped his head around, his silver fork

clanging into the plate. "Wild Bill's here in Dead-wood?"

Dacee June brushed her hair back out of her eyes, smearing a little butter on her forehead. "I saw him with my own eyes. His hair is long, his mustache is very neat, and he was the cleanest man on the stage. Jamie Sue said so. He is quite handsome. How old do you think he is?"

"Very old," Brazos insisted.

"Well, he seemed very polite," Jamie Sue added as she carefully sawed away on a thick piece of beef chop.

Louise Driver held a forkful of breaded okra and waved it over her plate. "I read that he got married this spring." She glanced over at Grass Edwards. "He married a widow lady eleven years older than him. Can you imagine?"

Grass swallowed hard and wiped his mouth on the back of his hand.

"I can imagine it," Thelma concurred. "Some men need a sensible and mature companion."

"I understand she's an acrobat in the circus," Jamie Sue offered.

"That sounds sensible and mature to me," Yapper Jim chuckled.

Louise Driver passed Grass a small glass bowl. "I brought over some of your favorite wild cherry preserves, Mr. Edwards."

Grass refused to look up at Brazos or the Jims. "Did Hickok's wife come with him?" he asked.

Jamie Sue wiped her mouth again before she spoke. "No, he was traveling alone."

Brazos picked a sliver of meat out from between his front teeth with his fingernail, then took another sip of coffee. "What does all of this have to do with Todd missin' supper? He didn't go play poker with Wild Bill Hickok, did he?"

"Oh, no. Actually, Daddy Brazos, there was also a man named Jacobson on the stage. He's a banker from Chicago who's thinking about opening a bank here in town."

"A Chicago banker? In Deadwood? Now, that is good news!" Grass Edwards tried to brush a spot of wild cherry preserves off his white shirt. "If we get eastern money investing in the gulch, we might have ourselves a fine town yet."

Yapper Jim reached clear across the table and forked a giant dill pickle. "I hope you told him which is the finest hotel in town."

Jamie Sue spread her napkin back across her lap. "Yes, I did. He wanted to have supper with someone who could tell him all about the economy of Deadwood. And who knows more about that than Todd? Every one of you has told me he's got the best business sense of any man in town."

"That's for sure. There are some days I reckon he doesn't have much competition," Quiet Jim piped up, his clean-shaven, thin face hidden mostly by a large coffee cup.

Brazos stretched his long legs under the table until they struck the barrel that held the tabletop. "I appreciate Todd's tending to civic responsibilities, but a family meal is extremely important. He should be here.

No business matter is that critical."

Jamie Sue pushed her fork into a heap of black-eyed peas. "I don't think he's skipping supper solely because of business," she murmured.

"Oh?" Thelma Speaker punctuated her response with raised eyebrows. "What's her name?"

"Why do women always assume it's some lady that distracts us men?" Yapper challenged.

"What's her name?" Thelma repeated.

"Mr. Jacobson brought along his daughter, Rebekah." Jamie Sue abandoned the black-eyes and ate a small bite of ham. "I believe she just graduated from a women's college in the East."

"You don't say?" Grass Edwards wiped his chin on the linen napkin. "Perhaps I should go welcome the . . ."

The sharp elbow of Louise Driver silenced Mr. Lawrence Edwards.

"I suppose Mr. Jacobson will be wanting to buy a home soon. So his wife can move out . . . ?" Thelma queried.

Jamie Sue nodded and resumed eating.

"He is married, then?" Thelma pressed.

Louise cleared her throat. "Don't be too obvious, dear."

Jamie Sue grinned. "I believe he did say he was a widower."

"Oh . . ." Thelma sat straight up. "That poor man. We'll just have to bake him a pie and steep some tea and welcome them to Deadwood. I'll need to tell them all about our lending library in the parlor."

Brazos spooned gravy over his okra. "Jamie Sue, did you see any signs of trouble coming in on the stage?"

"We didn't see a single Indian," Jamie Sue reported. "Of course, having a military escort helped. But it was as if every Sioux was busy somewhere else. It was ominous coming into town and seeing Main Street barricaded and guards posted. I'm glad Dacee June wrote to me and warned me what to expect."

Yapper Jim smothered his okra high with wild cherry preserves. "We know where a couple hundred Sioux warriors are."

Thelma put a spoonful of okra on her biscuit, then chomped down. "I heard just this afternoon that the Sioux retreated out of Spearfish Canyon," she mumbled.

Brazos pushed himself back from the table, then stood. "It's startin' to seem strange. It's as if ever' Sioux on the plains has somewhere else to go."

"I hope it's up in the British Possessions," Yapper added.

"If that's the case, we have a cliff to climb." Brazos strolled towards the back wall and turned up one of the kerosene lamps.

"You still figure on sendin' those coins to Juan and Tiny's kin in Cheyenne City?" Yapper Jim quizzed.

Brazos finished off one lamp, then stepped to the other. "Providin' the money's still there and we can find it. We'll let their families strike a deal with the Central Pacific or do whatever they want."

"Seems like the right thing," Quiet Jim added.

"What's the word from our soldier boy?" Yapper Jim

quizzed between bites of cheese-drenched scalloped potatoes.

Jamie Sue's eyes lit up. "Robert said the word came down from General Terry that the summer campaign would certainly take no longer than August."

"That's not quite as optimistic as Custer," Grass cautioned.

"Either way," Jamie Sue bubbled, "my Bobby will be home by the end of summer."

Brazos gazed at the entire group at the table. *Her Bobby? Nobody's called him that since you, Mamma. But, she's right, Sarah Ruth. He's her Bobby now.*

"What will you do after that?" Louise asked, picking at her food. The bite of potato on her fork was no larger than a dime.

"Robert expects to be transferred once the Sioux situation is taken care of," Jamie Sue explained. "If General Crook is sent back to Arizona, as is rumored, Robert is going to try to get transferred there."

"Arizona? Why on earth would he take you to such a God-forsaken, dangerous, and primitive land as that?" Brazos moaned.

"Are you implying that Deadwood is a safe bastion of culture and progress?" Quiet Jim challenged.

"We do have a lending library, and I'm considering forming an orchestra," Thelma Speaker asserted. "It will be a challenge, naturally, but, heaven knows, it is worth the effort."

"What I'm suggesting," Brazos's face relaxed into a smile, "is that I don't want Jamie Sue and Robert to be that far from us."

"Don't worry, Daddy Brazos. Robert's already talking about living in the Black Hills someday."

"He is?"

"Provided you don't up and move somewhere else in the meantime. Your boys will follow you to the ends of the earth, Daddy Brazos. You know that."

"All the boys, but one," Brazos sighed.

Jamie Sue dropped her head and stared at her plate. "I'm not supposed to tell you this, but Robert and I got a letter from Samuel."

"You what?" Brazos jerked off his spectacles and waved them in front of him. "Why aren't you supposed to tell me?" he fumed.

"Samuel said it just would stir you up."

"That's preposterous," he growled. "What does he mean saying something like that?" Brazos's voice was almost a shout. "He doesn't bother contacting his father since his mamma died, and then out of the blue sends a letter to you and Robert?"

"Daddy, just calm down," Dacee June cautioned. "You turn all red when you get upset. And you'll have heart pains."

"I most certainly will not," he barked, rubbing his chest with his right hand. He could feel his neck and face flush. "OK, perhaps I turn a little red." He took a deep breath and sighed. "What did Samuel say?"

"Somehow he heard about us getting married, so he sent his congratulations. He said he was doin' fine, and if some big deal went through he was going back to Texas to buy a ranch."

"That's all he said?" Brazos quizzed. "He didn't ask

about li'l sis . . . or me?"

Jamie Sue paused. "No."

"After three years of silence, that's not much."

"I think it's wonderful," Dacee June said. "It means Samuel's alive and thinking about family. That's good, Daddy."

"I believe that's a very mature attitude," Thelma commended.

Dacee June's eyes widened. "It is?"

Brazos glanced at his daughter. *She's right, Sarah Ruth. It was certainly more mature than 'Daddy Brazos.' Sammy's alive and well. Thank you, Jesus!*

"Robert said when the children are old enough for school we will need to settle down," Jamie Sue said.

Dacee June nearly exploded. "I knew it! You are going to have a baby!"

"Well, of course we'll have children someday."

"I hope they are all girls."

"Why on earth do you hope that?" Thelma asked.

"Boys can be such a bother," Dacee June sighed. "Take Carty Toluca, for instance."

"Oh?" Jamie Sue questioned.

"He kept trying for days to get me to go out into that old shed behind his house. Said he had something very unusual to show me."

"He did?" Brazos probed. "And just what did you say to such a proposition?"

Dacee June's eyes grew wide. "A proposition? It was hardly a proposition. He didn't even try to kiss me."

Brazos felt acid boil up in his chest and began to rub it again. "You went with him?"

295

"Yes, I told him I'd go if he promised not to talk to me for a week."

"You make tough demands," Louise said. "Just what did the young man want to show you, or should we ask?"

"A lousy chicken who lays blue eggs. That's the way boys are. It was dumb. Why make such a big deal over blue eggs? Robins do it all the time." Dacee June wrinkled her nose. "That's the last time I'm going out to a shed with a boy."

"It certainly is," Brazos agreed.

Dacee June glanced over at Jamie Sue. "You're going to just have girls, aren't you?"

Jamie Sue cleared her throat. "I don't think I can."

"Let me explain it to you, dear," Louise began. "First, at just the right time of the month . . ."

"No . . . no!" Yapper Jim protested. "Explain it to her some other time."

"Men sure do fluster easy." Dacee June ran her fork around the outside of an untouched mound of black-eyed peas.

Brazos had slept about two hours when he rose out of bed and began to pace the floor, barefoot. Finally, he turned on a lamp, tugged on his jeans, hunted for his spectacles, then plopped down in a dusty, green stuffed chair next to the window.

Not until his toes began to get cold did he look up from his Bible reading and stare across the shadows of his second-story bedroom.

Lord, I've been runnin' so long I've forgotten how to sit

still. I like the journey, but I'm afraid of the destination. That's why I keep sayin' that you're leadin' me on. I want to keep on the move. I thrive on immediate challenges.

How can I settle down here?

If this town turns routine, we'll push on to something more excitin'. I'll just pack up Dacee June ... and ... and Robert and Jamie Sue ... and Todd and ...

If Robert and Jamie Sue move to Arizona, maybe we'll all head that direction. Perhaps California, Lord. Is that where you want me?

Beneath the cross ... beneath some cross.

I've got to go where you want me, Lord.

That's not here.

Not in Deadwood.

No ranch. No farm. No acreage.

This can't be the place.

There's no Sarah Ruth to make it home.

But then, there's no Sarah Ruth anywhere. Is that what I'm lookin' for?

Brazos paced the floor in front of the darkened window.

Maybe every place is the same. Maybe there is no Dakota cross. Or any other kind of cross.

Maybe that's why I can't seem to settle down and sleep at night. I'm lookin' for something that will never come back.

He snatched up his Bible and continued to pace. He stopped near the table and held the open book to the lantern. "For I know the thoughts that I think toward you, saith the Lord, thoughts of peace, and not of evil, to give you an expected end." He plopped the book down on the unmade bed and resumed his pace.

That's what I'm ready for. Your expected end.

I've been lookin' for three years for my expected end to this saga.

And it's been like chasin' a mirage. The closer I get, the further it goes. And I'm tired.

I could have stayed in Texas.

I could have stayed in Cheyenne.

I could go to Arizona.

I could go to California.

It just doesn't matter.

The cross of Jesus.

That's the only cross that matters, and I already live under it.

Brazos flopped down in the green chair, leaned his head back, and closed his eyes.

Sarah Ruth, I've run as far as I can. I chased cattle, ranches, leads of gold, and business opportunities. I think I'll just sit a spell.

"Daddy, what are you doin' in the chair? Are you asleep? Did you sit there all night?"

Daylight was just breaking across the room as Brazos opened his eyes. His neck was so stiff he had to rub it before he dared turn it left or right. There was a sharp pain in the small of his back. His feet felt ice cold.

Dacee June pulled on his arm. "Are you feelin' all right?"

"There's never anything wrong with me that isn't cured by your smile, young lady."

"I brought you some coffee," she said.

"Where did you get the coffee?"

"I do know how to make coffee. Jamie Sue's going to help me make breakfast. We're goin' to cook all the meals from now on."

"Well, now I have two girls to look after me."

Dacee June stiffened. "No. She can cook and help with the housework, but I'm the only one who is going to look after you." She waltzed over by the window and stared out. "Mamma asked me to do it. When she was dyin' she said, 'Dacee June, you take good care of your daddy, because sometimes he gets to acting like a lost puppy.' And that's just the way you act sometimes. So I'm the only one in the whole wide world that's allowed to look after you!"

"That's what your mamma told you?"

"Yes, she did. And my mamma never lies."

Brazos hunted for his socks. "Well, you're right about that, Miss Dacee June Fortune."

"What are we going to do today, Daddy? Is it our turn to stand guard down at the barricade, watching for Indians? Or are we going to find that gold in Spearfish Canyon?"

"Neither." Brazos tugged on a long, brown sock. "Today, you and I are going to hike up on Forest Hill and see if we can find a suitable lot near Todd's to build us a house."

"A house? We're going to have a real house again?"

"Well, I don't intend to live above the store and entertain company on top of nail barrels the rest of my life."

"Can I have a round, cut-glass window in my room? And a full-length mirror, and my very own walk-in wardrobe closet?"

"I think most of that can be arranged."

Suddenly, Dacee June called out. "Daddy, come here! Come look! Look over there!"

Brazos sauntered towards the window, wearing only one brown sock. "What are you looking at?"

"Up on the hill, near White Rocks. The sun's reflecting off Big River's cross."

"No, I don't think so. I took all the silver off it so no one would steal it. It's just dull, rusty iron."

"No, really, Daddy. Get your spectacles. Look over there . . . it's shining!"

The morning sunlight had not yet dipped down into the gulch, but lit up the Ponderosas on top of the tallest mountains. From the opposite side of the gulch, a glimmering reflection seemed aimed right at their second-story window.

"It's Big River's cross, Daddy . . . really. It's a Dakota cross. Look, all of Deadwood is below the Dakota cross!"

"There is no way that dull, pitted iron cross could reflect that much sunlight."

"Well, it is . . . and it's coming right into our window. It's a sign from the Lord. This is our place. This is where God wants us to stay forever. Daddy, this is home."

"That might be, young lady. But that reflection is not from an iron cross."

"Don't you believe in signs and miracles, Daddy?"

"I sure do, darlin'. I see a miracle ever' day I look into your smilin' eyes. Now, go downstairs under the counter and fetch me my spyglass. Hurry, before that reflection dies down."

Brazos waited by the window as he heard Dacee June tromp down the wooden stairs. In a matter of moments, she burst through the room and over to the window, carrying the brass-cased telescope.

"Can I look first, Daddy?"

"Be my guest. But I'd search from the other window. You don't want to magnify that reflection right into your eye."

Dacee June put the brass eyepiece to her left eye and squeezed tight the right. "It's just got to be the cross, Daddy. I know it's the cross."

He walked over to her.

"Oh, no," she wailed.

"What do you see, darlin'?"

"A creep!"

"What?"

"It's that creep, Carty Toluca!"

"What's he doin'?"

"He's got a mirror in his hand, and he's shining its reflection right into our window on purpose! He's just tryin' to pester me. I wonder if I should go punch him in the nose?"

"Let me look," Brazos insisted.

Far across the gulch Brazos spotted the image of a teenage boy wearing ducking trousers, a white cotton shirt, and suspenders to his knees. In his hand, he cradled a small, round mirror. "Well, girl, you're getting to be mighty popular."

"But, I'm so disappointed I could almost cry," she

moaned.

"Why's that?"

"Because I wanted so much for this to be the place that is beneath the Dakota cross. I like living here, Daddy."

Brazos hugged her. "Maybe we are beneath the Dakota cross, darlin'."

"We are? Where is it? Can we see it from here?"

"Just look in your heart, darlin'. That's where the important cross is. It doesn't matter where we live. That cross is with us."

"Are we really going to stay in Deadwood and build a brand-new house?"

"Yep."

"Can I have my own enamel bathtub, just for me, and no one else can use it?"

"Sounds like a reasonable request for an eighteen-year-old."

"Oh, Daddy! I'm only twelve, and you know it!"

"You don't say? You seem much more mature than that."

"Do I get a tub for myself, please?"

"Have I ever turned you down?"

"Not yet," she grinned, and slipped her fingers into his.

Epilogue

At noon, on Saturday, June 24, 1876, three hours before the Battle at the Little Big Horn commenced, Lieutenant Colonel George A. Custer sent a battalion of 125 men under Captain Frederick Benteen to sweep the bluffs well south of the suspected Sioux encampment. Benteen tired of the scouting mission and turned north. He then received orders to bring up the packs carrying ammunition. While en route, he came upon the further divided and beleaguered forces of Major Marcus Reno. While suffering numerous casualties, the Reno-Benteen forces survived the Battle of the Little Big Horn. Sergeant Robert Fortune, serving in one of the three companies under Captain Benteen, sustained two broken ribs and contusions when his horse was shot out from under him. His injuries were not fatal.

Less than six weeks later, on Wednesday, August 2, 1876, at approximately 3:00 P.M., a previously unknown, shifty drifter named Jack McCall entered the Number 10 saloon on Deadwood's Main Street and shot James Butler Hickok in the back of the head as Wild Bill held a poker hand of black aces and eights.

Eighteen days after Wild Bill's death, on Sunday, August 20, 1876, Reverend Henry Weston Smith held worship services on the streets of Deadwood. After Sunday dinner he began a six-mile hike through the mountains to Crook City to hold similar services.

Hours later his murdered body was found, where it had fallen, along the trail deep in the woods. Neither a motive, nor a murderer, was ever discovered. The entire population of the northern Black Hills mourned the death of Preacher Smith.

Center Point Publishing
600 Brooks Road • PO Box 1
Thorndike ME 04986-0001 USA

(207) 568-3717

US & Canada:
1 800 929-9108